MURDER
WITH A
VIEW

MURDER WITH A VIEW

DIANE KELLY

St. Martin's Paperbacks

First published in the United States by St. Martin's Paperbacks, an imprint of St. Martin's Publishing Group.

MURDER WITH A VIEW

For information, address St. Martin's Publishing Group, 120 Broadway, New York, NY 10271.

www.stmartins.com

ISBN: 978-1-250-19748-1

Our books may be purchased in bulk for promotional, educational, or business use. Please contact your local bookseller or the Macmillan Corporate and Premium Sales Department at 1-800-221-7945, ext. 5442, or by email at MacmillanSpecialMarkets@macmillan.com.

Printed in the United States of America

St. Martin's Paperbacks edition 2021

10 9 8 7 6 5 4 3 2 1

To Gary Brown, a talented musician and songwriter I was honored to call a friend. You might no longer be with us, but you will be forever singing in our hearts.

ACKNOWLEDGMENTS

It took a village to make this book happen, and I am so grateful to all the villagers who played a part in bringing this story to life.

A big thanks to the fantastic and talented team at St. Martin's Press. Thanks to my insightful and hardworking editor, Nettie Finn. Your suggestions are always spot-on. Thanks as well to Allison Ziegler, Kayla Janas, Sara Beth Haring, Sarah Haeckel, Talia Sherer, and the rest of the St. Martin's staff for everything you do to get books into the hands of readers, reviewers, and librarians. Y'all are a great crew!

Thanks to Danielle Christopher and Mary Ann Lasher for creating such a cute cover for this book.

Thanks to my agent, Helen Breitwieser, for all you do to further my career.

An ongoing debt of gratitude to my good friend Paula Highfill, who suggested the house-flipping concept for this series.

A shout-out to all my writer friends who have encouraged me along the way and offered your invaluable input on my work. I wouldn't be here without you.

Thank you to my cousin Di Ann Chapman, who once told me a joke about going to a party in a pasture. That joke stuck with me and gave rise to the character's hit song "Party in the Pasture."

Thanks also to my friend and talented songwriter Carole Helm Pickett for suggesting the last name "Spurlock" for a character. I've given the last name to a singer named Lacy. Can't wait to hear the songs you write next.

Thanks to the wonderful readers on Facebook who helped me brainstorm lyrics for "Party in the Pasture." Y'all are a creative and clever bunch!

And finally, thanks to you readers who chose this book! Enjoy your time with Whitney, Sawdust, and the gang.

CHAPTER I

AUCTION ACTION

WHITNEY WHITAKER

It was barely sunup on a day in the middle of May when I was wakened by the sensation of my fluffy, buff-colored cat headbutting my cheek with his furry fore-head. *Who needs an alarm clock when you've got a cat to tell you when it's time to wake up?*

With a yawn and a sigh, I opened my eyes. Seeing that his efforts had been successful, my cat revved his motor and launched into a loud purr meant to further encourage me. I reached out my hand to pet my furry fellow. "All right, Sawdust. Mommy will get up and get your breakfast."

Sawdust trotted along next to me as I made my way out into the hall. On hearing our footsteps, my room-mate's long-haired calico kitten came skittering out of her bedroom at warp speed to join us. In her zealous-ness, the kitty overshot her mark, bouncing off the op-posite wall like a fuzzy pinball. Fortunately, she was no worse for the wear. I led them to the kitchen, split a can of flaked tuna between them, and gave them both a nice scratch behind the ears.

"You two behave yourselves today," I admonished them. "I'm off to buy some real estate!"

Later that morning, my cousin Buck and I walked into the Davidson County Courthouse with a spring in our steps, big ideas in our heads, and a certified check for ninety-five grand in my purse. Having spent much of our childhood together, Buck and I were as close-knit as siblings. We looked like siblings, too, sharing blond hair, blue eyes, and a tall stature. Buck's father—my uncle Roger—ran a carpentry business, and had taught us both the ins and outs of woodworking when we were young. We'd started off building birdhouses, later graduated to doghouses, and, these days, we'd partnered to flip houses made for human inhabitants. We'd recently earned a nice profit on the sale of a three-bedroom, two-bath Colonial we'd purchased and remodeled. We planned to plunk that profit down on another property and see if we could double or maybe even triple it. Flipping houses was a risky venture, though, like real-estate roulette. But we had nothing to lose—unless you counted our money, our solid credit ratings, and our confidence in ourselves. I chose not to.

The property we'd set our sights on this time was, ironically, not much to look at. The abandoned one-story motel dated back to the 1960s, when men with mutton-chop sideburns and women with bouffant hair-dos pulled into the place in their Chevy Chevelles, Plymouth Barracudas, or Ford Fairlanes. Currently, the place sported sea-foam green stucco and scratched pink doors, along with plastic tarps and plywood. Years had passed since anyone had paid taxes on the place, slept in its beds, or swum in its now-cracked pool. But with my mental crystal ball, I could envision the twelve motel rooms turned into six one-bedroom condominiums with contemporary conveniences and a charming retro façade that incorporated the guitar-shaped neon sign in the parking lot. With the property's prime location just across the Cumberland River from downtown Nashville, we could earn a huge gain—assuming we were the highest bidders at today's tax auction.

We checked in with the clerk at a table outside the room where the auction would be held.

"Name?" she asked, looking up at my cousin and me.

I spoke for us. "Whitney and Buck Whitaker."

She wrote our names down on a sheet of paper and held out a numbered paddle. "Here you go."

I eyed the paddle. Number 13. Call me superstitious, but I got a bad vibe. "Any chance we could get a paddle with a different number?"

The woman eyed the line forming behind us and sent me a sour look. "No. Sorry."

Buck pushed me forward into the courtroom and muttered, "You get what you get and you don't throw a fit."

"I wasn't throwing a fit," I said. "I just don't want to be jinxed."

But jinxed we appeared to be. There, in the front row, sat Thaddeus Gentry III. Even from behind, I recognized his stocky physique and thick, wolf like salt-and-pepper hair. His lupine resemblance didn't end at his hair either. He was a predator, slinking around the city as if it were his territory, searching for unsuspecting prey. Thad Gentry owned Gentry Real Estate Development, Inc., referred to as GREED Incorporated by those who disliked his tactics, including yours truly. Gentry was a ruthless real estate developer who swooped down on older, unsuspecting neighborhoods and rebuilt them, running off long-term residents in the process. Rather than rehabbing rundown areas in modest and affordable ways that would allow residents to remain, he strategically purchased plots, razing old homes and building new, bigger, upscale houses in their stead. Older homes would end up sandwiched between his expensive new structures, which caused lot values to soar. The neighbors would find themselves unable to pay the increased property taxes on homes they'd lived in for decades. Gentry would buy them out when they were forced to put the homes they could no longer afford on the market.

Buck and I had a much different philosophy about real estate. While we were in the house-flipping business to make a living, profits were not our sole concern. Our focus was on providing a safe, well-constructed, and visually appealing residence for the people who would someday call it home. The two of us also enjoyed the artistry involved in revisualizing an outdated eyesore, as well as the simple satisfaction that comes from physical labor.

Not long ago, Gentry and I had butted heads when he'd purchased the house next door to the one in which I now live. He'd attempted to have the adjacent property rezoned from residential to commercial, which would have caused the value of my house to plummet. He'd been suspected of bribing a member of the zoning commission, then settling the matter to prevent the truth from coming to light. I'd managed to beat him then, but could I beat him now? It was doubtful. Our funds were limited. Gentry's, on the other hand, were limitless.

I elbowed Buck in the ribs to get his attention and

jerked my head to indicate Gentry. Rubbing his side, Buck followed my gaze and frowned. He knew why Gentry was here. For the same reason we were. To put in a bid on the Music City Motor Court. Although the land on which the motel sat was a mere half acre, its location and skyline view made it a potential gold mine.

Buck and I slipped into the back row and put our heads together.

"We can't let Thad Gentry steal this chance from us!" I whispered.

"How can we stop him?" Buck asked.

I bit my lip and raised my palms.

Buck's eyes narrowed as he thought. "You think the Hartleys would make you another loan?"

Marv and Wanda Hartley owned Home & Hearth Realty, the real estate company where I worked part-time as a property manager. They'd generously loaned me the funds to buy the Colonial that Buck and I had recently flipped. They'd give me another loan if I asked, but I'd really hoped the arrangement would be a one-time thing, that Buck and I would be able to buy another property on our own this time, without help. My parents would gladly loan me some money, too, as would Buck's. But with me having reached the big 3-0 and Buck being on the backside of thirty, we were getting a little too old to run to Mom and Dad for money. We earned decent livings and could support ourselves, even save a little. But if we couldn't manage this on our own, maybe we were trying to bite off more than we could chew.

Before I could respond, the courtroom doors opened and in walked Presley Pearson on a pair of four-inch heels. Designer, no doubt, though I'd be hard pressed to identify any footwear brand not sold at Tractor Supply, where I purchased the steel-toed work boots I wore when making repairs at rental properties or helping out in the family carpentry business. Presley was smart and chic, with a short angular haircut that framed her dark-skinned face. Presley could be the solution to our problem—if she didn't still hold a grudge against me. She and I had a checkered past. I'd bought my current home from her former boss, and she'd been rightfully upset that he hadn't offered the house to her first. But by the time I'd learned she was interested in the property, the deal was done. Her boss was later found dead in the front flowerbed, so she'd dodged a proverbial bullet. Buck and I were now stuck with the unmarketable house. Nobody wants to buy a property where a person was murdered. Not without an enormous discount, anyway.

I stood and raised a hand to stop her. "Presley. Hi."

She turned my way and her face tightened. A reflexive reaction, I supposed. "Hello, Whitney," she said in a tepid tone.

"We'd like to talk to you."

Buck stood, too, arching a brow. "We would?"

"Trust me," I whispered to him. I held out a hand to invite Presley to sit next to me and Buck on the bench. Once we were all sitting, I asked, "Which property are you planning to bid on?"

She kept her cards close to her vest and turned the tables on me. "Why don't *you* tell *me* first?"

Unlike her, I exposed my hand. "The Music City Motor Court."

Her face sunk as she realized she had competition for the property she'd hoped to purchase.

I angled my head to indicate the front row. "See Thad Gentry up there? I have a hunch he's here to bid on the motel too."

She eyed the man and sighed. "Gentry Development is flush with capital. There's no way I could beat his bid."

"Neither can we," I said. "Not alone anyway. But what if we pooled our resources?"

She stared at me for a long moment, evidently engaged in a mental debate with herself, before asking, "How much were you going to bid?"

"Ninety-five thousand. You?"

"Sixty-eight," she said. "It's all my savings."

Now $163,000 would be chump change to Gentry, and we all knew it. Fortunately, a devious idea popped into my mind. I gave Presley a quick overview of our plans for the property, assuming we were lucky enough to land it.

"Condos?" she said. "That's a fantastic idea. They'd go fast and for a high price too."

She's in. I looked from Presley to Buck. "Are you two above pulling a fast one?"

Presley scoffed. "On Thad Gentry? Heck, no. He's a pompous you-know-what."

"So you've dealt with him too?" It wasn't surprising that Presley and Gentry would have interacted at some point. After all, Presley's former boss and Gentry were two major players in the Nashville real estate scene.

"He came to the office once," Presley said, "but he didn't even glance in my direction. I've only spoken with him on the phone. He was always rude and pushy."

Good. The fact that she hadn't dealt with him in person meant he wouldn't recognize her. He wasn't likely to recognize Buck either. As for myself, that was another matter. Thad Gentry and I had a run-in at our properties a while back, and there was no love lost between us. He'd probably recognize me, and he certainly wouldn't trust me.

We put our heads together and came up with a plan. Even after a property has been auctioned off in a tax sale, the county does not issue the winning bidder a valid deed until the expiration of the applicable redemption period. During the redemption period, the delinquent owner could redeem the property by reimbursing the purchase price paid by the bidder, as well as the delinquent taxes, penalties, interest, and court costs. Purchasing a property that was likely to be redeemed was a waste of time and would tie up funds that could be better invested elsewhere. If we could convince Gentry the motel was at risk of being redeemed, maybe he'd decide not to take a chance on it.

Buck took our #13 paddle, and he and Presley headed to the second row, taking seats behind Gentry. I, on the other hand, slid down to the end of the back row and slouched, doing my best to make myself invisible.

As the room continued to fill with people interested in placing bids in the tax auction, Buck and Presley made what appeared to be idle conversation, but that was actually full of fibs about the property. Though I was too far away to actually hear their discussion, based on our sneaky plan, I knew it went something like this:

Buck: *"No point in bidding on the Music City Motor Court. I met the owners when I was checking out the property yesterday. They're pulling funds together to redeem it."*

Presley: *"Are you sure?"*

Buck: *"Yep. Their new investors were with them. Couple of wealthy guys from Chicago. Flew down on their own private jet. Anyone who bids on that property is a chump. I've set my sights on that parcel off Lebanon Pike. There's an old farmhouse and barn on it now, but apartments are sprouting up all around that area. It's just a matter of time until a developer comes a-calling."*

Gentry turned his head slightly, clearly listening in on Buck and Presley's conversation. But if he overheard something they said and took it to heart, that was *his* problem, not ours. He shouldn't be eavesdropping on a private discussion.

A few minutes later, the room was full and the auction began. Several smaller houses sold before the auctioneer announced that the next property up for bid would be the one along Lebanon Pike. Several bidders raised their paddles, including both Gentry and Buck, who was toying with the tycoon. Others dropped out as the price went up. The auctioneer continued to raise the price by five-thousand-dollar increments until Buck bailed out at eighty grand.

As Gentry raised his paddle one last time, the auctioneer brought his gavel down. "Sold for eighty-five thousand dollars to bidder number eight."

Gentry cut a smug look back at Buck, who shook his head in pretend disappointment. I fought the urge to laugh out loud. Gentry was a smart man, but he was also a fiercely competitive one who didn't like to lose. He shouldn't have been so hasty. He'd just bought a worthless piece of land in the Mill Creek floodplain. Before it could be developed, expensive grading and flood control improvements would have to be made. *Sucker!*

His business concluded, Gentry stood and left the room to finalize the paperwork in the clerk's office down the hall.

The auctioneer announced the legal description of the next parcel of land, then said, "Otherwise known as the

Music City Motor Court." When he started the bidding, a dozen paddles shot into the air. *Darn!* Looked like we weren't the only ones who realized the property's potential.

Buck raised his paddle over and over as the price went from $100,000 to $110,000 to $120,000. About half of the bidders dropped out at that price, but several remained. The bid went to $130,000, then $140,000, and $150,000. By then only Buck and another man were still in the game. My intestines tied themselves in knots. We wanted this property—*bad*—and it looked like we might lose it!

The auctioneer raised the bid by only $5,000 this time around. "Do I hear $155,000?"

We had only eight thousand more dollars to go before we'd have to drop out. *Argh!* I crossed my fingers. For good measure, I crossed my toes too. Not easy to do in steel-toed boots.

Buck hesitated a moment before raising his paddle, a strategy to make the other bidder think twice about further raising his bid.

Seeing the hesitation of the remaining bidders, the auctioneer increased the bid by a smaller amount. "Do I hear $158,000?"

Both Buck and the other bidder waited a moment, before Buck slowly raised his paddle. The other man did likewise. I fought the urge to scream. I'd already visualized exactly what we could do to the property, had jotted down notes and sketched out some ideas. This man was screwing around with my plans, and I didn't like it one bit!

"Do I hear $160,000?" The auctioneer's head swiveled as he looked from Buck to the other bidder.

The other bidder raised his paddle and sent a scathing

look in Buck's direction. Buck raised his paddle as well.

"Can I get $162,500?" the auctioneer called, his eyes wide with anticipation.

The other man exhaled sharply, frowned in defeat, and shook his head. He'd reached his limit. Buck raised both his paddle and a victorious fist as the auctioneer brought his gavel down. "Sold to bidder number thirteen!"

Maybe 13 wasn't such an unlucky number after all. We even had $500 left over.

Buck and Presley stood and made their way down the aisle, both of them beaming.

I met them at the door, giddy over our win. "We did it!" I held up a hand and exchanged high fives with my cousin and our new business partner. I only hoped we could all work well together. Buck and I had developed a system. Adding another person to the mix could complicate things. But we'd cross that bridge if and when we came to it.

We headed down the hall to the clerk's office and stepped up to the counter beside Thad Gentry. He did a double take when he recognized me. I gave him my best smile. He frowned and turned away.

The matronly clerk took the approved bid from Buck and said, "You bought the Music City Motor Court, huh? I stayed there once back in the day. Got sunburnt out by the pool. Had a fun time, though."

Gentry's head had snapped in our direction when he overheard the woman mention the motel. His eyes narrowed as he looked from me to Buck and back again, seeming to notice the family resemblance.

I offered him a smug smile. "Didn't your mama tell you not to trust in rumors?"

The man skewered me with his gaze and chuckled mirthlessly. "Well played, Miss Whitaker."

Well played, indeed. Thad Gentry might not like me, but at least now he respected me.

CHAPTER 2
SITE VISIT

Buck, Presley, and I decided to celebrate over an early lunch at a café near the courthouse. I ordered a bottle of prosecco, a more affordable alternative to champagne. We'd spring for champagne later, once we'd sold the units.

I held up my glass. "To a successful partnership."

Buck and Presley clinked their glasses against mine, and we all took a sip.

After toasting our good fortune with sparkling wine, we worked out the particulars of our arrangement over our meal.

Presley looked from me to Buck. "Tell me more specifics about your plans."

I told her that we planned to improve the grounds, renovate the exterior, and finish out one spec model before tackling the additional units. "Once the spec unit is ready to show, we'll pre-sell the other units and use the down payments to finance the completion work."

"Smart," she said. "That way, our up-front expenses are minimized."

Fortunately, Presley agreed to leave the details of the renovation up to my cousin and me. "I don't like to get my hands dirty. I'll come by to check on things now and then, but for the most part I'll be a silent partner." Recognizing that, in addition to our monetary investment, Buck and I would invest sweat equity by performing much of the construction work ourselves, she agreed to accept 30% of the net profit as full payment for her share in the venture, with payment due upon sale of the last condominium unit. We jotted the details on a napkin, signed our names to it, and sealed the deal with handshakes. An attorney would cringe at our lackadaisical approach, but if Presley was going to trust Buck and me to do a good job on the remodel, I'd trust her to keep up her end of the bargain too.

After enjoying our meal, Presley dabbed at her mouth, lay her napkin on the table, and sat back in her seat, eyeing me. "If someone had told me yesterday that you and I would end up partners in a real estate deal, I would've told them they were crazy."

"We might have gotten off on the wrong foot," I said, "but you and I are a lot alike." It was true. We were both ambitious and determined, with an affinity for realty.

"Cat people, you mean?" The glimmer in her eye said she being facetious, but she nonetheless pulled out her cell phone and showed me several pics of an orange tabby she called Tangerine.

The adoring way she looked at the photos told me she felt the same way about her cat as I did about mine. "She's beautiful."

"Isn't she, though?" She returned her phone to her purse. "How's your little guy? Sawdust, right?"

This sounded like an invitation to reciprocate with kitty pics of my own. I retrieved my phone and showed her photos of Sawdust with Cleo. "He's got a new little buddy. She follows him everywhere, like a calico shadow."

Buck joined in too. There'd been three cats in Sawdust's litter, born to a stray in my uncle Roger's and aunt Nancy's barn. Sawdust had been the runt. While my aunt and uncle kept the mama cat, Sawdust ended up with me and his two siblings had gone to Buck and his brother Owen. My cousin held up his phone, his enormous tomcat filling the screen. "This guy lives with me." Buck jokingly referred to his cat as his roommate, and insisted the two were confirmed bachelors. Lately, though, I'd sensed Buck's commitment to his bachelor status waning.

After lunch, Presley headed off to her job, while Buck and I swung by the motel to prioritize our to-do list. The property sat on North 1st Street, not far from the sprawling football stadium where the Tennessee Titans played. The dilapidated inn was also within walking distance of the pedestrian bridge that spanned the Cumberland River. The bridge connected the east side of the river to downtown Nashville and the South Broadway tourist area. SoBro, as locals called it, encompassed a variety of restaurants, shops, and honky-tonks, as well as the Predators' hockey rink, the Country Music Hall of Fame, and the Ryman Auditorium where the Grand Ole Opry had been launched decades ago. The location would appeal to well-heeled singles or couples who enjoyed the downtown scene.

We parked on the street beside the L-shaped motel and stood side by side on the sidewalk, looking through the flimsy wire fencing that had been erected to keep people off the property. The asphalt parking lot was cracked, the rooftop HVAC units were rusty, and colorful graffiti decorated the pocked sea-foam green stucco exterior. Faded curtains hung askew in what few windows hadn't been covered with plywood or plastic tarps. All sorts of trash lay scattered about. Fast-food and candy wrappers. Soda cans. Broken beer bottles. Cigarette butts, both with and without telltale lines of lipstick encircling the filter. The seedy motel was a far cry from the Ritz-Carlton, but with some hard work we'd transform this derelict lodge into a place anyone would be proud to call home.

"First thing we do," Buck said, "is get that sign fixed." He pointed to the guitar-shaped neon sign. "We light that up and people will be curious about what's going on over here, start talking about it."

"Can't hurt to generate some buzz," I agreed. "Maybe we should string up a banner, too, one that says Coming Soon—Music City Motor Court Condominiums."

"Good idea."

We circled around the parking lot, and Buck reached down to lift up a loose edge of the flimsy wire fencing. We bent down and ducked under the flap to access the property.

As he let the fencing fall back into place, he said, "We'll have to find a better way to secure this place. That lightweight chain link isn't gonna cut it."

The bent fencing, the graffiti on the building, and the broken windows evidenced vandals having come onto the property. We'd have to do something to keep trespassers out. We couldn't afford to have our building materials stolen or someone getting hurt on the premises and filing a lawsuit.

I made a suggestion. "What if we install decorative

iron fencing around the place? It'll be useful now, and prospective buyers will like the added security too." Not that we were going for snob appeal, but the gate would also add an air of exclusivity.

Buck cocked his head. "You got a guy who will install a fence at reasonable rate?"

"Of course I got a guy," I said. "I always got a guy." Working as a property manager, I knew more than my share of people in the construction and repair trades. Plumbers. Electricians. Flooring installers. Fencing specialists. Painters and landscapers too. My contacts came in handy in our house-flipping business. Many of the contractors would cut me a good deal in return for sending business their way. The funky smell wafting from the green guck at the bottom of the cracked swimming pool reminded me we'd need a pool guy too. I pointed this out to Buck. "If we waited too much longer, those things wriggling and writhing in the muck might grow into full-sized swamp creatures."

"Well, then, you'll fit right in," teased Buck, though he nodded to show he knew this should be a priority.

As we proceeded along the walkway in front of the rooms, Buck stopped in front of the door to Room 9, which sported plywood over its window. Buck pointed to the door. The metal was bent around the lock. "Someone took a crowbar to this frame." He reached out a hand and pushed the door open.

Sunlight streamed from behind us into the room, casting our shadows across the space. Dirt specks sparkled within the bright beams like magic fairy dust. As our eyes adjusted, we peeked into the space to see a red Kawasaki motorcycle with studded faux-leather saddlebags parked on the far side of the king-sized bed, a book lying open and facedown on the nearest nightstand, and a sizeable lump under the worn covers. An instant later, the lump sat up, becoming a fortysomething man with shaggy brown hair, a burly beard, and a smile as bright as the sunlight. "Good morning, folks!"

Instinctively, I took a step back. Two thoughts ran through my mind. The first was *This guy sure does wake up happy.* The second was *What the heck is he doing here?* One glance about the room answered the second question for me. The man was living here. A bottle of water, a tube of toothpaste, and a toothbrush sat on the pink Formica bathroom countertop that spanned half of the back wall. Fast-food wrappers filled the plastic trash can. A stack of clean, folded clothing lay atop the other nightstand, which also featured an old-fashioned coin-operated vibrating bed massager.

Buck and I exchanged a glance. I was so taken aback I wasn't sure what to say. Luckily, Buck handled the matter. "I'm Buck," he said, responding to the man in a similarly friendly manner. He hiked a thumb at me. "This is my cousin, Whitney. As you can see, I got the looks in the family. She got the karate skills."

Karate? While I'd sawed many a board in half over my years in carpentry, I had none of the skills needed to break a board in half with a chop of my hand or a kick of my foot. But maybe Buck's bluff would discourage the guy from trying any monkey business.

"My name's Jimmy," the guy said. "Nice to meet you." As he relaxed his arms, the bedspread slid down his chest and settled around his waist. His well-developed pectoral muscles and six-pack abs said he worked out regularly. The tattoo on his left pec with an anchor and the letters USN said he was ex-Navy.

Buck gestured to the broken lock. "Did you do that?"

"Nah, man," Jimmy said. "That's not like me. It was already broken when I came along."

I joined in the conversation. "We just bought the place. Mind telling us what you're doing here?"

"Putting the motel to use," he said matter-of-factly. "Seemed senseless to look for a campground outside of town when there's a perfectly good bedroom right here that nobody's using."

The motel was far from "perfectly good." It wasn't perfectly anything. The electricity and water were turned off, and it was anyone's guess the last time the bedding and towels had been laundered. But the condition of the place wasn't really the main issue at the moment. "Are you homeless?" I winced a bit at my bluntness but knew the question had to be asked.

"Yes," he said, "but by choice, not circumstance. I spent the last twenty years on ships sailing all over the world. Saw more of other countries than I ever had of my own. When I left the Navy, I decided to spend a year or two on dry land traveling through the good old U S of A. Now, I go wherever the winds blow me."

"Like a trailer in a tornado," Buck said.

Jimmy snorted. "Exactly, bro."

So the man was a drifter, a modern-day hippie, a nomad. I was just the opposite, a homebody whose favorite place to be on a Saturday night was rooted on her couch with her cat curled up beside her. But who was I to question this man's choices? It takes all kinds to make the world go round. "Sounds like an interesting life."

"It is," he said. "You never know who you'll meet or what you'll learn." He made a circular motion with his hand. "Mind turning around while I put some clothes on? I'm in my skivvies."

I turned away. Buck, on the other hand, kept a loose eye on Jimmy lest things turn ugly. The guy seemed harmless, but for all we knew he could be a crazed axe murderer. It would be stupid for both of us to turn our backs on him, despite my purported karate skills.

Shortly thereafter, he came to the door in a pair of rumpled cargo shorts and a brightly colored Aloha shirt featuring cartoon sharks hula dancing in grass skirts. "Could you two keep an eye on my things while I pop across the street to use their bathroom? There's no running water here."

Buck swept his arm to indicate the Poison Emporium, the combination liquor and tobacco store half a block down. "Have at it."

The man jogged across the parking lot, deftly dove under the bent fence flap, and scurried to the store.

Turning to my cousin, I asked, "What do we do about this? Call the police to have him removed?"

"I'd hate to get him in trouble," Buck said, "especially since he's a veteran. Chances are he's planning to be on his way soon."

When Jimmy returned, I told him that we planned to start cleaning out the property that coming weekend.

Buck added, "You'll need to wrap up your stay by then."

"Darn," Jimmy said. "I'd been hoping to hang around a bit longer. Nashville's a nice place. I'm not quite done exploring the city."

I couldn't blame the guy for wanting to stay. With its beautiful rolling hills, friendly folks, and thriving arts and music culture, it was a charming city.

He rubbed his chin, pensive, before his face brightened. "Any chance you'll need some help with the cleaning and such? I could use some cash before I move on."

Another set of hands could really come in handy, especially hands that were at the ends of such muscular arms. Buck looked my way and I shrugged. We'd take a chance on the guy. Of course, I'd keep my large wrench in my pocket for self-defense purposes, just in case.

"Fifteen dollars an hour," Buck offered. "It'll involve some heavy lifting, demolition, stuff like that."

"No problem." The man stuck out his hand and, for the second time that day, we sealed a deal with a shake.

CHAPTER 3
KITTEN CLASS

SAWDUST

Whitney's roommate Emmalee had brought a tiny kitten home recently and Sawdust was immediately smitten with the fuzzy calico fur ball the humans called Cleopatra.

He'd been slowly showing Cleo the ropes—kitten lessons—teaching her how to live her best life in the cozy cottage they called home. He'd shown her where their water and food bowls were kept on the kitchen floor, as well as how to sniff the food, back off, and meow if she hadn't been served her preferred meal. He'd shown her to their litter box in the bathroom beside the claw-foot bathtub, along with the roll of toilet paper nearby that made a fun spinning toy. He'd even tried to show her the great view from the top of the cat tree in the front window, but she was still too small to make the climb to the highest perch. It was his favorite place to nap and watch the world, but he'd gladly share it with his new friend once she grew big enough to scale its summit.

At the moment, the two were playing in the warmth of a wide sunbeam coming through a window in the living room. Cleo swatted at his tail as he swished it playfully behind him for her entertainment. She pounced and held his tail to the floor, looking thrilled to have captured and conquered her prey. But when she bit into him—*Mee-ouch!*—it was time for another lesson, one of tough love. He whirled on her and she dropped his tail and crouched, looking up at him with big, frightened eyes. He hadn't meant to scare her, only to get her to stop treating him like a stuffed mouse filled with catnip. He gave her a stern look before swiping her forehead with his tongue, letting her know all was forgiven. She purred and rubbed up under his chin. *How had he ever lived without his little friend?*

CHAPTER 4

QUEEN-SIZED DEAD

WHITNEY

Late Saturday morning, I was lounging on the couch in the living room, entertaining Sawdust and Cleopatra with a stuffed toy mouse hanging from the end of a fish pole toy. My two roommates and I were sipping coffee, watching a recording of *The Bachelor* we'd missed earlier in the week, and making predictions on which women would be awarded a rose by the attractive, as-yet-unattached guy and which would be sent home in shame.

Emmalee sat curled up in her Papasan chair, still in her pajamas. Her skin was dotted with freckles, and her hair was a shade that a carpenter like me would describe as *mahogany*. She pointed to a busty blonde sobbing on the screen. "She's definitely going home. No guy likes that much drama."

Colette, who was not only my roommate but also my best friend, disagreed from the other end of the couch, shaking her ebony curls. "He'll give her a rose. Men are suckers for damsels in distress. It makes them feel big and strong."

The two turned to me with expectant faces. Before I could break the tie, my phone pinged with a text from Buck. *I'm up. Let's roll.* Sliding my phone into the pocket of my coveralls, I stood from the couch and hedged my bets. "I think she'll get a rose in *this* episode, but not the next."

As I walked over to hand the cat toy to Emmalee, Cleopatra pounced on my steel-toed work boot, digging in with her front claws and kicking the side of the boot with her tiny back feet. I raised my own foot and the kitten came with it. "Behold the mighty hunter."

Emmalee reached out and scooped up her kitten, cradling the floof to her chest. "She's ferocious." As if to prove the point, Cleo growled. Unfortunately, the only one she managed to scare was herself. She mewed and hid her face in Emmalee's armpit.

After packing Sawdust into his carrier, I bade my roommates goodbye and carried my cat out to my SUV. I picked up Buck at his trailer, which was nestled on a serene and secluded three-acre lot in the woods north of Nashville. We drove to the rental facility to fetch the twenty-six-foot truck we'd reserved. It was the biggest one they offered, a behemoth of a vehicle. Thank goodness Buck was driving it instead of me. I could never maneuver something that big without taking out a traffic light. I followed safely behind him in my SUV.

Immediately after speaking with Jimmy at the motel earlier in the week, I'd arranged to have the utilities turned on so he could live more comfortably in Room 9 until he finished working for us and was ready to move on. When Buck and I pulled into the parking lot, we saw the veteran sitting by the pool on a cheap wooden chair he'd dragged outside from his room. He wore what seemed to be his civilian uniform of rumpled shorts and a Hawaiian-print shirt, this one covered with cartoon palm trees and smoke-spewing volcanoes. He was basking in the sunshine and eating jelly doughnuts out of a waxed paper bag. The gate that had hung cockeyed from the crumbling brick wall enclosing the pool area had come entirely free from its hinges and leaned back against the exterior. Likewise, the flimsy fencing around the motel looked even worse today than it had earlier in the week. A section along the front had been wrested free from the support pole and lay twisted back, part of it lying flat on the parking lot, providing easy access to the property.

I slid out of my SUV as Buck climbed down from the truck. Buck gestured to the fencing. "What happened here?"

"No idea, bro," Jimmy said. "The fence was like that when I got back here last night. The gate too."

Had vandals knocked it over, or had it fallen of its own accord? There was no telling. I only knew it was a good thing my fencing guy was coming Monday to install an iron fence and security gate around the place. The last thing we needed was someone falling into the empty pool and cracking their skull. Besides, the bent chain link didn't much matter at the moment. If anything, whoever had moved it had saved us some trouble. We would've needed to pull back the temporary barrier to drive the truck into the parking lot anyway.

My cousin gestured to the bag in Jimmy's hands. "Gonna share those doughnuts?"

"Heck, yeah," Jimmy said. "I got enough for everybody." He tossed the bag to Buck, who removed a lemon-filled variety before handing the bag off to me.

I pulled the bag open and looked inside to find a chocolate-frosted cake doughnut and a glazed blueberry, my favorite. I pulled out the blueberry and secured it between my teeth before chucking the bag back to Jimmy. As I did, I noticed the butt of a cigar near Jimmy's chair. I hadn't realized he smoked. He hadn't smelled of cigars or cigarettes when we'd spoke with him earlier in the week.

Multitasking, I ate the doughnut while opening the cargo bay of my SUV and rounding up both my cat carrier and my toolbox.

Jimmy called, "Whatcha got there?"

"Only the best cat that ever lived." Okay, so maybe I was a little biased. But Sawdust was as sweet as they come. Smart too.

Jimmy came over and bent down to look into the carrier. "Hello, there, furry fella." Sawdust returned the greeting with a polite mew and extended his paw through the metal slats on the door of his carrier. Jimmy chuckled and took Sawdust's paw, giving it a friendly shake before turning his eyes on me. "Your cat has good manners."

"His mama raised him right."

Buck had brought a spare pair of lightweight coveralls for Jimmy, and handed them over. Jimmy slid them on over his clothes. Meanwhile, Buck plugged a radio into one of the outdoor outlets and tuned it to his favorite local country-western station to provide some entertainment while we went about our work. Beats singing "Heigh-Ho." He gestured to the room at the far end.

"Why don't you start down there, Whitney? If you'll take the bed frames apart, Jimmy and I will load the truck."

"Works for me." I'd be more than happy to leave the heavy lifting to them.

Heading for Room 1, I carried my toolbox in one hand and the cat carrier in the other. Some of the rooms had queen-sized beds, while others housed kings or two full-sized units, side by side. All in all, I had sixteen bedframes to disassemble. That would keep me busy for a while. In the meantime, the men would remove the mattresses, box springs, and furniture, and Sawdust would enjoy exploring the motel rooms. He was a curious kitty, and he enjoyed coming on excursions with me. Of course, I could only bring him along when we wouldn't be performing tasks that could pose a danger to him or where he might get in the way.

I set my tools and cat down on the walkway in front of the door to Room 1. I reached out and tried the door, but it didn't budge. "Hey, Buck!" I called. "This room's locked."

"Not for long." Buck came over and used a hammer to pull out the nails holding the graffiti-covered plywood in place. Once he finished, he finagled the wood from the window, leaned it against the exterior wall, and hopped up onto the window sill. Swinging his legs over, he dropped into the room and walked over to open the door from the inside. He held up a spring-style doorstop. "Found this on the floor."

I reached out and took it from him. "I'll fix it."

After leaning the plywood back against the window to prevent Sawdust from escaping, I carried my cat and tools inside with Jimmy following behind me. The room smelled musty and dusty. One of the bulbs in the overhead fixture was burned out, the remaining bulb providing only meager light.

I knelt down in front of Sawdust's carrier. "Okay, boy. It's safe for you to come out now." I released the latch and Sawdust sashayed out into the room, glancing about as if trying to decide which part of the space to explore first.

Buck pulled a quarter from his pocket and held it up in one hand, pointing to the coin-operated bedside massager with the other. "What say we give her one last go?"

"Count me in." Jimmy flopped backward onto the far side of the king-sized bed, raising his hands over his head as if about to take a drop on a roller coaster.

"Why not?" I flopped down in the middle of the bed. Not to be left out, Sawdust jumped up between Jimmy and me.

Buck dropped down next to me. "Ready. Set. Go." He slid the quarter into the device and turned the crank.

After a soft *clink* and *clank*, the mechanism under the bed kicked on. *Whirrrrr.* Sawdust hissed and crouched on the vibrating bed, digging his claws into the bedspread and hanging on for dear life.

I wrapped an arm around him to let him know he was safe. My voice wavered in an involuntary vibrato when I spoke. "I-I-It's o-o-o-kay, boy-y-y!"

Despite my reassurances, Sawdust wasn't having it. He leaped from the bed to the dresser and turned around to watch three humans jiggle like gelatin on the bed, his head cocked in curiosity.

"Aaaaah," Buck said on an exhale. "This is-s-s everything-g-g I dreamed it would be-e-e."

"Dream bigg-gg-gg-er, bro." Jimmy rolled off the bed and stood. "My bunk on the *Mustin* shook like this every time the captain started the engines. I prefer a bed that stays still."

"Party poo-oo-oo-per," I said.

Buck and I continued to jiggle and jostle until the timer ran out and the bed went quiet again.

Buck sat up. "Party's over."

"Not yet." I levered myself to my knees, grabbed a pillow, and whopped my cousin upside the head with it, just like I used to do when we were kids. *Whop!*

"Oh, it's on now!" Buck grabbed his pillow and whopped me back.

Jimmy scoffed. "Aren't you two a little old for a pillow fight?"

Buck and I exchanged a knowing glance and set our sights on Jimmy, swatting him with the pillows until he cried, "Okay! Okay! I surrender!"

Having vanquished our target, we tossed the pillows into the corner and got to work. I pulled the bedding off the bed and piled it atop the pillows. Buck and Jimmy grabbed the old, concave mattress and carried it out to the truck. They did the same with the box spring and furniture before disappearing through the adjoining door to Room 2 and closing the door behind them.

As my cat sniffed around the old-fashioned A/C unit, I knelt down and inspected the baseboard behind the entry door. A chunk of it was missing and the drywall behind it had crumbled. Someone had attempted to screw the doorstop directly into the sheetrock, but it hadn't held, being too soft to endure such demands. Fortunately, I could move the doorstop over an inch or two and insert it into the remaining baseboard so it could serve its purpose for the time being.

As I screwed the doorstop into the wood, the ever-curious Sawdust came over to see what I was doing.

When I stood, he sniffed the doorstop, twitched his whiskers, and took a step back. He reached out a tentative paw to touch the rubber end. When he realized he could make the device move, he batted it harder with his paw. *Boingggg! Boingggg!*

I reached down and ruffled his ears. "That's some fine entertainment, isn't it, boy?"

Boingggg!

While Sawdust batted and battled the spring, I set to work on the bedframe and quickly had it separated into manageable pieces. Keeping a close eye on the cat lest he try to slip outside, I set each of the pieces on the sidewalk out front where the guys could grab them and add them to the accumulation of furnishings on the truck. We continued this pattern until we reached Room 9, the one Jimmy was staying in.

As Buck grabbed one side of the mattress to remove it, Jimmy cast him a hopeful look. "Any chance I can hang on to that mattress for a few days until I head back out on the road?"

Cradling my cat in my arms, I stepped up next to Jimmy. "We can do you one better. Buck and I ordered you a new platform bed."

Jimmy's face brightened. "Really? I don't have to sleep on that lumpy mattress anymore?"

"Nope," I said. "You've got a memory foam mattress coming. New pillows and bedding, too, along with a dresser and nightstand. It will all be delivered this afternoon." It was the least we could do for a veteran. Plus, we'd found the ensemble on sale for a great price. The furniture store was trying to get a jump on its competitors' upcoming Memorial Day sales.

Smiling, Jimmy looked from me to Buck and back again. "You two are all right."

Not wanting to be mistaken for a softie, Buck said, "We were planning to furnish the model unit anyway. Besides, if your back hurts, you won't be able to work as hard for us."

Jimmy saw through Buck's bluster, issuing a soft snort. "Sure, man. Whatever you say."

In addition to the bedroom furniture, we'd also purchased a couch, a coffee table, a credenza, and an oval dinette set, as well as two oversized framed mirrors. We'd keep those pieces under wraps for now. Jimmy didn't need them, and we didn't want to risk them getting scratched or dirty while we did our work.

Buck turned to me. "Before we can start on the next room, we'll need to make a run to the dump, get rid of what we've loaded so far."

I stepped over to the window and pushed back the curtains to get a look at the truck. The bay was nearly full. Beyond the truck, on the Cumberland River a quarter mile away, the tall, red-tipped smokestacks and striped awnings atop the General Jackson Showboat moved slowly along, followed by its enormous red paddlewheel, as it cruised underneath the pedestrian bridge. The boat ran twice a day during peak tourist season, providing meals, a scenic ride, and some lively song and dance for those aboard. My fifth-grade class had taken a field trip to ride the boat two decades ago and, years later, my parents had taken me on the boat again to celebrate my graduation from college. This stretch of river marked the cruise's halfway point. After offering passengers a view of downtown and the Riverfront Park, the boat would hook a tight U-turn and backtrack down the water to the dock where it had started.

My stomach growled as I let the curtain fall back into

place. The morning's blueberry doughnut was a distant memory by then. "Pick up some burritos on your way back."

"Good idea," Buck said.

He and Jimmy loaded the bed and dresser onto the truck, rolled the bay door down with a raucous rattle, and headed off, leaving me and Sawdust behind. I set Sawdust down on the carpet, and he immediately trotted over to Jimmy's motorcycle to give it a through once-over. He reached up to try his claws on the saddlebags, but stopped when I wagged a finger at him and said, "No no, boy!" His compliance earned him a nice scratch under the chin.

After vacuuming Jimmy's room to ready it for the furniture deliverymen, I made my way back through rooms 1 through 9, where I took down the shower curtains and removed the dusty framed prints from the walls. The artwork featured enlarged photographs of local tourist spots.

One of the photos featured the Ryman Auditorium, a redbrick building built as a church but later repurposed as an entertainment venue. In the early 1900s, before women even had the right to vote, an industrious young widow named Lula Naff leased the space and scheduled shows, putting big names on the stage. She went on to manage the place for over three decades, to much success. Not only did she prove that women could have a good head for business, but she also brought the people of the city together, literally. One of the earliest entertainment venues to integrate, the auditorium served as the original home of the Grand Ole Opry. When the Opry moved to its new location, the Ryman fell into a state of disrepair. The iconic place had nearly been torn down a few decades earlier, but some dedicated people saved and restored it, and the auditorium now hosted a regular lineup of concerts and performances.

Another picture showcased the city's full-scale Parthenon replica, constructed in 1897 for the Tennessee Centennial Exposition in what was now known as Centennial Park. Another piece of artwork featured the Hermitage, former home of President Andrew Jackson, as well as hundreds of enslaved men, women, and children. "The Star-Spangled Banner" might have been named the national anthem during Andrew Jackson's reign as president, but the slaves at his home certainly weren't living in "the land of the free."

The final photograph portrayed Belle Meade Plantation, the historic home of a successful horse-breeding operation. Savvy builders installed gas chandeliers fueled by methane generated by the horses' poop. *Talk about polishing a turd.* While the prints had faded with time, someone might still be interested in them, or at least in the frames. I used a hand towel to wipe off the dust, then stacked the artwork outside so we could take it to a charity thrift store for donation.

I tried the door that connected Jimmy's room to Room 10, but found it locked from the other side. I stepped outside and walked over to the exterior door for Room 10. *Hmm.* The deadbolt was not engaged and the rusty doorknob hung loosely, the circular plate, or "rose," askew, revealing part of the hole behind it. With the handle off-kilter, the latch barely reached the strike plate and it took only a firm tug to open the door. Just as when Buck and I had opened the door to Jimmy's room earlier in the week, my eyes spotted a form on the bed. *Probably the old pillows tangled up in the bedding.* With the curtains drawn and the lights off, it was difficult to make out much. A lone cowboy boot lay on the floor at the end of the bed. *Who leaves a motel wearing only one boot? Hopalong Cassidy?*

I was about to step into the room when a squeal and the hiss of brakes sounded behind me. The delivery truck had pulled into the motel's parking lot. I closed the door and raised a hand in hello to the driver. He raised a hand back and unrolled his window. "Got your furniture." His gaze scanned the front of the motel. "Which room's it going in?"

I pointed to Jimmy's door. "The bedroom suite will go in Room Nine. The living and dining pieces can go in Room Eight."

He cut the engine and climbed down from the truck. His helper followed suit. In minutes, the bed was set up and ready to be made. The nightstand, lamp, and dresser were also in place. The mid-century-style headboard, nightstand, and dresser bore glossy white paint, and their legs were angled outward in the typical design of the time, as if the furniture were performing squats. Of course everything sat upon threadbare carpet for the time being, but we'd soon replace the worn carpeting with lightly stained hardwood flooring and a nice rug. Jimmy's room set up, the men proceeded to carry the other pieces into Room 8.

When one of the deliverymen reached out to remove the protective plastic covering, I put out a hand to stop him. "We'll remove the plastic later." Best to keep everything covered for now, to prevent dust from settling on it. I handed each of the men a tip, thanked them, and saw them out to their truck.

Once they'd gone, I returned to my SUV for the new bedding. I allowed Sawdust to explore Jimmy's room while I made his bed with the fresh sheets, pillows, and spread. The print was also a mid-century design, mustard-yellow diamond shapes against a bold turquoise backing. I stepped back to admire the look. *Not bad.* Of course we still had a long way to go before we'd have a model unit ready to show, but these touches had made a substantial difference already.

I looked down at my cat, who was curling himself around my ankles. "What do you think, boy?"

He responded by leaping up onto the bed and turning to announce his approval. *Meow.*

Two quick taps of a truck horn—*honk-honk*—let me know that Buck and Jimmy were back with the burritos. I headed outside, but not before ruffling Sawdust's ears and telling him, "Wait here, boy. I'll be back in a bit."

After rounding up drinks from the cooler we'd brought, Jimmy plopped back into the chair he'd been sitting on when we drove up this morning. Buck and I took seats on the concrete steps that led down into the empty pool.

"Head's up!" Buck called, tossing me a paper-wrapped burrito.

"Thanks, cuz." I unwrapped the crinkly paper and took a big bite. The burrito was the perfect blend of warm beans, savory spices, and fresh veggies. *Yum.* As I chewed, I gazed around the pool area, visualizing various ideas in my mind's eye. A vaulted pergola with built-in benches along the back and sides would provide both shade and a place for people to sit. Colorful string lights along the trim would provide both illumination and a party-like atmosphere. *Should the pergola be stained or painted?*

As I pondered paint versus stain, my eyes spotted what appeared to be a set of wide footprints approaching the green sludge that had accumulated around the clogged drain at the bottom of the pool. Oddly, they grew darker as they approached the sludge, disappearing into the puddle of muck. A wide smudge appeared between them. *That's weird.* Earlier, I'd pondered the seemingly ridiculous idea that the wrigglers could evolve into a swamp creature and emerge from the puddle. But had some type of equally ridiculous devolution occurred? Had a human disappeared into the slime?

I gestured to the bottom of the pool. "Does that look like footprints to y'all?"

"No," Buck said. "It looks like *shoe* prints."

I rolled my eyes. "They're the same thing."

Buck continued to needle me. "You're saying a foot and a shoe are the same thing? That's crazy."

Ignoring my cousin, I turned to Jimmy. "Did you walk down there, Jimmy?"

He leaned forward and looked down into the pool. "No. Wasn't me. Maybe whoever messed with the fence climbed into the pool."

"Could be skateboarders," Buck said. "They like to ride around in empty pools and do tricks and whatnot."

"But if someone had been skating down here, wouldn't there be wheel marks too?"

Buck shrugged. I supposed it didn't much matter who'd done it so long as they didn't do it again. Empty pools could be dangerous.

In the distance behind my cousin, a woman with long, pale blonde hair appeared on the pedestrian bridge, stopping in the center of the span and turning our way. Other than the football stadium, there wasn't much to see on this side of the Cumberland River. The real view was to the west. Maybe she was simply enjoying the breeze on her face, or maybe she was curious to see a rental truck and workers on site at the old motor court.

A cloud drifted by overhead, casting a shadow over her and drawing my eyes upward. *What a view.* The bridge and downtown skyline offered a sophisticated backdrop for the motel, and would definitely be a selling point once we were ready to market the units. When the outside was finished, we should take a photo from this angle to include in our promotions. Maybe even one photo taken in the daytime and one taken at night, when the colorful lights of SoBro would make the city sparkle.

We finished up our burritos and tossed the wrappers in a trash can we'd situated beside the pool. I angled my head to indicate Jimmy's room. "Come take a look, you two."

They followed me into Room 9. Sawdust stood up from the bed where he'd been sleeping and lifted his rear end in a deep stretch that approximated the yoga downward dog position.

Jimmy looked around, his head bobbing in approval. "Big improvement." He walked over and sat down on the bed next to Sawdust. Jimmy bounced a little to test the mattress, and the cat crouched instinctively to steady himself. Lying back onto the bed, the former seaman sighed in bliss. "I could get used to this."

"Get used to it later." Buck waved for us to follow him. "We need to get the rest of the furniture moved out and return the truck by five o'clock or we'll owe another day's rental fee."

Buck led the charge next door. I scooped Sawdust up off the bed and carried him along as I followed my cousin. As Buck entered the room, he spotted the errant boot that had caught my eye earlier. He picked it up, looking it over. "Where'd this come from? It's not dusty, so it can't have been here long."

I shrugged. "Must've been left by a vagrant."

"Doubt it," Buck said. "These are Luccheses. See?" He turned the boot so that I could see the telltale stamp on the sole. "This brand don't come cheap."

"Maybe the vagrant got them secondhand," I suggested.

"I suppose that's possible," Buck said, "but from the look of these I'd say they're near new."

"They're not the type of footwear worn for skateboarding either." *Exactly how many people have been traipsing about this motel?*

I carried Sawdust with me and set him down on the queen-sized bed where I could keep an eye on him while the men picked up the dresser. Once they'd crossed the threshold with the battered piece, I closed the door behind them and walked to the bed to gather up the bedding.

Sawdust had climbed atop the pile and was playing with something that stuck up from the blankets, batting it back and forth.

"What have you got there, boy?" I leaned in. To my surprise, a doorstop stuck up from the top of the covers, like a flagpole on a mountaintop. To Sawdust's dismay, the bedding around it prevented it from making the satisfying *boing*. But what was a doorstop doing in this pile of bedding? Had someone tossed the bedspread and sheets onto the floor and not realized the doorstop had been caught up in them when they picked them back up and piled them on the bed?

I reached and plucked the doorknob from the pile, surprised to feel some resistance before it came loose. A gummy, dark substance coated the screw on the end of the device. *What the . . . ?*

Apparently, Sawdust also had questions. He clawed

at the covers, pulling them back a few inches. Short, honey-brown curls appeared and, instinctively, I took a step back. *That's a stuffed animal, right? It has to be! A teddy bear, or maybe a play poodle.* But when Sawdust clawed the covers back farther to reveal a pale, pallid face, there was no denying it. A dead man lay on the bed, his blue-gray eyes seeming to stare at a water spot on the ceiling, his mouth hanging open as if in song.

CHAPTER 5

COVER UP

SAWDUST

This doorstop had been no fun at all. When Sawdust swatted at it, it didn't make the same funny *boinggg* as the other one that had been screwed into the wall. But here was something new to investigate. A person lay under the covers. Sawdust had uncovered his head. His skin was stiff and cool, not at all like Whitney's warm, soft body that Sawdust liked to curl up against in their bed when he slept.

He lowered his nose and sniffed at the man's face and hair. His sensitive nose detected smoke. He didn't like that smell. The house where he and Whitney lived had once caught on fire and he'd been terrified, not only by the smoke but by the demon on the ceiling that let out an earsplitting shriek. *BEEP-BEEP-BEEP!* No demon was shrieking now, though, and this smoke didn't smell fresh.

His cat curiosity got the better of him, and he had to see what else was under the sheets and blanket. He extended his claws and reached for the covers again.

CHAPTER 6

BODY OF EVIDENCE

WHITNEY

Horror wrapped its hands around my throat, choking off my scream. Sawdust clawed again at the bedcovers, pulling them back to reveal a light blue Western shirt with pearlescent buttons and musical notes embroidered in contrasting navy blue thread along the yoke. A small bloodstain darkened the snap-flap pocket.

The door opened behind me and I turned to Buck and Jimmy, opening my own mouth in a futile attempt to warn them of what they were about to see. But all that came out was a garbled cry. I circled my arm, pointing in the general direction of the bed.

Buck stepped forward first, staying a few feet back from the bed but stretching his neck out for a better look. "Holy sh—" He clasped a hand over his mouth in shock, effectively stifling himself.

Jimmy craned his neck to look too. "Is that a body in the bed?"

I nodded and he took an involuntarily step back. He grasped his hair in his fingers, as if trying to pull the image out of his head. His voice was high when he spoke again.

"Was he here while I was sleeping next door last night?"

"Must've been," I said softly, finally finding my voice.

Buck's eyes narrowed and he moved to the foot of the bed to get a better look. "I think I know this guy."

I gasped. "You do?"

Buck turned my way. "Not *know* him, know him. I mean I recognize him. I could be wrong, but I'm pretty sure this is Beckett Morgan. I saw him sing at Tootsie's a couple years ago, before he hit big and was still busking for tips."

"Beckett Morgan?" Jimmy's brows rose. "The guy who sings 'Party in the Pasture'?"

"You know the song?" Buck asked.

"Everybody knows that song. They play it on the country stations and the Southern rock stations too. You couldn't avoid hearing it even if you wanted to."

Jimmy had a point. The crossover hit had wide appeal, and Beckett's debut album had gone platinum in near-record time, even though the other songs on it were mediocre at best. That single song had made the singer a pretty penny. But what in the world would Beckett Morgan be doing here, at a seedy, shutdown motel? Of course, the man's identity and reason for being at the motel weren't nearly as important at the moment as summoning the authorities here to take charge of the situation.

I whipped my cell phone from my pocket and dialed 9-1-1. "My cat found a body," I told the dispatcher, my brain still discombobulated by the discovery. "We need help."

She asked for my location and dispatched an ambulance and police. After setting the wheels in motion, she asked whether the person could be alive. Though his color and rigidity told me there was no way he could still have any life left in him, I nonetheless motioned to Buck, pointing to the body in the bed and then pressing my free hand to my neck, silently directing him to check for a pulse. Cringing, Buck put his fingers to the guy's neck and held them there for a few seconds before looking back at me and shaking his head.

"No," I told the woman. "There's no pulse. He's stiff too." Not to mention he'd had a doorstop stuck in his chest.

The wail of a siren sounded in the distance, coming closer. Buck headed to the door. "I'll go out front and flag 'em down." Jimmy followed him.

After ending the call with emergency dispatch, I rounded up Sawdust and returned him to his carrier. My cat safely restrained, I called Detective Collin Flynn. Collin was a homicide investigator with the Nashville Police Department. We'd met on an earlier investigation. We were also currently dating, though it was much too soon to put a label on our relationship. At this point, we were like Jimmy, just seeing where things took us.

He answered on the third ring. "Hey, Whitney."

"Sawdust found another body."

There was a pause as Collin processed the information. "That cat's got a knack for uncovering corpses. Where are you?"

"At the motel."

"I'll be there ASAP."

I jabbed the button to end the call and slid my phone back into my pocket. By then, the ambulance was pulling into the motel. I carried my cat out front and stood by as Buck directed them to the room. Jimmy returned to his wooden chair, watching the paramedics hustle about, their movements quick and practiced as they slid from the back of the ambulance and grabbed their gear. Setting the carrier down next to me, I took a seat again on the edge of the pool, resting my feet on the top step. Buck joined me a moment later.

We watched through the open door of Room 10. In a repeat of Buck's earlier performance, the EMT felt for a pulse on the man's neck and found none. She confirmed her conclusion by sliding her stethoscope between two pearl buttons of his shirt and taking a quick listen. She looked to her male partner and shook her head.

She walked to the door and ran her gaze across the three of us. "Do y'all know the deceased?" After we'd indicated that we were not familiar with him, she said, "If you ask me, he looks a lot like Beckett Morgan. You know, the singer?"

Buck concurred. "I thought the same thing."

Jimmy leaned forward, resting his forearms on his knees. "What would a guy like Beckett Morgan be doing at a place like this?"

All Buck and I could do was shrug.

The EMT shrugged too. "Might just be a doppelgänger."

A Nashville PD cruiser pulled into the parking lot. At the wheel sat the dark-haired, dark-eyed Officer Hogarty, a no-nonsense woman who'd served as Detective Flynn's training officer back in the day. She never let him forget it either. Her similarly dark-haired but much younger female partner sat in the passenger seat. I'd met them months ago when I'd first met Collin. They climbed out of their cruiser and came over.

Hogarty pointed to Room 10. "Body in there?"

I nodded.

She and her partner stepped over to the door and peered through. Hogarty glanced back at me and Buck. "This victim is the spitting image of Beckett Morgan."

Buck let out a loud breath. "We're not so sure it isn't him."

"Beckett or not," she said, "the man's days of partying in a pasture are over." She instructed her partner to round up the cordon tape, and spread her arms as if shooing chickens as she stepped toward us. "We need to establish a perimeter. Move back past the fence." She turned and called to Jimmy. "You! In the chair! I need you to move outside the fence with Buck and Whitney."

He stood and gave her a salute. "Yes, ma'am."

She turned back to Buck and me. "Who's that?"

"Jimmy," I said, realizing I didn't yet know his last name and that I needed to get a W-9 form from him so I'd have his full moniker and social security number to report his earnings to the IRS.

"He work for you two?"

"He does," I said. "Started today."

She cut him a second glance before asking under her breath, "Where'd you find him?"

"Right here," I said. "At the motel."

"Squatting?"

Although I'd had the same thought when we'd first met him, I didn't like the way the term sounded now. I countered with, "Putting underutilized resources to use."

She frowned. "Uh-huh. That how he put it to you?"

"Yeah."

As Jimmy walked up to stand beside us, Officer Hogarty stepped up close to him and gave him a not-so-subtle once-over. Her cohort did the same, like an understudy learning her role. I had to admit, he looked a bit scraggly, what with the unkempt beard and wild hair. But heck, he was on an extended vacation. Lots of men took a break from shaving when they were on vacation. Besides, he'd had to wear his hair short and his face clean shaven all those years in the navy. No one could blame him for wanting to let his hair grow out for a change.

Hogarty jerked her head to indicate the room. "The motorcycle in there with the Florida plates. That yours?"

"Yes, ma'am," Jimmy said.

"What brings you up from the Sunshine State?"

He raised his hands to the sides, palms up. "Just taking a road trip to see America. I served my country in the Navy for two decades. Figured I ought to get to know her."

"Is that so?" Hogarty's tone was skeptical, but that was nothing unusual. She seemed to trust no one.

Our conversation was interrupted by Detective Flynn's arrival. He pulled up behind Hogarty's cruiser in his plain sedan. After climbing out, he headed straight for me and took me gently by the arm. "You all right, Whitney?"

I was anything but all right. I was rattled, shaken, and totally creeped out. Still, I was alive, which was more than we could say for the guy in Room 10. "I'll be okay."

Reassured, he nodded in greeting to Buck. I introduced him to Jimmy and the two shook hands. "Jimmy's been staying at the motel," I said. "We've hired him to help with some of the moving and cleanup."

Collin gave Jimmy a through once-over, too, though he was much subtler than Officer Hogarty had been. "Stick around. After I take a look at the room, I need to get some information from all of you."

He pulled a pair of latex gloves from his pocket and slid them on as he walked to the door. There, he whipped a pair of blue paper booties from his pocket as well, and slipped them on over his loafers. He spoke quietly with Officer Hogarty before disappearing into the room. He ventured back out a few minutes later and came over.

"Were you able to identify the victim?" While I felt awful for whoever lay in that bed, I knew it would be far worse for me and Buck if the man truly was the country-western superstar rather than a mere lookalike. Word would spread like wildfire that our motel was the sight of the singer's violent demise, and our plans to profit off the place could disappear just like his killer. It was a selfish thought, and I felt ashamed for thinking it, even if it were true.

Collin nodded. "I was."

Buck's brows shot up. "So is it Beckett? Not just a lookalike?"

"It's him. The ID in his wallet confirmed it."

Buck and I exchanged glances. He said out loud what I had the sense to keep to myself. "It would've been much better for us if the body had been a nobody."

I cut him an edgy look. "Nobody's a nobody, Buck."

"You know what I mean," he said. "Besides, you were thinking the same thing."

I couldn't deny it.

Collin attempted to allay our worries. "Police scanners have been encrypted for several years now, so civilians can't monitor our communications. Officer Hogarty and her partner know not to speak about an ongoing investigation, and the EMTs can be trusted to be discreet too. I'll do what I can to keep the location of Beckett's murder from being disclosed, but there's no guarantee. Information sometimes has a way of slipping out." He turned to Jimmy. "Speaking of ID, would you happen to have any on you?"

"Sure do." Jimmy pulled his wallet from the back pocket of his faded jeans and opened it, removing his Florida driver's license. He held it out to the detective.

Collin took the license and held it up, signaling Hogarty over. "Do your thing," was all he said, but it didn't take a genius to figure out he was asking her to run a background check on Jimmy, to see if he had a criminal record or any outstanding warrants. He pointed to where we were standing and addressed Jimmy. "Hang here. I need to talk to Buck and Whitney in private."

"Okay."

While Jimmy stood in wait as he'd been instructed, Collin led me and Buck far enough away that our conversation couldn't be overheard. Once we were out of earshot, he stopped, huddled close, and said, "I need to see what your security system caught."

I cringed. "It didn't catch anything."

"Why not?" Collin asked.

"Because we haven't installed it yet." I pointed to my SUV. "The components are in my cargo bay."

Collin exhaled sharply. "Haven't I advised you that security should be your top priority? Empty buildings attract crime."

It was true. Building sites tended to attract unsavory folks looking for materials or tools to steal, and empty structures made good places to conduct drug deals or dump bodies. Besides, after a murder victim had been found at an earlier house we flipped, the detective had admonished me that changing the locks and installing security systems should always be our first tasks.

Buck came to my defense. "This is the first day we've

put in any physical labor here. I planned to install the video cameras once we got the rooms cleared out. Time's ticking on the truck. Besides, we figured Jimmy staying here would be a deterrent."

That assumption turned out to be wrong in a big way.

"All right," Collin said, seeming to realize there was no point in further arguing the matter. "Tell me everything you know."

We filled him in on the day. When we'd arrived. How we'd found the outer fence bent and the pool gate completely off its hinges. The work we'd done. The body in the bed. The blueberry doughnut our temporary tenant had offered me.

He cut his eyes to Jimmy. "What do you know about Jimmy Weber?"

"Weber?" I repeated. "That's his last name, then."

Collin gaped. "You didn't even know his last name and you let him stay on your property?"

Buck scowled. "Well, when you say it like that . . ."

Collin had a point, but Buck and I had trusted our guts. I piled on, "It's not like we were staying here with him. We only see him during daylight hours. Besides, he's a veteran."

"That doesn't necessarily mean he's a good guy," Collin said. "He could have been dishonorably discharged, or maybe lying about his service to get on your good side. How do you even know he served? Got any proof?"

"Yes," I said. "He has a U.S. Navy tattoo on his chest."

He gaped a second time. "You've seen his bare chest?"

Buck came to my rescue. "We both did. He wasn't wearing a shirt when we found him in the bed in Room Nine earlier in the week."

"So he was trespassing," Collin said.

I told him the same thing I'd told Officer Hogarty, though I couched it in different terms. "The motel was just sitting vacant. He didn't see any harm in making use of one of the rooms for a few days."

Collin exhaled a loud breath. "You need to be more careful, Whitney."

I pointed to my cousin. "I've got Buck to protect me. I've also got this." I pulled out the large wrench I'd taken to carrying in my pocket and held it up. Some people defended themselves with a Remington or Winchester. I defended myself with a Craftsman.

Collin turned to Buck. "You need to be more careful too." Having finished chastising us, he asked how Jimmy had reacted to seeing the body in the bed.

I thought back, replaying the discovery in my mind. "Jimmy seemed just as surprised as we were."

"Was he the first to identify the deceased as Beckett Morgan?"

"Buck was first," I said, "but Jimmy knew who Beckett Morgan is." *Or was.*

"I'm curious that Weber was familiar with Beckett," Collin said. "Might mean he knew him somehow. With Mr. Weber staying here last night, it means he would have had an easy opportunity to kill Beckett too."

"But if Jimmy killed the guy," Buck asked, "why would he stick around? He's got to know that being at the scene would make him look guilty."

"True," Collin said. "But what would make him look even more guilty?" He tilted his head in question.

I ventured an answer. "Leaving the scene."

He pointed his ballpoint at me. "Bingo."

I thought out loud. "But even if Jimmy had the chance to kill Beckett, he'd also need a motive and the intent to kill." Dating a detective had taught me a few things.

"Why would Jimmy want to kill Beckett?" A good enough motive often gave rise to intent, but I simply didn't see why Jimmy would want the singer dead.

"Let's see what he might tell us." Collin turned to Jimmy, motioned with his hand, and called the guy over. "Mr. Weber! Come over here, please."

Jimmy saluted Collin, perhaps out of habit. "Yes, sir."

Once Jimmy had joined us, the detective launched into his interrogation. "Did you know Beckett Morgan?"

"Only from his songs," Jimmy said. "Didn't know him personally. Saw him on television once or twice. My mother likes country music. I saw photos of him on the covers of the tabloids, too, after he jilted Lacy Spurlock."

Before recording "Party in the Pasture," Beckett Morgan had recorded a love ballad with the popular female singer. "The Warmest Kiss" hadn't hit number one on the charts, but it had a respectable run and gave Beckett his first recording credit. The song had also led to rumors that the two singers were romantically involved—a shining star and a rising star, both bright. Beckett and Lacy had performed the duet live at the Country Music Awards show, which was televised. As the song concluded, Lacy leaned in for an impromptu, unscripted kiss. Beckett couldn't have jerked his head away any faster. When the live audience burst into gasps and nervous laughter, he seemed to realize he'd humiliated the star who'd given him a leg up, and he stepped forward to envelop her in a hug. It was too late, though. The damage had been done. The tabloids had a field day with the situation, milking it for all it was worth with headlines like "Spurned Spurlock Shamed on Stage," "No Warm Kiss for this Couple," and "Morgan Gives Spurlock the Cold Shoulder."

Collin asked Jimmy when he'd left Florida, where he'd stopped along the way, where he'd stayed and for how long, and what he'd done in each of the cities and towns. Jimmy provided an oral travel diary of his adventures, starting in Coral Springs, Florida, a month prior. He'd meandered along the Atlantic coast of the state, checking out the bars and beaches. He'd then ventured into Georgia, spending some time in Atlanta and nearby Stone Mountain, before venturing farther north to Amicalola Falls. His next major stop had been Chattanooga, and from there he'd rode his motorcycle through the scenic Smoky Mountains before heading west through Knoxville and then into Music City. It was like Gulliver's travels, minus the Lilliputians and Yahoos.

Collin made notes as Jimmy spoke. "How are you funding your travel?"

"Mostly from savings," Jimmy said. "I didn't earn a lot in the navy, but I didn't spend much either. Sent most of my paycheck home to my mother to help her pay her bills."

I cut Collin a look that said *See? He's a nice guy.*

Collin cut me one back that said *Don't believe everything you hear. This could all be made up.*

Jimmy continued. "I've done some odd jobs along the way to make a little bank." He gestured around the motel. "I got this gig here. I earned some cash back in Georgia helping a farmer clear some brush from his land. Helped a woman in Florida power wash the decks on her beach house."

"May I take a look at your arms?"

Jimmy raised his arms out in front of him, like a mummy on the prowl. "Look away."

Collin ran his eyes over the back and inside of

Jimmy's arms and hands before meeting his eyes again. "Whitney says you've got a navy tattoo?"

Before we knew what was happening, Jimmy had pulled his Hawaiian-print shirt up and over his head, and stood there, bare chested. I couldn't help but once again admire his muscled physique, and was unconsciously doing so until Collin cleared his throat, cutting me an annoyed and accusatory glare.

My face flamed, but I covered with, "See? There's the tattoo."

Collin returned his attention to Jimmy. "Where'd you serve?"

"Most recently, I was assigned to the destroyer USS *Mustin* as a maintenance engineer."

"Honorably discharged?"

"Yes, sir." He reached into his back pocket, pulled out his wallet again, and removed another card. "Here's my military ID if you'd like to see it." He held out a card that included a military seal and his photo. With his short buzz cut and no facial hair, the man in the photo was hardly recognizable as the same man who stood before us. I suppose my thoughts must have been written on my face, because he chuckled. "I clean up pretty good, don't I?"

Collin snapped pics of the front and back of the ID card. "Tell us what happened last night."

"Be happy to," Jimmy said, "though after my sixth whiskey things got a little hazy." He went on to tell us that he'd walked across the pedestrian bridge into So-Bro around seven o'clock, ate dinner at a brew house, and proceeded to bar hop up and down Broadway. "Left the last place around two o'clock or so, and took a walk along the waterfront, watched the river go by for a bit. Then I walked back across the bridge and came right back here, to the motel. I noticed the fence had been pushed back, but nobody was around and my bike seemed okay, so I figured either some drunks had fooled with the fence, or maybe the wind had caught one of the signs posted on the fence and pushed it back. The thing wasn't too sturdy to begin with. I went to my room, brushed my teeth, and went to bed. Slept like a dead man"—he cringed at his inadvertently poor choice of words—"until I woke up around nine this morning. Took a shower, rode my motorcycle to a doughnut shop, and came back here." He gestured to me and Buck. "These two showed up not long after, and I've been with them the rest of the day."

Collin asked, "Did you hear any noises from Room Ten last night?"

"No," Jimmy said, "but, like I said, I'm a heavy sleeper. Learned to be when I was in the navy. The bunks aren't spacious, and they aren't quiet either. There's a dozen guys around you, most of them snoring. The engines are loud too. I could sleep through a tornado."

"You said nobody was on the motel property when you returned," Collin said. "Did you see anyone after you came over the bridge?"

Jimmy looked up in thought. "There was one fella," he said. "We crossed paths at the corner." He pointed to the closest intersection a half block down. "Don't remember much about him, but he wore a shiny belt buckle. It caught the streetlight and got my attention. It had an animal footprint on it," He raised three curved fingers. "Like a bird claw."

"Did you two exchange words?"

"Maybe a 'hey,'" Jimmy said. "Can't say for sure. It was late and I was on autopilot."

"Did you see his face?"

"No. He was wearing a cowboy hat. With the way the light fell on him, it shaded his face."

"Was he white? Black? Latino?"

"White, I think." Jimmy shrugged. "But don't hold me to it. It was too dark to tell for sure."

"Tall? Short? Fat? Thin?"

Again, Jimmy shrugged. "He must not have been too much one way or the other or maybe I'd remember."

"Did he get into a vehicle?"

"Couldn't say. I just passed him and moved on, didn't look back."

"Were there any vehicles parked nearby?"

"Could have been," Jimmy said. "Don't know for certain."

"Have you seen the man around here before?"

"Don't think so."

The detective returned to something Jimmy had said earlier. "You said you had six whiskeys."

Jimmy nodded. "That's right. I know because I went to three different bars and had two at each place."

"That's a lot of alcohol."

Jimmy chuckled. "Tell me about it. The headache I had this morning told me it was too much, especially for a guy my age. I'm not that young sailor on shore leave anymore."

"Exactly how drunk were you when you came back to the motel last night?"

Jimmy snorted. "What you're really asking is whether I was drunk enough to kill someone and not remember it."

Collin owned up to it. "Pretty much, yeah."

"No," Jimmy said. "I wasn't that drunk. I didn't black out. Besides, I'm not an angry drunk. I'm a happy drunk. Ask anybody."

"All right," Collin said. "Who should I ask? Was anyone with you last night at the bars?"

"Not exactly," Jimmy said. "I flirted with a few ladies, but I didn't get any of their numbers."

"That's mighty convenient."

Jimmy didn't rise to the bait and merely shrugged rather than arguing.

Collin held his pen at the ready above his pad. "Which bars did you visit?"

"Well, shoot," Jimmy said. "I'd have paid more attention if I'd known there was going to be a quiz." He looked up in thought, scratching his head. "The first had a bunch of license plates on the wall. The next one had a bar made to look like a big horseshoe. I ended the night at that place with the rooftop bar."

Collin frowned. "Half of the places on SoBro have rooftop bars."

It was true. When all of them were in full swing, it sounded like a battle of the bands taking place over your head as you walked down the street.

"That last one was next to a boot shop. That should narrow it down, shouldn't it?"

"Not really," Collin said. "There are several boot shops along that stretch of Broadway."

Jimmy rubbed his chin as he tried to remember more details. "I think it was owned by a singer. That help?"

"Again, no," Collin said, irritation in his voice. "Jason Aldean and Dierks Bentley both own places on SoBro."

Jimmy rubbed his chin again before raising his index finger in the air. "Ah! I remember it was next to a karaoke place. I went by on the sidewalk and heard someone caterwauling inside. I wondered how in the world they'd gotten a gig with that voice. That's when I noticed a sign in the window saying it was a karaoke bar and I realized the person singing wasn't a professional."

"All right," Collin said. "That should narrow it down."

Officer Hogarty stepped over with Jimmy's driver's license. She cast the man a glance before handing the card to the detective. "He's clean."

"Thanks." Collin photographed the front and back of Jimmy's license before returning it to him. "What's your cell number?" Collin jotted it down as Jimmy rattled it off. "Stick around town a few days," Collin told him. "We might have some follow-up questions."

"Can I stay in my room here?"

"That's up to Whitney and Buck. We'll need a few hours to process the scene, but we should be done by evening."

Jimmy looked to Buck and me. We both nodded. I was 99% sure Jimmy wasn't guilty, but it was still a possibility. Maybe he had totally screwed us over by killing a celebrity at our motel. But how could we find out? An adage came to mind: Keep your friends close and your enemies closer.

CHAPTER 7

IFS, ANDS, AND BUTTS

WHITNEY

A crime scene van arrived a few minutes later and erected plastic curtains around the perimeter of the property so nobody could see exactly what was going on at the motel, including me, Buck, and Jimmy. Buck called the truck rental company and extended the lease for another day, blowing that line item on our meticulously prepared budget.

Collin effectively but politely told us to get lost. "No need for y'all to stick around right now. I'll text Whitney when we're done here."

With several hours to kill—*ugh, bad choice of words*—Buck, Jimmy, and I decided to go to the home improvement store and order the materials we'd need to finish the interior of the spec unit. At some point, I'd have to call my parents and let them know what had happened, but I'd wait to see what Collin and the crime scene team found out first. If they could determine right away who had ended Beckett's life and make a quick arrest, it would be much easier. If the killer was not identified and caught, my parents would worry. I'd hate to put them through that.

We swung by my house first so I could drop off Sawdust. The driveway was empty, my roommates elsewhere, probably running the usual weekend errands. While Jimmy and Buck waited in my SUV, I carried Sawdust inside. Cleo peeked out from under the couch. When she realized her best buddy was back home, she bolted out from under it, rushing over to pounce on Sawdust as he emerged from his carrier. He played along, flopping over onto his side as if her teeny, tiny tackle had taken him down. Sawdust was nothing if not a good sport. I ruffled their ears. "Behave, you two."

I returned to my SUV and we aimed for the store. I'd taken measurements earlier in the week and roughed out a sketch for the spec unit. The plan was to turn each pair of adjoining motel rooms into a two-room condominium. One of the adjoining rooms would remain a large bedroom with a bathroom. The other room would be gutted and reconfigured as a combination living room and kitchen.

We walked into the store and stepped aside so I could show them the sketch in my notebook. I pointed to the kitchen area at the rear of the room. "We'll arrange the kitchen in a U shape to make it easily accessible, and leave the center open for a dining table." While colored appliances were the rage back then, a mid-century style could be achieved with neutral white appliances featuring the rounded edges popular in the period. Shiny white subway tiles would create an eye-pleasing backsplash, while speckled white quartz countertops and flat-front cabinets in a bold paint would complete the look. The spaces would be lit by hanging chrome lights in a funky starburst design. "To unite the rooms, we'll use the same flooring throughout. I'm thinking hardwood stained light gray and laid in a herringbone pattern."

I showed Buck and Jimmy the pages I'd created with ideas and photos of kitchens I'd found in magazines and online, and we selected materials that would fit the bill, choosing the least expensive options that would achieve the desired look.

Once we'd placed orders for the larger materials, including the security doors and windows, we headed to the paint section. I looked over the sample cards, and selected several possibilities for the cabinets. "What colors do you two like best?"

My sample cards contained various vivid shades of orange, pink, blue, and green. No shy pastels here.

Jimmy ran his gaze over the samples. "So, basically, we're picking a color of sherbet?"

I couldn't deny he had a point. "These were common colors in the fifties and sixties."

After some debate, we chose lime green for the kitchen and turquoise for the bathroom to match the bedding we'd already bought. We'd paint the walls a neutral gray and place colorful accent pieces about to bring out the colors.

Buck gestured to the paint samples. "What about the exterior?"

"Let's lean in," I said. "We can use all of these colors outside." I pointed to three especially bright shades of orange, blue, and pink.

Buck's lip quirked. "Won't that look tacky?"

"It'll be authentically kitschy," I said. "We want this place to look different. That's the whole point."

He acquiesced. It didn't mean he agreed with me, though. It only meant he knew paint was relatively inexpensive and that we could repaint the place in more neutral shades if it ended up looking like a cheesy Vegas casino or beachfront souvenir shop.

As we left the store three hours later, I checked my phone. The detective still hadn't texted to say they were done. I looked up at Buck and Jimmy. "How about dinner?"

"I could eat," Buck said. "Call Colette. See if she wants to join us."

My best friend and roommate, Colette Chevalier, was a chef at the Capitol Grille in the fancy Hermitage Hotel downtown. While she often worked on the weekends, she had tonight off. "How'd you know she wasn't working tonight?"

He shrugged. "She must have mentioned it."

"When?"

He shrugged again.

I narrowed my eyes at him. I'd suspected for a while now that my cousin and my best friend shared a mutual attraction, yet neither had openly acknowledged their feelings. Maybe they didn't want to put me in the middle and make things awkward if the attraction was one-sided or short-lived. With Buck being my cousin and business partner, and Colette being my best friend and roommate, there'd be no way for them to avoid each other later if things didn't work out. But it was ridiculous for the two of them to keep dancing around like this. I put Buck on the spot. "You've got a thing for her, don't you?"

Buck frowned. "I'm just being nice. She works hard cooking for other people all the time. Only seems right she gets a night off now and then when someone else cooks for her."

Jimmy snorted. "Dude. I barely know you and I can see right through that BS."

Buck cut him an edgy look. "You want to find another place to sleep tonight?"

Jimmy raised his palms in surrender. "All right, bro. I must've been mistaken."

Whether Buck had feelings for my friend or not, his suggestion was a good one. With our busy schedules, Colette and I hardly ever saw each other, despite living in the same house. We were the proverbial ships passing in the night. I pulled out my phone and called Colette. "Buck, Jimmy, and I are going to dinner. Why don't you join us?"

"I'd love to," she said. "Where are you headed?"

"Where would you suggest?" I asked. Being in the restaurant business, she always knew the best places to eat or new eateries to try, and she always knew just what to order from the menus too.

"Has Jimmy been to Puckett's?" she asked.

Puckett's Grocery and Restaurant was designed to look like a general store, after the original location of the same name in a little town nearby called Leipers Fork. The place was popular with both locals and tourists alike, and a great place for good old-fashioned Southern cooking. I asked Jimmy whether he'd tried the place yet. When he said no, that sealed the deal.

"See you in thirty," I said.

As usual on Saturday evenings, there was a line waiting for tables at Puckett's. Buck spoke to the hostess and had her put us on the list, and we waited outside for Colette. A light breeze kept things pleasant. Country-western music wafted through the doors each time they opened. A few minutes later, we saw my friend walking up Church Street. Buck and I raised our arms and waved.

Dressed in a ruffled light blue sundress and girlie sandals, Colette put my jeans and tee to shame. Her dark curls were pulled up in an adorably messy pile atop her head, though one had broken free and hung down by her left ear, bouncing with each step. Once she'd reached us and Buck and I had greeted her with a fist bump and a hug respectively, I introduced her to Jimmy.

"Wow." He held out his hand. "You look like you stepped right off the screen of a rom-com."

She laughed, taking it as the compliment it was intended to be. Buck, on the other hand, scowled.

I leaned toward her and whispered, "Guess what."

"Don't tell me Sawdust found another body." She grinned at her joke until she saw my face, then hers fell as well. She repeated her words, but in a tentative, anxious tone. "Don't tell me Sawdust found another body."

I looked around to see who might be listening, but the others waiting seemed engrossed in their own conversations. Still, I cupped my hand around her ear, as if playing the telephone game. "It's Beckett Morgan."

She gasped, pulled her head back, and mouthed *Beckett Morgan?* "Are you freaking kidding me right now?"

"I wish I were."

"Please." She held up a hand. "No details until I've had a glass of wine."

Colette had always shied away from horror movies and novels. Though she handled raw meat on a regular basis on the job, she had little tolerance for human gore.

"Buck?" called the hostess, standing on tiptoes as she scanned the crowd.

Buck raised a finger to signal her. "That's us." He put a hand possessively on Colette's lower back to guide her inside.

Behind them, Jimmy eyed Buck's hand before turning to me, a smug smile on his lips. "I called it."

"Yeah, you did." The only question now was, when would one of them be brave enough to act on their feelings? I wasn't sure if I should encourage either of them. What if the feelings were unreciprocated? I'd make either my cousin or my roommate feel uncomfortable. Did I even want them to be together? Part of me was selfish, realizing that I'd likely see less of my friend if they started dating. But another part of me realized the two of them together could be perfect. They were complementary in many ways. Colette liked to cook, while Buck like to eat. Colette collected kitchen tools, while Buck collected hand tools. Colette could be tentative, averse to change, while Buck was braver, took more chances. Besides, if they ended up together, she'd be officially part of my family, my cousin-in-law. We'd get to spend some of the holidays together for a change. I'd love that.

Once we'd been seated and a round of drinks had been served, Colette swallowed a big gulp of wine and set her glass back on the table. She leaned in. "Okay. I'm ready now."

In hushed tones, I told her about Sawdust jumping up on the bed and toying with the doorstop that was stuck in the man's chest. When she recoiled in shock, Buck reached out and put a reassuring hand on her shoulder.

I continued to fill her in. "Sawdust pawed at the covers and pulled them back. The last thing I'd expected was to see a face looking up at me."

She shuddered involuntarily just as Beckett's big hit began to play from the speakers overhead. The lyrics were campy and nonsensical, but that was part of the song's charm.

It might be past your bedtime,
You might be past your prime,
You might have passed your exams or passed a
    kidney stone,
You might have passed some tears,
You might be passed a beer,
But it's always the right time for a party in the
    pasture.
Grab your boots,
It'll be a hoot!
You might be past your limit,
Past your curfew,
Past your expiration date,
Past your quota,
Past your comfort zone,
But just put on your blue jeans,
It'll be past your wildest dreams.
There's never a wrong time for a party in the
    pasture.
Grab your boots,
It'll be a hoot!
Girl, I can't see past your eyes,
Let's get pasture-ized,
Baby, please just listen,
It's not past your comprehension,
It's a party in the pasture.

Buck, Jimmy, Colette, and I exchanged glances, each
of us cringing, especially when the song came to the line
about being "past your expiration date."

We didn't speak throughout the song, remaining
respectfully and collectively silent in implied agreement.

When the song was over, Colette said, "Do they have any suspects?"

Jimmy scoffed. "Just me."

"You?" Colette's eyes widened. "Why?"

"Because I slept at the motel last night," Jimmy said. "I'm not worried, though. They'll clear me, eventually. I didn't know Beckett Morgan. Why reason would I have had to end his life?"

Turning to more pleasant matters, I said, "When I was taking the bed frames apart this morning, I got an idea. What if we held a grand-opening celebration to launch the sale of units at the motel? We could invite realtors, potential buyers, maybe the media. We could take bids on the units afterward."

Buck concurred it was a smart idea. "If we had a good turnout, it might drive the prices up."

Higher prices meant higher profits, not only for us, but for our silent partner Presley, as well. *Oh my gosh.* I'd totally forgotten about Presley! I'd have to tell her about Beckett before the news broke. *Ugh.* I dreaded the task. In the meantime, I turned to Colette and made a proposition. "How would you like to provide the hors d'oeuvres for the grand opening? We'd pay you for expenses plus a catering fee."

Working as a chef where she prepared someone else's dishes night after night didn't quite satisfy my friend's creative culinary ambitions. Colette also loved preparing foods for our social events, and took an occasional small catering gig for extra income. She always came up with the perfect menu.

"I'd love to!" She tapped a finger to her chin, the wheels in her head already turning. "You know what would be perfect? Appetizers from the same time period as the motel. Back in the fifties and sixties, they were big on anything you could skewer or stick a toothpick in. Stuffed tomatoes and peppers. Dips and spreads. I've got a hundred ideas already."

The server arrived with our food then. Good thing, because Colette's talk about appetizers had made me hungry.

Over dinner, Jimmy regaled us with tales of his years in the navy, from harrowing stories of storms at sea to amusing anecdotes about various ports of call. He'd seen the northern lights from the ship, as well as various forms of sea life in their natural habitats, including whales, dolphins, and sharks. "I saw a mermaid once too. She surfaced, gave me a wink, and disappeared."

"Let me guess," Buck said, his head cocked in skepticism. "That was after you'd gone bar hopping in Tokyo?"

"All that hot Japanese sake had nothing to do with it," Jimmy said. "I know a mermaid when I see one."

Colette, naturally, grilled him about the foods he'd eaten as he traveled the globe. While he couldn't quite stomach the dinuguan, or blood soup, that many ate in the Philippines, he enjoyed their fried noodles known as pancit guisado. He'd also tried a delicious Egyptian lentil and rice dish called koshari, though he'd discovered it at a café in the United Arab Emirates.

When we'd finished our meal, Buck grabbed the check. "We talked about the motel and made plans for the grand opening. That makes this a deductible business dinner, doesn't it?"

"Heck, yeah," I said. We'd need all the deductions we could get.

We walked Colette back to her car before returning to

my SUV. As I slid behind the wheel, my phone pinged with an incoming text from Collin. *We've cleared the scene. Have questions for the three of you.*

After texting the detective to let him know we were on our way, I drove us back to the motel. The construction debris now littering the ground around the bin told me they'd dug through it looking for evidence. The cordon tape and temporary curtains had been removed, along with the pool gate, and the crime scene van had gone. Officer Hogarty's partner was gone, too, her shift completed, though Hogarty still hung around. It was unclear whether she was merely being nosy or Collin had asked her to stay. I feared it might be the latter, that he expected to make an arrest shortly and wanted backup on site. *Has he found some concrete evidence to implicate Jimmy in Beckett Morgan's murder?*

After we climbed out of my SUV, Collin walked over. Hogarty stepped up beside him, holding a small nylon duffel bag printed with the blue and gold Metro Police logo. The zipper was open. Collin addressed Jimmy. "Just a few follow-up questions, Mr. Weber."

"All right," Jimmy said.

"Do you smoke?" Collin asked.

"No," Jimmy said.

"So you haven't smoked any cigarettes or cigars here at the motel?"

"No," Jimmy said. "I've tried cigarettes a few times, a cigar once or twice, even smoked something that maybe wasn't a hundred-percent legal when I was a dumb kid. But have I smoked recently? Here? No. You thinking that cigar butt that was by the pool might be a clue?"

"You noticed it?" Collin asked.

"Yeah," Jimmy said. "Didn't think much about it,

though. Just figured someone walking by had tossed it.
People treat this place like a garbage can."

It was true. Cigarette butts, food wrappers, aluminum
cans, and broken beer bottles lay all about the motel
property. Or at least they had this morning. The parking lot was much cleaner now, some of the trash apparently seized as potential evidence.

Collin reached into the duffel bag Officer Hogarty
was holding and pulled out the cigar butt enclosed in
a clear evidence bag. "Is this the cigar you saw?" The
cigar butt included a gold and black band with red lettering and a gold fleur de lis.

Jimmy eyed the bag. "Looks like the same one, but I
didn't pay it much mind."

"You said you didn't smoke it, but did you touch it
at any point?"

"No," Jimmy said. "Didn't bother picking it up
because I figured we'd be sweeping up the parking lot
once we finished with the rooms."

"Did you notice any other cigars or cigar butts
around?"

"Not here at the motel, no. There's always a few
around the store down there." He pointed to the Poison
Emporium down the street. "They sell all sorts of cigars. Got a humidor and everything."

"Good to know." Collin dropped the cigar back into
the duffel bag and gestured to the wooden chair Jimmy
had placed beside the swimming pool. "I see you
brought a chair out here. Did you get into the pool at any
time since you arrived here?"

"No." Jimmy's forehead bunched. "Why would I?
There's no water in it."

Rather than answer Jimmy's question, Collin moved
on. "You mentioned that you noticed the fence was

pushed back when you returned to the motel last night. Were any of your things missing from your room?"

"Not that I've noticed," Jimmy said. "I didn't have much to begin with, and nothing was worth much. I don't take anything valuable on the road."

"Other than your motorcycle."

"Well, yeah." Jimmy's tone implied a distinct *duh*.

Unfazed, Collin said, "It's a nice bike."

Jimmy glowered, realizing the statement could be a backhanded compliment, an implication that maybe he'd killed someone to defend his property. "There's nicer."

"Sure," Collin said. "But it would be understandable if you came across a guy out here last night, thought he was coming for your bike, and the two of you got into an altercation."

"It might be understandable," Jimmy said, "but it didn't happen."

Collin kept on, undeterred. "Cooperation, a confession. They can go a long way in getting a suspect a reduced sentence. The prison sentence for involuntary manslaughter can be as short as one year, even less in a plea bargain. If you want to come clean, it's one of those better-sooner-than-later scenarios. The more time law enforcement has to put into this case, the less likely we'll be to go easy on you."

Jimmy's jaw flexed, his whiskers bristling. "I'm not going to confess to something I didn't do."

The two men stared each other down for a long moment, as if performing some type of Jedi mind trick.

The detective finally broke the silence. "All right if Officer Hogarty takes your prints? That way we'll be able to identify them if they show up on anything we dusted."

Jimmy lifted a shoulder. "Fine with me."

Hogarty pulled an ink pad and a stiff paper card from

a plastic box sitting atop the closed trunk of her cruiser. She motioned Jimmy over and proceeded to take his prints, rolling his fingers on the ink pad prior to repeating the motion on the card. When she was done, she handed him a wet wipe to clean his hand.

"All right," Collin said. "We're done here." He turned to Buck. "Need some help getting that fencing back in place?"

"I'd appreciate it," Buck said.

We moved the cars from the parking lot onto the street, leaving the moving van in the lot. The three men wrangled the bent fencing back into place as best they could. Once Jimmy had ducked back through, they sealed the fence with zip ties.

Through one of the links in the fence, Buck handed Jimmy a pair of needle-nose pliers and more zip ties. "If you need to get out, you can use the pliers to cut through the plastic, then resecure the fence with the ties."

"Take this." Collin handed Jimmy his business card and gave the man a pointed look. "Don't leave town without checking with me first."

Jimmy chuckled. "Grounded, huh? You sound just like my dad back when I was in high school." When he saw the pointed look on Collin's face, he changed his tune a bit. "Don't worry. I won't skip town."

Buck and I bade Jimmy goodbye, and he headed back to his room.

Now that Jimmy was gone, Collin jerked his head to indicate his car. "We need to have a private discussion."

Officer Hogarty slid into the passenger seat, while Buck and I climbed into the back.

Over the next few minutes, Collin gave us a quick rundown of the evidence they'd collected and the conclusions they'd reached. "We won't have the autopsy results for a few days, but based on what we saw here today, it looks like Beckett suffered a severe closed-head injury. We didn't find any sort of weapon on site that might have been used to bludgeon him, but we noticed a green substance on the back of his shirt and pants. The footprints and the wide smudge in the bottom of the swimming pool tell me someone knocked Beckett backward into it, then went down into the pool to drag him out."

A-ha! That explained the odd footprints. The person wasn't walking *into* the sludge, they were *backing out* of it. Beckett being dragged also explained how his boot had fallen off in Room 10.

"Could you get any information from the footprints?" I asked. "Maybe a shoe size?"

"No," Collin said. "The person had dragged their feet, so it's impossible to pinpoint a size. The shape of the most discernable prints make it look like the person was wearing boots, though. There's a space between the ball of the foot and the heel. We found another cigar butt in the sludge. Same brand. Could be trash that rolled into the pool or got tossed into it, or it could be a clue. Can't tell at this point. Anyway, the address on Beckett's license was for a high-rise in the Gulch. His car is still parked in the garage there, so he either walked here or someone else gave him a ride."

My gaze moved to the pedestrian bridge in the distance. "If he walked here, he would have come over the bridge."

"Looks that way," Collin concurred. "According to his tour schedule on his website, he played a gig at the Ryman Auditorium last night. Warmed up for Armadillo Uprising."

I was familiar with the band. They'd started as

the musicians and backup singers for another young superstar named Brazos Rivers. After Brazos had been sent to jail for tax evasion a few years back, they'd regrouped, appointed a new lead singer, and been reborn as Armadillo Uprising. True to their name, they'd been rising up the charts ever since.

Collin reached into the duffel bag lying on the console between him and Officer Hogarty. He pulled out a clear evidence bag that contained a mobile phone and held it up. "Beckett's phone was in the sludge too. It's still running, which was a surprise. Only problem is the screen's shattered, probably from his fall, and it's got a fingerprint lock. I tried, but couldn't get it to open."

In other words, he'd used the dead man's stiff finger in an attempt to open the device. The thought sent an icy spike up my spine, and I shivered involuntarily.

Collin dropped the phone back into the duffel. "I'll see what the lab can do. Maybe they can put a new screen on it, get it open so I can check his call history. I can get the information from the phone company if I have to, but that always takes longer. We'll also canvass the area, see if anyone saw anything, talk to Beckett's family and friends, take a look at video footage from the businesses nearby. I'll let you two know what I find."

I put my hand on the door handle, preparing to climb out. "Anything Buck and I can do?"

"Yeah." Collin gave me a pointed look. "You can be careful around Jimmy Weber."

CHAPTER 8

YOUR ATTENTION, PLEASE

SAWDUST

Sawdust was sitting atop his cat tree late that evening when he saw Whitney pull her car into the driveway. *Hooray! She's home!* He climbed down from the carpet-covered perch to meet her at the door. It had only been a few hours since she'd brought him back home, but that was at least eleven cat naps ago and felt like forever.

The door opened and Whitney stepped inside, carrying her noisy toolbox with her. It jingled and jangled as she turned to close the door behind her and set it down on the floor. "Hey, boy." She reached down and gave him first a scratch behind the ears and, when he turned his head and leaned into her hand, a nice scratch under his cheek. *Aaaaah.*

Colette and Emmalee came out of their rooms and the three women took seats on the living room furniture, talking in tones that varied from hushed near-whispers to loud exclamations. He had no idea what the three were talking about, he only knew he was being totally ignored. *How could Whitney be so cruel?*

The two felines exchanged glances. Cleo was being ignored by Emmalee too. The situation called for desperate measures.

Cleo followed him as he went over to the couch and rubbed himself along Whitney's ankles. When that got him nothing, he forced his way between Whitney's calves and the sofa behind them. Whitney hardly seemed to notice. She just kept on talking to the other humans. *What topic of conversation could possibly be more important than her cat?* He leaped up onto the sofa beside her. Cleo was still too little to jump so high. She reached up and dug her claws into the fabric in an attempt to climb it.

Atop the couch, Sawdust mewed and nudged Whitney's hand, but instead of petting him with it, she reached out and picked up a tall glass from the coffee table. It was one of those glasses with the flat circular bottom, a skinny middle, and a wider cup on top to hold the liquid. Sawdust knew from experience that those types of glasses were easy to knock over, much easier than a shorter, sturdier glass.

As Whitney took a sip, he realized he had to escalate matters. He went for a DEFCON 4 maneuver and headbutted her elbow. She cried out as the red liquid in her glass spilled onto her chest. He felt sorry for upsetting Whitney, but at least he had her attention now. She set her glass back down on the coffee table. *Good. Surely she'll pet me now.*

Except she didn't. Instead, she picked him up and set him back down on the floor, breaking his heart and wounding his pride. *How could she reject him like this?*

Cleopatra looked over at him from where she hung

on the couch. The pity in her eyes was too much for him to bear.

Whitney was normally an attentive and affectionate kitty mommy. Sawdust had never activated DEFCON 1, intentionally biting Whitney to teach her a lesson, and he'd rarely had to go to DEFCON 2, raking his claws over her skin. But tonight was an exceptional night. He prepared for a DEFCON 3 move. Still, maybe he could get her attention by merely threatening the action rather than doing it.

He gracefully hopped up onto the coffee table, swishing his tail to catch her eye, but still Whitney's attention was on the other women rather than him. *Swish-swish.* He took a step closer to her glass, then another. *Swish-swish.* Still no response. He'd have to do it.

He raised his paw and looked at Whitney. *Hello? See what I'm doing here? Aren't you going to stop me by picking me up and petting me on your lap? Hello?*

But she didn't stop him. He stretched out his paw and gave her glass a gentle tap.

Clink.

The glass fell over, the liquid spilling out and running over the edge of the table and onto the rug.

"Sawdust!" Whitney stood, righted the glass, and shook a finger at him. "Naughty boy!"

He followed her as she gathered up a dish towel from the kitchen and returned to wipe down the table and blot the rug. When she finished, she tossed the towel onto the table and finally picked him up, setting him on her lap and running a hand over his back. Whitney was nothing if not forgiving. He started his motor and purred in appreciation.

CHAPTER 9

THE BOYS IN THE BAND

WHITNEY

In the early afternoon on Sunday, I took a deep breath to steel myself, then called Presley to share the dreadful discovery. "I have something bad to tell you," I said in an attempt to prepare her for the blow I was about to deliver. "We found a body in one of the rooms at the motel."

She hesitated a moment before asking, "A *dead* body?" She likely already knew the answer to her question. Nobody refers to a living human being as a "body."

"Yes," I said. "Unfortunately, it's going to be big news. The person we found was Beckett Morgan."

She gasped. "The 'Party in the Pasture' guy?"

"That's the one."

Needless to say, she was both shocked and distressed. "What happened? Was it an accident? An overdose? He didn't take his own life, did he?"

"He was murdered." I'd spare her the details. Heck,

I wished I could forget that bloody doorstop and the vacant look in Beckett's eyes, his lone boot lying on the floor.

"Oh, my gosh!" She paused, as if processing the information. "Do they know who did it?"

"Not yet. The police are working on it." *So am I.* My efforts had been instrumental in resolving earlier investigations. Maybe they'd be useful again. I didn't just build homes, I also built cases. Collin was a crackerjack detective, but who couldn't use some help?

"Is it safe for you and your cousin to keep working on the motel?"

It was nice of Presley to be worried, especially when she must surely be regretting going into business with us. "We're taking precautions."

She sighed. "Beckett's fans will be so upset when they find out he's gone."

"For sure."

"I hate to say this," she said, "but this is going to seriously cut into the property value."

I couldn't deny it was a distinct possibility, but I was trying my best to be optimistic. "It will," I said, "if word gets out that he was killed at the motel. The detective working the case said he'd try to keep the site where Beckett was found under wraps."

"Good luck with that. All it would take is one person with loose lips and the news will spread like wildfire." She had a point. The ease of communication on the Internet was both a blessing and a curse. "I could lose every penny I invested in that place, couldn't I?"

Knowing she'd been saving up for years to invest in her first property, I felt my guts wriggle in guilt. "Buck and I will do everything we can to prevent that from

happening. We put all the money we have into the motel too."

While she'd have every reason to turn on my cousin
and me then, she didn't. "We're in this together. I might
have resented you before, but I saw how hard you
worked. I wouldn't have gone in with you if I didn't
trust you. I know you'll do what you can to protect our
investment."

I appreciated her vote of confidence. "I was thinking we should hold a grand opening celebration once the
first unit is complete. We could invite realtors and potential buyers, let them see the place and tour the spec
unit. It could generate interest, maybe even drive the
prices up. My roommate's a professional chef. She's
agreed to make appetizers for the event."

"Those appetizers will have to be darn good if they're
going to make people forget a murder took place at the
motel. But I agree. An open house is a good idea."

I promised to keep her informed of any progress in
the investigation. When we ended our call, I took another deep breath to steel myself and called my parents.

"Hi, hon!" Mom said. "I'm going to put you on
speaker so Dad can hear you too."

After exchanging the usual preliminaries, I said, "A
body turned up in one of the motel rooms."

"Whitney!" my mother snapped. "That's not funny."

"Believe me, Mom,"—my voice quavered with emotion—"I know it's not."

She gasped. "You're serious? Again?"

"Yes." Empty buildings tended to attract crime,
sometimes violent crime. Beckett wasn't the first body
we'd found. After swearing them to secrecy, I said, "It's
Beckett Morgan."

"Beckett Morgan?" my father said. "Now where do I know that name from?"

"The radio," my mother said before I could fill him in. "He's the boy who sings that 'Party in the Pasture' song."

It said a lot that my parents knew his name. They rarely got their pop culture references right. Not that I blamed them. They had their own favorite singers and bands, mostly the ones they'd enjoyed in their younger days who were still making music.

"I know that one," Dad said, "That song comes over the speakers a half dozen times a day, at least."

My father was an otolaryngologist, and my mother assisted on a part-time basis at office. Like most businesses in the city, they played country music radio over the speakers in their office. The tunes helped keep the patients' minds off the pain in their ears, noses, and throats.

"Collin's working the case," I told them. "We're hoping he'll sort things out soon."

"I sure hope so," Mom said. "In the meantime—"

"I know, I know," I said. "Be careful. Watch my back. Keep my wrench handy."

"Exactly," my parents said in unison.

The bad news delivered, I kissed Sawdust on the head and told him to look after Cleo while Mommy went to work for a bit. Shortly thereafter, as I approached the turn to the motel in my SUV, my eyes spotted someone standing alone at the rail near the eastern end of the pedestrian bridge. The woman had long corn silk–blonde hair pulled into a braid and wore a black dress. *Is she the same woman I saw yesterday?* Could be. Then again, lots of people used the bridge and identifying anyone from this distance would be nearly impossible.

I pulled into the motel to find that my cousin had beat me there. Buck's van was parked next to the moving truck.

"About time you showed up!" he called as I climbed out of my SUV.

"A woman needs her beauty sleep," I said in my defense.

"Looks like you should have stayed in bed a few hours longer, then," he teased.

Buck, Jimmy, and I spent the afternoon clearing the rest of the rooms, but only after first installing the security system. We placed cameras under the eaves at either end of the L-shaped building, with six more cameras situated over the doors to the odd-numbered rooms. We also put a camera over the double doors to the lobby, which was positioned in the right angle formed by the legs of the L-shaped structure. When we finished, I texted photos of the cameras to Collin, along with the login details so that he could access the feeds online. He replied with a thumbs-up icon.

Thankfully, the bloodstained bedding that had covered Beckett Morgan had been taken as evidence, so we didn't have to deal with that. Even so, the three of us were sufficiently creeped out when we disassembled the queen-sized bed that Beckett had died in.

Though I hated to bring up an uncomfortable subject, I felt that Collin's accusations had to be addressed. I eyed Jimmy as I handed him a dusty lamp. "Thanks for giving the police your fingerprints last night. That will help Detective Flynn move things along. He's a fair guy who just wants to get to the truth. I hope you know he was just doing his job."

"It's difficult not to take being accused of murder personally," Jimmy said, "but I supposed if I were in his place, I'd suspect me too."

"So no hard feelings?"

"No hard feelings."

By half past six, the rooms were emptied and ready for demolition. As Buck and I packed up our tools, a news report came over his radio, announcing the "unexpected death of popular singer Beckett Morgan." The deejay went on to say that the death had been deemed suspicious and a police investigation was underway.

When the next song cued up, Buck turned the radio off. "At least they didn't say where it happened."

"Looks like Collin was able to keep that information under wraps, after all." *Thank goodness.*

We bade goodbye to Jimmy and headed out.

Monday morning, I stopped by Home & Hearth Realty to handle some of my property management duties. I'd left Sawdust at home today. Buck, Jimmy, and I would be handling the demo work later, and it could be dangerous. No way would I put the furry little love of my life at risk. Besides, Cleo was smitten with her big brother and Sawdust clearly returned the sentiment. I didn't feel quite as guilty leaving him at home when I knew he'd have company.

My bosses, Marv and Wanda Hartley, sat at their side-by-side desks. Both were in their early sixties with the gray hair and rounded physique that often come with age. But while Mr. Hartley's thinning hair barely covered his scalp and let some pink skin peek through, Mrs. Hartley's hair hung in thick, loose waves about her face. They looked up in unison and greeted me with warm smiles.

"How are things at the motel?" Mr. Hartley asked. "Everything humming along?"

"We got a lot accomplished over the weekend." I took a seat in one of the wing chairs that faced their decks. "But something extremely unfortunate happened."

Mrs. Hartley's face scrunched in concern. "What was it? Did the roof collapse? Broken water pipe? I hope it wasn't another fire."

"Did you hear about the singer Beckett Morgan being found dead?"

"Oh, dear!" Mrs. Hartley cried, her hand clutching invisible pearls at her throat. "Tell me he wasn't found at the motel."

"If I told you that," I said, "I'd be lying."

Mr. Hartley groaned. "That's some bad luck, for the both of you. Do the police have any idea who did it?"

"Not yet," I said. "Detective Flynn is working on it."

"You be careful," he warned. "They say the guilty often return to the scene of their crimes. I'd hate for you to be in any danger."

"Don't worry." I pulled the wrench from my pocket and held it up. "I keep this with me at all times."

Mr. Hartley frowned. "That'll come in handy if the killer wants you to fix his plumbing."

"I've got pepper spray too."

"That's not much better."

"It'll be a moot point soon," I said. "My fence guy is coming this afternoon to install a security fence around the property. Nobody will be able to get in or out without the passcode."

"Good to hear."

I moved to my workspace and got down to business. I typed in names and dates on a lease for a three-bedroom

duplex, and sent it to the new tenant via e-mail for signature. I forwarded a current tenant's move-out notice
to a property owner, advising that I would schedule a
final walk-through and list the availability of the unit
online. Finally, I arranged for the installation of a new
oven vent in a small ranch home.

My duties there done, I returned to my car and made
my way to the motel. Again my eyes spotted a blonde
woman by herself on the closer end of the pedestrian
bridge. She wore black again, another dress. Like before,
she was looking in the direction of the motel.

As I returned my eyes to the road in front of me and
rounded the corner, I realized what she might be looking at. A throng of people filled the sidewalk in front of
the Music City Motor Court. *What the heck is going on?*

I pulled up to a crowd of two dozen or more people
milling about. My first thought was that they were pro-
testing the renovation of the motel for some reason, but
then I noticed that the cheap chain-link fencing was
adorned with flowers, ribbons, balloons, and cigars.
Some had even placed six-packs of canned and bottled
beer at the makeshift shrine, no doubt a nod to a lyric in
the late singer's hit. *We'll share some laughs, and share
some beers, shed our worries, and shed our fears.*

"Darn," I muttered to myself. "Looks like the cat's
out of the bag."

Young women in boots, blue jean shorts, and tank
tops gathered in groups, consoling one another. Two
thirtyish men strummed guitars and sang a soft, slow
ode to the star that shined no more.

The crowd made no effort to move aside as I pulled
up. Buck was helping his father and brother on a carpentry project this morning and had not yet arrived, so I

whipped out my cell phone and called Jimmy. "How long has this been going on?"

"Since sun-up this morning," he said. "I've been hiding out in my room."

Word must have gotten out that Beckett's body had been found at the motel. But who had leaked the information? The only ones who knew were me, Buck, Jimmy, and the first responders. "Can you come open the fence and let me in?"

"I'm on it."

I returned the phone to my purse. The door to Room 9 opened and Jimmy stepped out, a shirt with cartoon crabs on his back and a pair of pliers in his hand. I eased forward, unrolling my window and calling "Excuse me, y'all! I need to get through!" When that didn't work, I tapped lightly on my horn. *Beep-beep.* And when that didn't work, I was forced to take drastic measures, blasting my horn and speaking without contractions. *HOOOONK!* "You all move, please!"

The crowd cast me nasty looks. Never mind that they were trespassing on private property.

Jimmy cut through the zip ties and pulled the fence back just enough that I could ease through without scratching my paint.

Hoping to avoid questions, I parked as far away from the fence as I could. No such luck. The instant I stepped out of my SUV, someone called, "Who are you people?" Another shouted, "What are you doing?" Someone else hollered. "You shouldn't be in there! This is a man's grave!"

There was no sense in pointing out that Beckett Morgan wasn't buried here. He'd only died here. It was splitting hairs. Besides, they were here to show respect for an entertainer they'd admired and enjoyed. I couldn't blame them for that.

An idea came to me. Just like we planned to hold a grand opening once the outside and spec unit had been fully rehabbed, maybe we could hold a vigil here for Beckett Morgan, give his fans the sense of community and closure they sought.

I walked over to the fence and raised a hand in greeting. "Hey, y'all. It's wonderful that you want to honor Beckett, and I'd like to give you the chance to do that. Problem is, a fencing contractor will be arriving in less than an hour, and the crew's going to be working along here. What would y'all say to holding a candlelight vigil here tonight instead? Maybe start at seven? You can bring lawn chairs and hold it in the parking lot."

The group issued murmurs of agreement.

The two guys with the guitars came up to the fence. The taller one said, "We played in Beckett's band." He hiked a thumb at himself. "I'm Sawyer." He turned the thumb on his shorter, stockier cohort. "That's Wylie. Okay if we perform a tribute at the vigil? Maybe two or three songs to kick things off, and another one to wrap things up at the end?"

Looked like I was now in charge of hosting the impromptu wake.

"Of course," I said. "That would be real nice." As they turned to go, it dawned on me that they might have relevant information about Beckett and who might have wanted the singer dead. I raised a hand and called after them. "Wait!" When they turned around, I asked, "Did y'all play with Beckett Friday night at the Ryman?"

Sawyer nodded. "Sure did."

"Were you with him after the show?"

Wylie spoke now. "We were."

"Can you stick around a minute?" I asked. "The detective handling the case might want to talk to you, see if you can help him out."

They exchanged curious looks and shrugs.

Sawyer said, "I don't have anywhere I need to be."

"Me, neither," Wylie said. "Least not until one o'clock. Then I'm due at the studio."

I stepped away to phone Collin. When I told him members of Beckett's band were at the motel, along with untold numbers of groupies, he said, "I'll be right there."

While waiting for the detective, Jimmy and I gathered up the things Beckett's fans had left and piled them against the crumbling brick wall that surrounded the pool. We wrangled with the fencing, removing it and storing it behind the big trash bin we'd rented and parked at the far end of the lot to hold the building debris.

"What now, boss?" Jimmy asked.

I rounded up an assortment of screwdrivers from my toolbox. "Go through all the rooms and remove the covers from the light switches and electrical sockets." The task was one of the few demolition duties a person could do by themselves.

Jimmy took the tools and gave me a salute. "Aye, aye, captain."

As Jimmy headed to Room 1, Collin pulled up to the motel in his unmarked sedan. By then, the crowd had dispersed other than the two musicians and five sobbing young women who stood in a circle with their arms draped around one another's shoulders. As I turned to speak to Collin, my gaze lit on the blonde on the bridge in the distance. She turned and walked away, disappearing from sight as she headed toward downtown.

I met him at his car and accosted him as he climbed out. "How did these people find out Beckett was killed here?" I whispered. "Nobody knows except the first responders. Could one of them have leaked the information?"

"It's doubtful," Collin replied softly. "Besides, there's another person who knows."

"Who?" I asked.

"The killer."

"Oh. Right." I gulped. "You think the killer tipped these people off?" If so, the killer might be closer than I'd expected. Heck, the killer might even be among the people who'd come by this morning.

"It's possible the murderer might have inadvertently spilled the beans," Collin said. "Or maybe they did it on purpose, thought it would muddy the waters or distract the police for all these people to show up here." He looked at me from under his brows. "And don't forget that Jimmy knew too."

I considered it highly unlikely that Jimmy would have leaked the information. Why would he want all of Beckett's fans traipsing around his temporary home? "Did you find any fingerprints on the pool gate?"

"Yes," Collin said. "None were Jimmy's."

"Does that mean he's off the hook?"

"Not in the least. He could have worn gloves or wiped his prints off, or maybe he didn't touch the gate with his hands. Maybe he kicked it, or bumped it with his backside as he was dragging Beckett from the pool. That could explain why it was off its hinges."

Though I believed Collin was off base where Jimmy was concerned, I wasn't going to argue with him about it. He was the professional investigator here. All I really had to go on was my gut. Guts could be wrong, couldn't they? Mine certainly was the time it told me I should try a ghost pepper. It had been like eating pure fire.

Our private exchange concluded, I walked Collin over to Sawyer and Wylie, and introduced the three.

After they shook hands, Collin angled his head to indicate me. "Ms. Whitaker said you two were with Beckett on Friday night?"

"That's right," Sawyer said. "We're session musicians. I play guitar. Wylie plays guitar too, as well as bass and mandolin."

Letting his guitar hang from the strap over his shoulder, Wylie stuck his hands out at waist level and made picking motions. "Don't forget the dobro."

Collin pulled a note pad and ballpoint pen from his breast pocket. His eyes moved from one of the men to the other and back again, like one of those Kit-Cat Klocks. "Tell me about Friday night. I understand you two played with Beckett?"

"We were the opening act," Sawyer said. "It was a great show. Our performance went off without a hitch, and the entire audience was on their feet when we wrapped up with 'Party in the Pasture.' Warm-up bands don't usually get an encore, but we did. Sang the song a second time and the crowd went nuts all over again. We stuck around when we were done and watched Armadillo Uprising from backstage. Seemed like a stellar night."

"Until after," Wylie said.

"Yup," Sawyer agreed. "That's when the poop hit the fan."

"Oh, yeah?" Collin cocked his head. "What kind of poop are we talking about?"

"Major ruckus." Sawyer let out a whistle, shaking his head. "Gia Revello came around and started a nasty squabble with Beckett."

Collin's brows knit. "Who's Gia Revello?"

Wylie filled him in. "She's an executive with Cumberland River Records. They've produced all of Armadillo Uprising's albums. Produced Beckett's first album too."

Sawyer said, "We were standing outside the backstage doors with Beckett at the time. He was signing autographs for fans, letting them take photos and snap selfies. Then Gia Revello barged up and took him to the woodshed, right there in front of everyone."

After jotting down the woman's name, Collin asked, "What was the argument about?"

Sawyer's shoulders lifted. "Hard to say, exactly. I believe it had something to do with their contract."

"That's how I took it too." Wylie grimaced. "She was brutal, said that without her Beckett would be a 'one-hit wonder' and that he had 'more ego than talent.'"

Collin rubbed his chin, mulling over what he'd just been told. "Any idea why she'd say those things?"

"No," Sawyer said. "She just started spouting off. Didn't really say why."

Wylie concurred. "I don't know what got her so riled up, but Beckett kept telling her to talk to T-Rex, that he'd sort it all out."

"T-Rex?"

"Rex Tomlinson," Wylie said. "T-Rex is his nickname. He manages Beckett Morgan. Or, *managed*, I suppose I should say. He manages lots of other bands, too, including Lacy Spurlock."

"Yup," Wylie said. "Rumor has it he's the one who suggested Beckett and Lacy do the duet together. Guy's a genius when it comes to the music industry."

Sawyer frowned. "Just wish he could've convinced Beckett to hire us on permanent."

Collin's expression remained neutral, but that ever-so-slight narrowing of his eyes told me he was assessing the guitarist. "What do you mean?"

"Session work isn't exactly what you'd call stable," Sawyer explained. "Sometimes, your phone's blowing up with people wanting to hire you. Other times, you're eating store-brand cornflakes for dinner and wondering if you'll be able to make rent."

Wylie concurred with an *mm-hmm*. "Sawyer and I played pretty regular for Beckett when he was in town. Went on the road with him sometimes too. We hoped he'd make us a deal, give us some kind of long-term contract, maybe form an official backup band. T-Rex talked to Beckett about it, but Beckett said he wanted to 'keep his options open.'"

"Keep his money was more like it." Sawyer's frown deepened. "Beckett would have had to pay us more if he hired us full-time." As if remembering why he was at the motel in the first place, Sawyer straightened, erasing his frown. "I suppose we can't blame the guy, though. I mean, there's hundreds of musicians just as good as us around Nashville. He could've had his pick. We were lucky he hired us at all."

Wylie scoffed. "Speak for yourself, dude. I've played for Willie, Dolly, and Kelly Clarkson. Beckett was lucky to have me playing for him."

Collin's eyes flashed. *Had Wylie just implicated himself?*

Evidently, I wasn't the only one who'd noticed. Sawyer's jaw flexed, and he sent a silent message to his friend, dipping his chin and looking at him from under his brows. "Regardless, we appreciated the gigs and had a lot of respect for Beckett. Didn't we, Wylie?"

Wylie took the hint. "'Course we did. We wouldn't be here, otherwise. Beckett played his fingers to the bone getting where he did, paid his dues and then some. Had a great voice too. Incredible range. My grandmother said he sounded like Tom Jones or Nat King Cole. She came to hear me play for Beckett once, and I feared she'd toss her granny panties onto the stage." He punctuated his words with a nervous chuckle.

Collin readied his pen. "Who else played with Beckett Morgan on Friday night?"

Sawyer rattled off the name of a pianist who also played an electric keyboard. "A drummer too. Gabriel something-or-other." When he pulled the musicians up in his contacts list to provide Collin with their phone numbers, I caught a glimpse of his screen. The drummer was listed in his contacts as Gabriel Somethingorother.

Collin returned to the argument between Beckett and Gia Revello, making a circular motion with his finger. "Go back to the squabble between Beckett and the lady from the record company. How'd it end?"

"Beckett stormed off," Wylie said. "Went back inside the auditorium."

"Gia Revello stormed off, too," Sawyer added. "Didn't see her again, so I guess she left the Ryman then."

Collin's head bobbed as he processed the scene in his head. "Did you see Beckett later that night?"

"We did," Sawyer said. "Gave him a few minutes to

cool off, then went to his dressing room and asked if he wanted to go for a beer. He said he'd love to, so long as we didn't talk business."

"And?" Collin prodded.

"We went next door to Tootsie's," Wylie said.

Tootsie's Orchid Lounge was a popular landmark named after its original owner and the shade of purple paint her contractor had chosen for the place. The bar was popular with tourists and locals alike. It featured cold beer and live music, and sat right around the corner from the Ryman Auditorium.

"Gotta say," Wylie went on, "it was darn near the best night of my life. Girls see you hanging with Beckett Morgan, you go from a six to a ten."

"*Six?*" Sawyer snorted. "Dude, you're a four, at best."

"*Four?* Kiss my—"

"Guys!" Collin said. "You're at the bar, talking to women . . ." He made the circular motion again, telling them to move the story along.

"Right," Sawyer said. "Girls kept throwing themselves at Beckett all night, too, but he wasn't having it. Couldn't seem to shake the run-in with Gia Revello. Just turned his back on the groupies and nursed his beer. Around one in the morning, Beckett said he'd had enough. So we left Tootsie's and walked to our cars. Beckett has a place downtown and he'd hoofed it to the Ryman for the show, but he came with us anyway. Said he needed a cigar real bad."

"Where were you parked?"

"Free lot thataway." Sawyer pointed down the street to the parking lot south of the Titan's football stadium. It sat just this side of the footbridge and offered parking at no charge, a more economical option than the pricey paid lots near the tourist traps across the river. He then turned his finger to point in the other direction. "Last we saw Beckett, he was headed up there to the Poison Emporium to buy a cigar."

"A cigar?" Collin repeated. "Just one cigar, you mean?"

Sawyer shrugged. "That's how he put it. But I can't say I've ever seen him smoke more than one in a row."

"Me, neither," said Wylie. "Matter of fact, I heard him mention he had a one-cigar limit. Said any more might damage his vocal chords and he wouldn't take the risk."

"You two ever smoke with him?" Collin asked.

"One time." Wylie grimaced. "About a year ago. Couldn't stomach it."

Collin looked to Sawyer. "How about you?"

"Couple of times," Sawyer said. "I can stomach cigars, but I don't much like them. It's just as well 'cause I can't afford them. Not the good ones, anyway. Those Montecristos Beckett smokes are imported from Nicaragua. They cost nearly twelve bucks apiece."

"How do you know that?"

Sawyer shrugged. "Suppose Beckett must have mentioned it."

Collin's head bobbed. "Know anyone else in Beckett's circle who smokes cigars?"

"Regularly?" Sawyer said. "No, I mean, the other guys join Beckett now and then. It kind of makes you feel special when he offers one to you, like you're part of his inner circle, you know? But I can't recall anyone else who smokes cigars on their own."

"Yeah," Wylie agreed. "Musicians are more of a drinking crowd."

Collin jotted a note before looking up again. "Besides

Gia Revello, do either of you know anyone who might have had a beef with Beckett?"

The two exchanged a knowing glance before Sawyer turned back to Collin. "Ladies," Sawyer said. "More'n you can count."

CHAPTER 10

FOOTAGE

WHITNEY

"Any ladies in particular?" Collin asked.

"Shoot," Sawyer said. "I can name at least three off the top of my head."

"Then do it," Collin said, putting his pen to his pad.

Sawyer rattled off the names of three women Beckett had allegedly dated and dumped. Wylie added two more to the mix before saying, "And that's just the ones we know of. There's probably more. Beckett was a ladies' man, but he'd never commit. He's what my grandmother would call 'fickle.'"

"Fickle is what guys like us would call 'lucky.' Am I right?" Collin gave the guys a grin that only someone who knew him better, like me, would realize was forced. He seemed to be making an attempt to connect with the two, to get them to let down their guard.

"Heck, yeah," Wylie said. "Luckiest man I ever knew."

Collin chuckled. "How'd y'all know to come here to the motel this morning?"

Wylie said, "Saw a post on Facebook. Beckett's fan page."

"Who made the post?"

Wylie scratched his hand. "Can't quite recall. One of his fans, I suppose."

Sawyer lifted his chin to indicate the other musician. "When he saw the post, he texted me. Decided we should come pay our respects."

When he seemed to have gleaned all he could from the two, Collin dismissed them with a "Thanks for the information." Once the two had left the motel, Collin and I huddled to discuss what they'd told him.

I mused aloud. "Sawyer and Wylie seemed upset that Beckett wouldn't hire them on to be official members of his band. Think one or both of them might have been angry enough with Beckett to end his life?"

"It's certainly possible. They knew where Beckett was headed Friday night, and were among the last to see him alive. Would've been easy to confront him on the empty street after he bought his cigar." He lowered the pen, holding it like a dagger. "That doorstop that was stabbed into Beckett's chest?" He made a stabbing motion with his pen. "That tells me the killing was personal, that whoever did it was furious at Beckett for one reason or another." He returned the pen and notepad to his breast pocket. "It also tells me it wasn't premeditated. If someone had planned to kill Beckett, they would have brought a weapon with them, not improvised with whatever they happened to find available."

"So no chance it could have been random?"

"I'd never say never, but it seems highly doubtful. His wallet wasn't taken, so robbery doesn't appear to be a motive." He cast a glance at Jimmy, who'd come out of Room 6 with a stack of plastic socket covers in his hand

and was headed to the dumpster to ditch them. Under his breath, Collins said, "I still say it could have been Jimmy Weber. If he thought Beckett was trying to steal his motorcycle, he might have been angry enough to stick a doorstop in the guy."

Jimmy had been nothing but laidback and jovial since I'd met him, not the type of guy who'd easily fly off the handle. "I'm still not feeling it."

"Agree to disagree." Collin stuffed his hands in his pants pockets and rocked back on his heels. "At least he was honest about being a happy drunk."

"Oh, yeah?"

Collin angled his head to indicate his cruiser. "Come check out Exhibit A."

I followed him over to his plain sedan and slid into the passenger seat. He booted up the laptop affixed to the dashboard mount and started a video feed. It showed a crowd of people performing a country line dance on a rooftop to music we couldn't hear. Jimmy swayed right in the middle of them. He had one hand raised above his head. The other was at his chest, clutching a glass. His mouth hung partway open in a relaxed smile as he took a few steps to the right en masse with the others, kicked out his foot, and switched directions to move left. After a turn and hop, they repeated the simple moves. When the song finished, he and the woman dancing next to him headed over to the railing, where they looked out over the Cumberland River. Jimmy said something to the woman, and she threw her head back and laughed. He laughed too. He couldn't have looked less like a vicious killer if he'd had an oversized lollipop in one hand and a teddy bear in the other.

My focus shifted from the screen to the detective. "The fact that you have this video footage tells me how you spent your day yesterday. Tracking Jimmy's movements Friday night."

"That's right," Collin said, "but only after I first drove up to Bowling Green, Kentucky, to speak in person with Beckett Morgan's family."

Beckett's hometown sat an hour north of Nashville, pretty much a straight shot up Interstate 65. I'd been to Bowling Green years ago, while on a day trip with Buck and his family to visit Mammoth Cave. Buck's parents, my aunt Nancy and uncle Roger, looked after me for a few weeks each summer when I was a kid, while my parents went off on vacations abroad. Aunt Nancy often invited me to come along on their less glamorous but more adventurous family vacations, saying she'd have no fun without some female company. Buck, his brother Owen, and I had a blast exploring the huge cave.

I reached out and put a supportive hand on Collin's shoulder. "I can't imagine how hard it must've been to have to give them the news."

"It goes with the job," he said matter-of-factly, but the hard swallow told me it had taken a toll on him. He might be a homicide detective, but that didn't mean dealing with death didn't affect him. "I questioned his parents and siblings, but none of them had any idea who might have killed Beckett. By all accounts, he was having the time of his life here in Nashville, and everything was going his way."

In other words, they'd provided no leads for the detective to follow up on.

"What about Beckett's phone?" I asked. "Any clues there?"

"Lab's still working on it."

Knowing that murder victims were often killed by

someone they were intimately involved with, I asked, "Did Beckett's family tell you about anyone he was dating? Maybe one of the ladies Sawyer and Wylie mentioned?" Or maybe even two or three of them. Maybe one had found out he'd been stringing others along, too, and she'd killed him in a jealous rage.

"They told me Beckett had dated his high school sweetheart up to the time he moved to Nashville last year, but that things cooled off quickly thereafter. She was in nursing school at Western Kentucky University, and they were too busy to find time for each other anymore. His parents said she was a sweet girl, but that she didn't seem entirely supportive of his music career. They believed she was holding him back, so they were relieved when the two split up."

"And there's been nobody serious since?"

"Not to their knowledge," he said.

"So, what's next?"

He pointed down the street to the Poison Emporium. "Gonna take a look at their security feeds."

I gave him my most winning smile. "Can I come with you?"

He eyed me suspiciously. "Why?"

Truth be told, I fancied myself a bit of an amateur sleuth and thought I might be of assistance to Collin. Even so, I didn't want to insult the guy by implying he wasn't up to handling the task on his own. He was the professional, after all, and had been trained in investigation techniques. I, on the other hand, had been trained in carpentry techniques, including joist notching and how to use a sliding bevel. Not exactly the most helpful skills for solving homicides, but I had to admit it made me nervous that he was so intensely focused on Jimmy. And, like me, the detective was a sucker for cats. He was Daddy to two of the demanding beasts, a gray tabby named Copernicus and a black-and-white tuxedo cat named Galileo. Needless to say, Collin was also an astronomy buff. I tried to use his love of furry creatures to my advantage. "I'm curious," I said, "like a cat. You know you can't leave a cat's curiosity unsatisfied."

"You know what they say about cats," he said. "Curiosity kills." A macabre sentiment, but at least he didn't say no. I took that as acquiescence. I climbed out of the car and called out to Jimmy, who'd come out of the motel with another armful of junk plastic to toss in the bin. "I'm going down the street with the detective. I'll be back in a bit."

"Okay, boss." He tossed the junk over the top of the bin and said, "What should I do next?"

"Interior doors. Taken them off the hinges." The heavy old doors were scuffed and scratched beyond repair, their hinges rusty and barely holding on. We planned to replace them with lighter-weight doors inlaid with frosted glass. With windows only on the front walls of the units, natural light would be at a premium. A glass interior door would allow the rooms to share light, but the frost would provide sufficient privacy. I gestured to my toolbox. "Help yourself to any tools you might need."

He gave me a thumbs-up, and Collin and I strode off down the street. In no time, we'd reached the Poison Emporium. At this time on a weekday, business was slow, and only two cars sat in the lot. The store's slogan, *Pick Your Poison*, adorned the front window. Just like Buck and I had decided to lean into the retro motel vibe, this place, too, had leaned into its truth, proudly proclaiming to be exactly what it was, a purveyor of toxic substances.

Jing-a-ling! The bells on the door announced our arrival to the clerk, a skinny, sixtyish man who stood at the front end of the third row, stocking bottles of Jack Daniel's whiskey on an end cap. He wore jeans and a bright red knit shirt emblazoned on the chest with the Poison Emporium logo. "Howdy, folks. Help ya find somethin'?"

Yeah, I thought, *you can help us find a murderer.* But I had the sense not to share my thought aloud.

Collin, on the other hand, replied with a vague, "I hope so."

We walked past the sole customer, a man in a business suit who stood in front of a display of Kentucky bourbon, his eyes scanning his options.

The clerk stepped down from the stool to stand before us, an expectant look on his face. Collin introduced himself, showed the man his badge, and offered him a business card.

"A police detective?" The man looked down at the card in his hand. "This can't be good."

Poor Collin. Nobody was ever happy to see him. Except me and his cats, that is.

"You're in no trouble," Collin said. "I'm just investigating a crime that happened nearby. I need to take a look at your security feed, see if it picked up anything that might help."

The man pointed out the window. "This about the body that was found at that seedy motel over yonder?"

Before I could hold my tongue, I blurted, "It won't be seedy for long."

The man looked at me before looking back to Collin. "Who's she?"

Collin cut a look my way, telling me I could speak for myself.

"I'm the new owner of the motel." I stuck out my hand. "Whitney Whitaker. My cousin and I are turning the place into upscale condominiums."

His brows rose as he gave my hand a shake. "Is that so? Glad to hear it. Could be good for business."

Once Collin had the man's attention again, he asked, "How'd you know a body was found at the motel?"

"I was here Saturday evening. Between the cop cars, cordon tape, and the coroner's wagon, it wasn't exactly a mystery. It was Beckett Morgan that was found, wasn't it?"

Collin's jaw flexed as he confirmed the man's supposition. "It was. How did you know it was him?"

"His fans have been coming in all morning, buying his favorite cigars. I thought it was strange, everyone suddenly interested in the Nicaraguan Montecristos, so I asked one of the customers what was up. He told me Beckett had been found dead at the motel over the weekend. Such a shame. I'd seen the guy in here myself Friday night."

Collin went for his pocket and notepad again. "You did?"

"Well, technically, I suppose it was Saturday morning. We were open until two a.m. He came in not long before we closed."

Collin and I exchanged a glance. Jimmy said he'd left the last bar in SoBro around two o'clock, walked the riverfront, and then come back to the motel. That put him and Beckett in this area around roughly the same time. At least we now had a window for the time of death. If Beckett was in this store shortly before two, presumably he was killed not long thereafter, most likely while heading back past the motel to his residence downtown.

Collin returned his attention to the clerk. "What did Beckett buy?"

"His usual cigar and Kentucky bourbon."

"You said 'usual.' Does that mean Beckett came in here regularly?"

The man dipped his head. "He did."

Collin circled his pen in the air to indicate the store's inventory. "Can you show me which cigar and bourbon he bought?"

"Sure." The man led us over to the humidor and pulled out a cigar wrapped in clear, shiny cellophane. Just like the cigar butt Collin had shown to Jimmy, this cigar bore a gold and black band with a gold fleur de lis in the center of a circle. Red lettering arching over the top of the circle read MONTECRISTO, while gold text below spelled out NICARAGUA SERIES.

The clerk handed the cigar to Collin, who spent a moment carefully looking it over. He returned it to the man and asked, "What about the bourbon?"

The man put the cigar back into the humidor before pointing to a locked glass case behind the checkout counter where the more expensive liquor was kept. "Beckett drank Wild Turkey Decades."

"Ah," Collin said. "The good stuff."

"At a hundred-and-forty-nine bucks a bottle, it better be good," the man said. "Couldn't tell you one way or another, though. Never had a taste of it myself."

The upscale liquor shared the secured display with cartons of cigarettes and other tobacco products that were both pricey and easy to surreptitiously pocket. No doubt they were stored behind the counter to prevent pilfering.

"Speaking of wild turkeys," Collin said, "you ever

notice Beckett wearing a belt buckle with a bird foot printed on it?" He raised his hand to form three talons, just as Jimmy had done when he mentioned seeing the man with the belt buckle.

"Can't say that I have," the man said.

"Another customer, maybe?"

"Don't recall ever seeing such a thing, but people come in here wearing all kinds of getups. 'Specially the tourists. They're all hat and no cattle." He snorted a laugh. "'Course from behind this tall counter I mostly just see people from their belly up."

Until this exchange, it hadn't dawned on me that the man Jimmy had seen on the street could have been Beckett Morgan himself, before he was killed. But in light of the fact that Jimmy saw the man between the bridge and the motel, that would mean Beckett would have had to backtrack to the motel to meet his demise. I supposed it was possible someone had led or forced him back to the place, maybe wanting to get Beckett off the street where they wouldn't be seen.

Getting down to the matter at hand, Collin gestured to the security cameras mounted on either corner behind the checkout counter. "Mind if I take a look at your video feeds?"

"Sure, sure." The man waved for us to follow him. A door blocked access to the space behind the counter. The storekeeper pulled a keycard on a lanyard from inside his shirt and tapped the card to the keypad to unlock the door. A *click* told us the lock had been released. He opened the door and held it ajar so we could come through.

As the man sat down at a computer at the far end of the counter, Collin asked, "Did the fans say how they knew Beckett Morgan had been found at the motel?"

"Not that I recall," he said. "I didn't ask. I suppose it's been on the news, but the young folks today don't watch television like my generation does. Probably one of their parents caught a news report and filled them in."

It was doubtful. The police department had not revealed the location of Beckett's body to the media. More than likely, the news had spread like wildfire via text and social media, like Wylie had mentioned. But who had struck the match that started the blaze?

The man's fingers moved over the keyboard and mouse as he accessed the security feeds and brought an image to the monitor. Per the time and date stamp in the lower right corner, we were watching a feed from 1:37 Saturday morning. Like now, it was off-peak hours and the store was nearly empty, only two customers, a man and a woman, in the place. The couple stood shoulder to shoulder facing the far wall, their mouths moving and heads turning toward each other as they took various bottles off the shelf in an apparent discussion over the brand of tequila to buy and the size of the bottle. As the customers brought their bottle to the counter, the same man who sat in front of the computer screen now appeared on it as he stood from his stool behind the counter and stepped into camera range.

While the clerk rang up the couple, Beckett Morgan slunk through the door, his gray felt cowboy hat tipped forward as if he didn't want to be recognized. He was wearing the clothes I'd found him in —jeans and the light blue Western shirt embroidered with musical notes on the yoke. Of course, the shirt had no bloodstain on the snap-flap pocket . . . *yet*.

Beckett turned down the first aisle and pretended to be looking at the products until the couple left. Once they were gone, he stepped forward and waved hello to the clerk, who tossed him a key to the locked humidor that stood at the front end of one of the rows. The two seemed to have a routine. Clearly, Beckett was a regular here. He unlocked the climate-controlled glass case, reached inside, and removed a single cigar before locking the case again. He carried the key and cigar to the counter, returned the key to the clerk, and pointed to the Wild Turkey Decades on the shelf behind the man. The clerk rounded up a bottle, bagged it, and set it on the counter before ringing up the purchases. Beckett handed the man several twenties, and refused his change with a raised palm and a smile.

"Tipped me fifteen bucks," the clerk said. "Always pays in cash and tells me to keep the change. Wish all the customers were that generous. One of 'em cussed me out earlier because we didn't have his usual brand of scotch in stock. Ain't my fault the wholesaler shorted me on the last order."

Collin made a tapping motion with his finger. "Go back to where Beckett stepped up to the counter and pause the feed."

"All righty." The man went back several seconds and stopped the feed.

Collin leaned in as if looking for an important detail. His eyes were locked on Beckett's chest. I had a suspicion he was trying to determine whether the late singer had a second cigar already in his breast pocket. I leaned in too. There was no telltale end sticking out, no long cylindrical lump.

Collin turned to the clerk. "Did you happen to notice whether Beckett already had a cigar in his pocket when he came in?"

"Didn't notice one," the man said. He glanced at the

screen. "It would likely show if he did. They're too long to be completely hidden in most pockets."

I chimed in. "Could it be in one of his jeans pockets?"

The clerk scoffed. "Heck, no. That's a sure way to end up with a bent or broken cigar and a pocketful of tobacco flakes." The undertone of his words was *Any fool knows that*, but I chose not to take offense. What did I know? I'd never smoked a cigar. The one time I'd tried a cigarette in college, I'd nearly coughed up a lung.

Collin and I watched as Beckett walked out of camera range. The angle told us that we were looking at the feed from the camera in the front corner, which was angled toward the back wall. Pointing up at the other camera, which was situated in the back corner and angled toward the front of the store, Collin said, "Show me the feed from that one."

"Gotcha."

The man pulled up the second feed. The scene replayed itself from the other side, though this time we could see Beckett walk out the door. He took a couple of steps away from the exit, incrementally disappearing from view from top to bottom until only his feet, clad in leather boots, were visible. His feet stopped and stood still for a few seconds before the toe of another boot appeared just a short distance in front of his, as if someone were facing him. *Could it be the killer? Or was it merely another customer who recognized Beckett, maybe stopped him for an autograph? Could it have been the man Jimmy had seen, the one with the birdfoot belt buckle?*

As I watched, I mentally willed the person to step forward so we could see who it was. Unfortunately, they didn't comply. The resolution of the image wasn't high enough for us to get much detail from the toe of the boot. All we could tell was that it was either dark brown or black and was straight across the end. Not quite a square-toed boot, but not pointy either. Unfortunately, the style was popular with both men and women, so the image didn't help us narrow things down. The three visible boots were still for a few beats before they moved off camera at 1:41 a.m.

Collin turned to the clerk. "Do you have cameras outside?"

"Nope. If someone's gonna rob the place, they gotta come in here to do it. Doesn't much matter what happens out there in the parking lot."

It might have mattered that night, I thought.

Collin had the man play through the remaining feed at double time. No customers came in after Beckett. We watched the screen until it showed him locking the doors and sliding the metal security gate into place behind them. Whoever had confronted Beckett in front of the shop hadn't come inside afterward. But might they have come inside beforehand? Maybe still been hanging around the parking lot or elsewhere nearby?

Before I could raise the issue, Collin beat me to it. "Can you start the feed at midnight? I'd like to see who came in before Beckett."

The man rolled his mouse around and clicked a few keys. He ran the feed at double time until a customer appeared, then let it play at a real-time rate. Nothing seemed out of the ordinary. When Beckett reappeared on screen, the man clicked his mouse to pause the feed. "We done here? I've got some shelves to stock."

"Almost," Collin said, "and I appreciate your time. But I'm going to ask one more thing of you, if you don't mind." He pointed to the computerized cash register. "You can search your sales by product, right?"

The man nodded.

"I'd like to see data for any sale of a Montecristo Nicaragua Series cigar here in the last three months. Date, time, debit or credit card information."

"Just individual cigars, or full boxes too?"

"Both, please, sir."

The man did as asked. A printer situated on a shelf below the computerized cash register whirred to life and spit out around a dozen pages of information. When it stopped, the man handed the printout to Collin.

Collin doffed an imaginary hat. "Can't thank you, enough."

"Glad to help," the man said. "I hope you find who done Beckett in. Shame he went so young. He seemed like a good kid."

CHAPTER 11

VIGILS AND VIGILANTES

WHITNEY

Back at the motel, Collin and I parted ways. I stayed there to work on the demolition, while he headed off to follow up on the leads he'd gotten from Sawyer, Wylie, and the manager of the Poison Emporium. My fence guy showed up shortly thereafter, and his crew got right to work, installing a heavy-duty aluminum security fence around the perimeter of the property.

Jimmy and I were in the process of removing the bathroom countertop in Room 3 when Buck arrived. He came through the open door, puzzlement on his face. He gestured to the parking lot behind him. "What's with the flowers and beer and stuff?"

"Someone spilled the beans," I said. "Beckett's fans turned the place into a shrine." I told him about the vigil planned for that evening.

"You sure that's such a good idea?" he said. "It'll only draw more attention to the fact that the guy was killed here."

"True," I said, "but it'll also give his fans some clo-sure, maybe put the matter to rest quicker than it might otherwise."

"How'd they find out?" Buck asked. "I thought every-one was sworn to secrecy."

"Who knows?" I shrugged. "Could be the killer spread the news. Maybe the killer thought if a bunch of other people showed up here, it would draw the cops' attention away."

The mystery of who spilled the beans would remain a mystery, at least for now. Buck, Jimmy, and I had work to do.

We spent the rest of the day removing the counter-tops. Tomorrow, it would be bathtubs and toilets. We'd do Jimmy's room last. No sense deconstructing his bath-room and leaving him high and dry, literally, until we were ready to install the new fixtures in his room.

Though the vigil wasn't scheduled to start until seven o'clock, Beckett's most devoted fans began to arrive at a few minutes after five to ensure themselves a good spot. My fence guys called it a day. They'd worked fast, and had managed to install all of the fencing except the rolling gate for the drive-through entrance and the ac-companying electronic security keypad. They'd be back tomorrow to finish up.

Using a few cinder blocks, some spare two-by-fours, and a sheet of plywood, Buck and I set up a makeshift stage near the entrance to the pool area. We also cov-ered the entrance to the pool area with plywood and draped a gray tarp over the wall to discourage people from trying to enter the dangerous space. Beckett had already fallen into the pool and suffered major head trauma. We didn't need anyone else accidentally doing the same. I gathered up the flowers and placed them along the front of the stage. Not only would they look pretty there, they would hide the fact that the stage was cobbled together with spare construction materials.

By half past six, the parking lot was packed, Beckett Morgan's fans either sitting in chairs they'd set up in haphazard rows or standing shoulder to shoulder behind the seated mourners. Several had placed lit candles in glass jars among the flowers on the stage. With so many burning flames, the place resembled a Catholic church. Smelled like one, too, the various scents of the flowers and candles blending in an aroma not unlike incense. Between the candles and the crowd, the fire marshal would be none too pleased if he happened upon the scene, but at least the opening for the automobile gate would provide easy egress should there be an emergency. I also opened the two pedestrian gates located at either end of the fence, using large metal snap hooks to hold the open gates in place.

The murmur of the crowd was punctuated with an occasional high-pitched wail as a female fan gave in to her emotions. Men sniffled and shook their heads in sorrow, too, their honky-tonk hero gone. The pile of mementos and flowers grew exponentially, threatening to topple over. Eventually, when there was no more room to get inside, people began to line up outside the fence, looking in through the bars.

Buck and I slid out of our coveralls, revealing the nicer clothes we'd donned underneath.

Jimmy said, "Guess I better clean myself up too." He disappeared into his room, emerging a minute later in his most demure Aloha shirt, which featured pink and white plumeria flowers, the type used in Hawaiian leis.

Collin texted me at 6:45. *Help! On the street. Can't get through crowd.*

Fortunately, Buck and I had the forethought to place sawhorses along the sidewalk to form a barrier in front of the rooms, so we were still able to move along the walkway directly in front of the motel. I replied to Collin's text. *Go to the back door of the motel lobby. I'll let you in there.* While the new fence fully enclosed the area on the front of the inn, we'd left the back of the building unfenced so it would be accessible for meter readers and garbage collection.

I slunk down the walkway and entered what had once served as the motel's business hub. An incomplete set of room keys hung from hooks on a board behind the check-in counter, the blue plastic tags shaped like acoustic guitars. A padded stool with a cracked vinyl seat stood at an outdated electronic cash register. Bins under the counter held miniature bars of soap and tiny bottles of shampoo and mouthwash, along with dusty, ancient boxes of facial tissue. A mechanical pull-tab style vending machine stood along the back wall, a single peanut butter candy bar in a striped wrapper standing sentinel in one of the slots. Alongside it was a soda machine, glass bottles with aluminum caps filling two of the five holes. There were two doors along the right wall. One led to a powder room, the other to a room that had served as the motel's laundry facility and a storage space for the housekeeping carts and cleaning supplies.

Buck and I had debated what to do with the space. Fitness center? Clubhouse? Laundry room? We'd eventually settled on a combination of the latter two. After all, anyone who could afford one of these condominiums could also afford a fancy gym membership, but they'd need somewhere convenient to wash their clothes. Moreover, while the living space in the units would be able to accommodate intimate gatherings, a clubhouse would provide a nice space for residents to entertain larger numbers of guests.

I strode to the heavy back door and opened it. Collin stood there, wearing the same navy pants and white button-down shirt as earlier, though he'd added a tie and a gray blazer with a badge affixed to the chest to identify him as law enforcement. His face was tight in frustration.

"No luck with your leads?" I asked as he stepped through the doorway.

"None," he said, "though I did learn some things about boots and cigars."

I closed and locked the door behind him, and followed him to the counter. He pulled a piece of folded paper from his pocket and unfurled it on the countertop, smoothing it with his hand. I stepped up next to him. In front of us was a pictorial chart illustrating the various types of toes found on cowboy boots. Thirteen were shown, all named with letters of the alphabet, though some had common nicknames. The X toe was the classic style, what I'd always thought of as the "pointy-toed" kind. The E, H, and I toes were commonly called "squared-toe" boots. The C, P, R, U, and W toes were rounded. The D, E, N, and O styles were a combination of pointy and squared, with the boot tapering toward a squared-off end of various widths.

Collin stretched out a hand, inviting me to take a closer look. "If you had to guess which type of toe we saw on the video from the Poison Emporium, what would you say?"

My eyes scanned the options. I pointed first to the D, then to the N toe. "One of these. D or N."

"That's what I thought too." He folded the paper and returned it to his pocket. "Beckett wore a men's size ten.

I was hoping the forensics team could tell me what size the other boot is so I could at least narrow it down to a men's or women's boot. But with only the tip of it showing, they couldn't make an accurate assessment."

"So we still don't know if it was a man or a woman who stopped Beckett outside the store?"

"No. We don't know whether the person wearing the boot was alone either. Another person could have been standing out of camera range. Maybe more than one person."

In other words, the boot had been a dead end. *Well, maybe not entirely.* "You searched Jimmy's room after we found Beckett. Did you see any boots like that, with a D or N toe?"

"No. Jimmy had only a pair of cheap flip-flops and a pair of black biker boots with a rounded toe and knobby rubber sole."

I raised a brow to say *I told you he wasn't guilty,* but I left it at that. "What about the cigars? Any luck there?"

"No," he said. "I couldn't identify the customers who'd paid in cash, and the ones who paid with debit and credit cards were dead ends. Several were tourists who don't live here in town. A couple others were businessmen with no connection to Beckett, the music industry, or the SoBro scene. Another was a Cuban artist who collects cigar bands."

"Really? That's a thing?" I'd heard of people collecting bottle caps, stamps, coins, and even postcards, but never cigar bands.

"It was news to me, too," Collin said. "There's even a name for it—vitolphilia. The guy told me there's a cigar museum in Havana, Cuba, with an entire section dedicated to cigar bands."

"You learn something new every day, huh?"

Though I'd meant my words to be merely rhetorical, Collin said, "Too bad I didn't learn something useful. I'm not sure whoever smoked the second cigar even bought it at the Poison Emporium. There's a chance they bought it at another tobacco shop. You can even order them online. I still can't rule out that Beckett might have smoked both of them either. The lab has confirmed that his DNA was on the butt found by the pool, but they're having trouble with the one that was in the sludge. They said they'd keep working on it, though, and see if they can extract anything."

"If you're hoping to detect a cigar scent on anyone here tonight," I said, "you're probably out of luck. Between the flowers and the candles out there, it's impossible to smell anything else." Litter boxes aside, I'd rarely experienced such an olfactory overload.

Collin took the news in stride. "I suppose I'll just have to do my best. Maybe somebody will pull a cigar out to smoke, or have one tucked into their pocket."

"What about Beckett's phone?" I asked. "Has the lab been able to get that working?"

"They've cleaned it out and replaced the screen. It booted up for a few seconds but then died again. They'll keep trying. If they don't get it working again, I'll check with the phone company."

"What about the ladies Wylie and Sawyer mentioned?"

"I got in touch with all five of them. I told them about the vigil and asked them to find me afterward. I can get a more accurate vibe when I interview a person of interest face-to-face than I can get on the phone."

Though a woman could have easily shoved Beckett and caused him to lose his footing so that he fell backward into the pool, I had some difficulty believing a woman would be strong enough to drag him up out of it. Then again, adrenaline enabled people to do all sorts of things they might not normally be capable of. Besides, with all the physical work I did on my jobs, I could handle a sizable load. A strong woman like me might have managed to move him. He wasn't unusually large, after all.

Collin asked, "Have you or Buck accessed your camera feeds?"

"No," I said. "Didn't see a reason to." After all, by the time we'd installed them, Beckett had already been killed.

"I took a look," Collin said. "There was a young woman who came by here yesterday evening after y'all left. She stood on the sidewalk and stared at the motel for a few minutes, then walked back the way she'd come." He pulled another printout from his pocket, this one on photo-quality paper, and set it on the counter.

In the photo was a pretty young woman with long, pale blonde hair. She wore a black dress with black boots and a thick black choker necklace. The date and time stamp on the screenshot told me she'd come by at 7:03.

"I can't be certain," I told Collin, "but I think I've seen her. A blonde woman in a black dress was standing on the bridge yesterday, looking this way."

"The woman in the photo came from the direction of the bridge," Collin said. "Went back that way too."

My blood went cold as a realization struck me. "She knew Beckett was found here before anyone else did."

"Appears that way."

"She could be the killer, then."

Never one to jump to conclusions, even ones that seemed inevitable, Collin countered with, "Maybe.

Could be she was just interested in the motel for some other reason."

"Any idea who she is?"

"Not yet." He picked up the photo and slid it back into his pocket. "She might be one of the ladies Sawyer and Wylie mentioned. I'm going to look for her tonight, see if she shows up to the vigil. Help me keep an eye out, would you?"

"Of course."

We exited the lobby and took places next to Buck and Jimmy outside the door to Jimmy's room. Buck greeted Collin with a fist bump, while Jimmy ducked his head in hello.

Collin pulled the photo from his pocket. "Either of you seen this woman around the motel?"

They both craned their necks to get a look.

"Not me," Jimmy said.

"Me neither," Buck said. "A purty thing like that would have caught my eye."

I asked, "Did either of you notice anyone watching the motel from the bridge?"

"Nope," Jimmy said. "But I wasn't really looking."

"Me neither," Buck repeated.

Collin tucked the photo back into his pocket. "Help me keep an eye out for her tonight, okay? I want to talk to her, find out why she was interested in the motel."

Jimmy straightened, his face brightening. "Does that mean I'm off the hook?"

"Not in the least," Collin said. "I still consider you a person of interest."

Jimmy shrugged. "You're going to feel mighty foolish when you're proven wrong."

Collin lifted a nonchalant shoulder. "I can live with that. And if you want to prove me wrong, keep your other eye out tonight for the guy you saw Friday night with the bird-foot belt buckle."

Jimmy gave Collin a two-fingered salute in acceptance of his order.

Sawyer and Wylie pushed their way through the crowd, guitars in hand. My gaze shifted of its own accord to their feet. Both wore boots, and both looked like the toes could be either the D or N style we'd seen in the footage from the store.

"Okay if we take the stage now?" Sawyer asked me.

"Be my guest," I said, my focus shifting to his face. "In fact, why don't you handle the lineup? You're used to being on a stage in front of an audience. You'd do a much better job hosting this vigil than me."

He gave me a nod. "Will do."

As they turned to go, Collin raised a hand to stop them and pulled the photo from his pocket a third time. He held it out to them. "Is this woman one of the ladies you mentioned to me earlier?"

"No," Sawyer said, "but she looks familiar."

"Yeah," Wylie said. "I've seen her at some of the shows, hanging around. Couldn't help but notice a girl who looks like that. She always seemed shy, though. Never came up and talked to anyone. Most groupies ask for an autograph or selfie, but she hung back. She was always alone too. Usually groupies travel in, well, groups."

Collin thanked them for the information and they headed toward the makeshift stage, where they strapped on their guitars. The two stepped up onto the platform and Sawyer waved a hand in the air to get everyone's attention. The murmuring crowd erupted in shushes before going silent. Sawyer introduced himself and Wylie, and the two proceeded to play a couple of songs in tribute to Beckett. Both were lesser hits from his first album. Sawyer sang lead vocals on the first, with Wylie singing on the second. When they finished, Sawyer invited those attending the vigil to form a line if they wanted to speak or sing. The throng shifted as people pushed their way through to get in line.

"Whoa," Sawyer said on an exhale when he saw the long queue. "We've got lots of people wanting to pay their respects. Looks like we'll have to impose a time limit. No more'n a minute each, okay? When I wave my hand, it's time to get off the stage."

The first person to take the stage was a young woman with dark skin and dark hair. "Let's bow our heads and pray."

Buck, Jimmy, Collin, and I turned our faces downward. Collin and I exchanged a surreptitious and knowing look, and took advantage of the prayer time to eye the feet of the people around us. Many wore broad, square-toed boots, which was the most popular trend today. Still, there were some rounded and pointy-toed boots among them, and others that appeared to have the D or N toes we'd seen in the video. A good number of the women wore high heels that looked stylish but by but no means comfortable. While I owned a couple of pairs of heels for special occasions, I'd always been more of a steel-toed than a high-heeled kind of girl.

My eyes also roamed the crowd in search of a belt buckle bearing a bird's foot, but saw none. Of course, the crowd was so thick I couldn't see far.

When the prayer concluded, the woman left the stage, another taking her place. This woman had pale skin and strawberry blonde curls. "This poem is by the late poet Christina Rossetti. It's titled 'Song.'" She proceeded to recite the poem, which was perfect for this somber occasion.

> When I am dead, my dearest,
> Sing no sad songs for me;
> Plant thou no roses at my head,
> Nor shady cypress tree:
> Be the green grass above me
> With showers and dewdrops wet;
> And if thou wilt, remember,
> And if thou wilt, forget.

> I shall not see the shadows,
> I shall not feel the rain;
> I shall not hear the nightingale
> Sing on, as if in pain:
> And dreaming through the twilight
> That doth not rise nor set,
> Haply I may remember,
> And haply may forget.

Two men and one woman took the stage next. One of the men had an acoustic guitar, the other a cajón box drum. The woman carried a violin. Despite the just-recited poem's admonishment to sing no sad songs, the trio sang a very sorrowful tune, Luke Bryan's hit "Drink a Beer," about a man who'd lost his buddy. Someone rounded up the now-warm beers that I'd stacked against the wall and passed them out to the crowd. The *snap-hiss* of the pop-tops releasing punctuated the music, and the crowd held their beers up in tribute during the chorus.

Tears pricked at my eyes, and I wiped them on my sleeve. Next to me, Buck wiggled his nose, telling me that he, too, was fighting back emotion. Collin took my hand in his and gave it a squeeze. Like the song said, Beckett Morgan had gone too soon, and I vowed to myself then and there to do everything in my power to help put his killer behind bars.

The vigil continued smoothly until a chubby guy who'd evidently drank too many beers during the "Drink a Beer" tribute took the stage, raised a fist in the air, and said, "When we find out who killed Beckett Morgan, I say we rip him to pieces! Who's with me?"

When the crowd erupted in whoops and applause, Collin darted forward, leaped up onto the platform, and flashed his badge to the young man, ordering him to leave the stage. "Now!" Collin raised his palms to calm the crowd and called, "Metro police are doing everything we can to identify Beckett Morgan's killer and make sure justice is served. Vigilante justice is not the answer. You could end up in danger or facing charges yourself. If you have any leads, call me. I'm Detective Collin Flynn. The main switchboard will make sure I get the message. Understood?"

A few boos erupted among the less law-abiding members of the mob, but for the most part the group seemed to accept Collin's commands. The chastised crowd was quiet until the next speaker took the stage.

As Collin returned to my side, the sound of his silenced cell phone vibrating met my ears. He pulled it from the inside pocket of his sport coat and discreetly eyed the screen. Well, maybe not entirely discreetly. I'd leaned over so that I could take a look too.

Collin cut me a slightly irritated glance, but he nonetheless allowed me to read the screen. It was a text from the lab. He tapped the screen to read the message. The lab techs had managed to get Beckett's slimy, water-logged phone unlocked and had captured a screenshot of his recent calls. The ones listed in black indicated outgoing calls. The ones in red indicated incoming calls.

Per the screenshot, Beckett had placed his final outgoing call at 1:36 Saturday morning to someone identified only as J.C. The call lasted only 27 seconds, an unusually short amount of time. Had he actually spoken with J.C. or merely left a voice mail? Unfortunately, the phone didn't provide that level of detail for outgoing calls, only the length of time that elapsed during the connection between the two mobile devices.

Beckett's penultimate call was placed to a Rex Tomlinson at 1:24 a.m. *Wasn't Rex Tomlinson the name Wylie had given this morning for Beckett's manager?* Another screenshot provided information about the call. It had lasted only 53 seconds. Given that Beckett had entered the Poison Emporium at 1:37 a.m., he must have made these two final calls between the time he parted ways with Sawyer and Wylie at the free parking lot and the time he arrived at the tobacco and liquor store.

The as-yet-unidentified J.C. had subsequently placed three calls to Beckett's phone on Saturday morning, the first not long after daybreak, the others at two-hour intervals thereafter. Two calls had also come in from Rex Tomlinson on Saturday, the first at 6:22 p.m., the next at 7:14. Tomlinson had called Beckett a third time Sunday afternoon. The voice-mail screen showed that the earliest call from J.C. and all of Tomlinson's calls went to voice mail, unanswered, placed to a man who was no longer alive to take them. *If only they'd known . . .*

The lab sent a screenshot of his recent text message list, and the same names appeared. Other than J.C., Rex, and his mother, Beckett seemed to have little direct phone contact with other people. I supposed that might be normal for a star. Probably his manager handled most of his business communications, while Beckett would have interacted only with his manager and people he knew personally.

The phone vibrated again with a wrap-up text from the lab. *Full details on calls have been sent to your e-mail. We've pinged the phone belonging to "J.C." to the Music City Motor Court.* In other words, J.C. was right here, right now, one of the many faces in the crowd. But which one? How could we know?

Collin slid his phone back into his pocket. His jaw flexed as he returned his attention to the stage. My guess was he was champing at the bit to take a full look at the phone records and to speak to J.C. and Rex Tomlinson, but that he also realized he could follow up with those folks later and he needed to glean what he could from the other people here tonight. Too bad the lab techs couldn't clone him so he could be in two places at one time.

The night wound down with Sawyer and Wylie leading those gathered in a slow, sorrowful rendition of "Party in the Pasture." Many in the crowd lit taper candles that they held during the song, while others activated the lighter app on their phones and waved them in the air. Dozens of men lit cigars they'd brought, puffed on them to get them glowing, and raised them in the air, as well, the aroma of tobacco and smoke wafting over the crowd. So much for trying to pinpoint a single cigar smoker among them. *Did one of these men smoke a cigar with Beckett at the motel late Friday night? Is one of them his killer?*

Sawyer ended the event by looking skyward and saying, "Rest in peace, Beckett." His words were followed with murmurs of "Amen."

Collin jerked his head toward the lobby and implored me, Buck, and Jimmy to hurry out the back door and go looking among the attendees as they departed for a man wearing a bird-foot belt buckle. "Snap a pic if you can," he said. "Follow him and see if you can get a license plate number for me. But only if you can do so safely."

We scurried out the back and positioned ourselves strategically on nearby corners, where we'd be able to watch people go by. The crowd slowly began to disperse as people left, many heading down the street to their cars in the parking lot at the base of the bridge. As the people passed by, I put a hand to my forehead as if upset or suffering a headache, and eyed them from under my fingers so they wouldn't be able to tell that I was looking at their waists, searching for the buckle. I held my phone at the ready, poised to take a pic, but to the crowd it would appear as if I was reading my screen.

My eyes spotted a belt buckle with a black bear silhouette on it, another with a bucking bronco. A star. A two-toned cross. An eagle. An American flag. A woman wore one with a feminine floral and scroll pattern. My heart jumped up into my throat when I saw one that looked like a bird foot. On closer inspection it was merely two arrows crossed in an X pattern, the arrowheads pointing down, the feathered shafts above. *Could this be the belt buckle Jimmy saw? Did he mistake the arrows for feet, given that they had feathers on them? Could the man wearing the belt also be J.C.?*

CHAPTER 12

MISSING YOU

SAWDUST

Whitney had been gone all day and Sawdust didn't like it one bit. He missed her. He hadn't had an ear rub or a chest scratch all day. He hadn't gotten to tell her about his day—*meow, meow, meow*—and he'd had nothing but dry kibble to eat since breakfast.

When he missed Whitney like this, there was only one thing he could do to make himself feel better. Immerse himself in her scent.

To that end, he climbed into the laundry basket that contained her jumbled coveralls and other clothes she'd worn. He used his paws to arrange the garments around him, settled in, and breathed deep. *Mmm. Whitney.*

CHAPTER 13

FAMOUS LAST WORDS

WHITNEY

I raised my head and my phone and snapped a quick photo of the man wearing the belt buckle. His head was angled my way as he spoke to the curly-haired blonde next to him. He had an unremarkable, average face and build, which would jibe with Jimmy's statement that nothing in particular stuck out about the man. *Should I follow him?* I debated with myself for a few seconds. If I followed this guy, I could miss another man coming by in an actual bird-foot belt buckle. But if I didn't follow this guy, we might never be able to identify him. I turned to look at the remaining people approaching. The stream had lessened to a trickle. I figured the odds were best if I trailed him.

I stalked him to the parking lot, where he and the woman stopped at a silver Dodge Challenger. As they stood behind the trunk, the woman burst into sobs, putting her hands to her face, her curls quivering. The man stepped forward and wrapped his arms around her back to comfort her. I felt as if I was intruding on a private moment, so I quickly snapped a photo of the license plate before hustling back to the motel, eyeing waists along the way. No belt buckles with talons.

When I arrived back at the Music City Motor Court, Collin was speaking privately in front of Room 9 with a twentysomething woman. Her lively, golden blonde ponytail bounced off her back and shoulders as she nodded and gestured in an animated fashion. Two other attractive women in their twenties waited in front of Room 5, speaking with Sawyer and Wylie. I took it that Collin had already interviewed the other of the five ladies Sawyer and Wylie had mentioned. None of the three women still here were the woman I'd seen on the bridge, the same one who'd been standing in front of the motel in the photo Collin had shown us earlier. I wondered if either of the other two ladies Beckett had been keeping company with was her.

I cornered Jimmy and discreetly showed him the pic I'd snapped with my phone. "The man you saw near the motel late Friday night. Is this the belt buckle he wore?"

Jimmy squinted at the screen for a few seconds, raised his shoulders, and wobbled his head. "Maybe. I mean, it doesn't look exactly like a bird's foot, but the feathers might have thrown me off. All I got was a quick glimpse, an impression."

I swiped my screen to show him the photo of the man. The clarity wasn't great, especially when Jimmy flicked my screen with his fingers to enlarge it. "What about him? Is this the guy you saw?"

He wobbled his head again, grimacing. "Sorry, Whitney. I can't be sure. I want to help, but my memory's hazy."

"No worries," I told him. "I got the man's license plate. If he's the one, Detective Flynn will figure it out."

Jimmy straightened, relief relaxing his hunched shoulders.

A few people still hung around the parking lot, talking in small groups. A fortyish man splintered off from one of the groups and headed over to join Sawyer, Wylie, and the women. He wore black boots and jeans, paired with a shiny black leather belt, a well-pressed dress shirt, and a traditional straw cowboy hat. He had dark brown hair and a clean-shaven face, resembling George Strait from twenty-five years ago. Though I was curious who the man was, I didn't want to butt in. Instead, Buck, Jimmy, and I set about dismantling the temporary stage. We'd wait until all of Beckett's fans had gone to remove the tokens of affection they'd left him. To do otherwise would seem rude and heartless. Most of these people had probably never met Beckett in person, but his music had clearly meant something to each of them. Maybe they'd shared an unforgettable romantic moment while listening to "The Warmest Kiss," or maybe they'd once had fun with friends in a pasture and cherished those memories. Or maybe they'd just wanted to be part of something bigger than themselves, and the country music scene allowed them to experience that feeling.

I was bent over to pick up one of the cinder blocks when a male voice from behind me said, "Excuse me." I turned to find the George Strait lookalike standing there. Up close like this, I could see subtle but sure signs of middle age setting in, crow's feet around his eyes, thick laugh lines on either side of his lips reminding me of the hinged mouth on a ventriloquist's dummy or a marionette. But this guy was no dummy, no modern-day Charlie McCarthy or Howdy Doody. He was Rex Tomlinson. Beckett's manager.

And the next-to-last person Beckett had called shortly before his death.

He stuck out his hand in greeting and gave me a soft smile that deepened the laugh lines even further.

I shook his hand. "Whitney Whitaker."

"Sawyer and Wylie tell me you own this motel."

"I do," I said. "Along with my cousin Buck."

On hearing his name, Buck looked over from the stack of spare plywood. I motioned for him to join us, and introduced the two when he came over.

Rex shook my cousin's hand. "Tragedy, what happened to Beckett? For such a young guy with so much promise to die in a place like this . . ."

His unfinished sentence hung in the air, but it was clear what he meant. It was sad for an illustrious star to die in a shabby, derelict motel. I'd take offense if he was wrong, but he wasn't.

Picking up again, he said, "I can't imagine what Beckett was doing here."

I wasn't sure what details Collin would want to share with Tomlinson, so I didn't offer any. But I figured I couldn't go wrong with, "We're not sure either."

He exhaled a soft breath and said, "I could hardly believe it when I heard the news." He cleared his throat, apparently choked with emotion. "It just doesn't seem possible he's gone. Heck, I talked to him on the phone late Friday night. We'd planned to meet up for dinner at his favorite steakhouse Saturday evening. I wondered why he didn't show." He cleared his throat again. "For all I know, I might have been the last one to talk to Beckett. You know what his last words to me were? 'See ya over a glass of bourbon and a twenty-two-ounce rib eye.'"

At that, the man choked up completely, emitting a

half-cough, half-snorting sound. Instinctively, I reached out and placed a hand on his shoulder to comfort him.

When he gathered his composure, he said, "We were going to hammer out the details for his next recording contract, what demands he wanted to make, what the label would have to offer if they wanted to keep him. Guess we'll never know what could have been."

Behind Tomlinson, I saw Collin finish up with the ladies and engage in a quick conversation with Sawyer and Wylie. The three proceeded our way en masse, and I stepped back to give them room to join us.

Collin extended his hand. "Hello, Mr. Tomlinson. I'm Detective Flynn."

"Detective." The older man gave him a nod and took his hand. "Call me T-Rex. Everyone else does, including these crazy boys." He looked to Sawyer and Wylie and gave each of them a friendly, if small, smile, as well as a congenial pat on the back. "Good to see you two. That was a nice thing you did tonight, organizing this event to honor Beckett."

The vigil had been my idea, not theirs, but there was nothing to be gained by pointing that out. Besides, while it had been my notion originally, the two musicians had run the show.

"Happy to do it." Sawyer cringed when he seemed to realize his words sounded tactless. "I mean, not *happy* . . . I'd rather Beckett were still alive so we hadn't had to . . ."

Tomlinson took him by the shoulders and looked him in the eye. "Don't worry, son. We know what you mean." He released his grip. "Glad to see there was such a good turnout on short notice. Beckett deserved it."

Collin looked from Tomlinson to the musicians.

"Unless y'all have some pressing matters, could I speak to you privately, T-Rex?"

"Of course," the man said. He turned to the musicians one last time. "You two take care now. I'll be in touch."

Realizing they'd been dismissed, Sawyer and Wylie said their farewells and walked off, carrying their guitar cases with them.

Collin addressed me. "Mind if T-Rex and I use the lobby for a few minutes?"

"Be my guest, Detective."

Collin held out an arm to invite Tomlinson to accompany him to the lobby. I turned to see Jimmy watching them, his eyes slightly narrowed.

"What's the matter?" I asked Jimmy.

"Nothing, really," he said, still watching the men go. "Tomlinson's just not my kind of guy."

"What do you mean?"

"Too fancy, talking about steaks and demands and labels." He shrugged. "Guess we're just different types of folks."

That was putting it mildly. Jimmy was the type of impulsive free spirit who'd squat in an abandoned motel while on an itinerary-free motorcycle trip across the country. Rex Tomlinson was a wheeler-dealer in the country music industry with schedules and agendas and dinner meetings with clients. Also, Tomlinson likely owned more than three pairs of underwear. Judging from the two pair I'd seen hanging to drip dry over the shower curtain rod in Room 9 this morning, Jimmy had brought only a trio of boxers with him on his road trip. Not that I was paying attention to things like that, of course.

Now that everyone other than T-Rex had gone, Buck, Jimmy, and I began to gather up the items the fans had left. I saved the poems, cards, and photographs to give to Collin so he could pass them on to Beckett's parents. They hadn't come to the vigil, but that wasn't a surprise. It was at most forty-eight hours since they'd received the heartbreaking news, too little time to come to grips with their loss and face an overwhelming crowd of their son's admirers. Besides, Collin had said they planned to hold a small, private ceremony back at the Morgan ancestral plot in Kentucky. Tonight's event had been designed for fans, not family.

Jimmy gathered up the remaining beer, scooping up an armful of six-packs. "No sense letting all this beer go to waste." To that end, he carried them into his room and stacked them on the dresser.

Taking Jimmy's lead, Buck said, "No sense wasting these expensive cigars either." He gathered them up in a spare plastic bucket.

I followed suit, using an empty five-gallon paint bucket to collect the bouquets left behind. The competing scents of the various blooms was cloying, but I could separate them out back at home and put some in each room so that Colette, Emmalee, and I could enjoy them. I didn't want to be disrespectful, but it seemed like someone should make use of the flowers. Beckett's fans had spent a small fortune on them and most were still fresh.

A few minutes later, Collin and T-Rex stepped out of the lobby, their business concluded. T-Rex pulled his keys from his pocket. I noticed he kept them on an elliptical keychain with openings on either end. He must use the keychain to open bottles of beer. He should enjoy some of the beer Beckett's fans had brought, shouldn't he? After all, per Sawyer and Wylie he was the man who'd launched the young star's career.

Before Jimmy could grab the last six-pack of bottled beer from the collection and take it to his room, I scooped it up. "Here." I held the beer out to T-Rex. "Beckett would have wanted you to enjoy this."

The man took the bottles from me and gave me a little smile in return. "Thanks, Whitney. That's very thoughtful of you."

Buck held out the bucket of cigars. "Would you like to take a few of these too?"

T-Rex held up a palm. "No, thanks. I don't smoke. Tried to get Beckett to quit, as a matter of fact. I was afraid the habit would damage his vocal chords."

A moot point now, sad to say.

As the man turned to go, Collin stopped him with, "One last question, T-Rex."

When he turned back around, Collin asked, "Do you know anyone who might have had a beef with Beckett?"

He flinched, as if it pained him to reveal his knowledge. "Yeah, I do. Guy by the name of Shep Sampson."

"Who's Shep Sampson?"

"Banjo player," Rex said. "One of the best in the business. Plays harmonica and a mean accordion too. He played with Beckett for a while, but Beckett fired him."

"Why?" Collin asked.

Rex exhaled a sharp breath. "Because he accused Beckett of the worst thing you can accuse a singer of."

"Which is . . . ?"

"Stealing his song."

CHAPTER 14

DOUBLE VISION

WHITNEY

T-Rex went on to illuminate us about the music industry. "In rap and hip-hop, it's a point of pride for the recording artists that they write their own songs. It's nearly unheard of for a rap or hip-hop artist to sing a song written by someone else. Anyone who does is seen as inauthentic, a phony. Drake got a lot of flak a few years back for singing some songs other artists had a hand in writing. Things are evolving, though. Collaborations are becoming more common. Country-western music has always been more of a mixed bag. Many country artists buy songs from professional songwriters, and the practice is considered perfectly acceptable. After all, vocal skills and songwriting skills don't necessarily go hand in hand. Some people are one-trick ponies. Besides, some good songwriters and vocalists just aren't made for a stage. They lack that star quality that makes a good performer."

I understood what he was getting at. I'd seen singer-songwriter shows on several occasions at the Bluebird

Cafe, the Listening Room, and other venues around the city. While the shows were always entertaining, some of the performers were a much better fit for an intimate venue than an auditorium or arena.

Tomlinson went on to say that other country singers, such as crossover artist Taylor Swift, wrote their own lyrics exclusively, sometimes with a cowriter, and were blessed with across-the-board talent in songwriting, vocals, and stage presence. "They know how to write a song *and* put on a show. Lady Gaga's the same. She can write and sing. Same with Ed Sheeran."

Regardless, Beckett Morgan had claimed in many an interview that he'd partied in pastures in his small hometown in rural Western Kentucky, and that the experiences had provided fodder for his breakout hit, "Party in the Pasture."

Collin asked, "Could there be any truth to Shep Sampson's accusation?"

"Truth?" T-Rex issued a *pshaw.* "Not an ounce. Shep's a struggling musician who's never attained the level of success he thinks he's due. Still, he could've made trouble for Beckett, so I did what I had to do as Beckett's manager, to save his reputation."

"Which was . . . ?" Collin asked, prodding the man to be more specific.

"Convince Beckett to buy Shep off," T-Rex said, matter-of-factly. "It was best to keep Beckett's name out of it, though, and to make sure there wasn't a paper trail leading to him either. So I paid Shep twenty-thousand dollars out of my own pocket to keep his lying mouth shut."

Interesting. I wondered if T-Rex was right, that Beckett hadn't stolen the song. Maybe Shep was a slick opportunist who saw a chance to extort money from a rich but inexperienced recording artist. But could it be possible that the opposite was true? That Beckett had indeed stolen the song from Shep, and knew the guy would be powerless against his substantial resources? Either way, Collin would suss things out, figure out the true story. Not only was it his job to do so, he was darn good at it. Especially when I chipped in and helped.

T-Rex added, "I hate to sound crass, but twenty grand was a drop in the bucket compared to what I earned managing Beckett. Now I've got to cancel the rest of Beckett's tour. So much for the management fees I would've made. Whoever killed Beckett didn't just cost that young man his life, he cost him and me a nice chunk of change." His voice hitched as he said softly, "I'm going to miss that kid. He could've gone far, and I could've helped him get there."

Collin concluded his interview and T-Rex headed off with a tip of his hat and a "Goodnight, folks" to the lot of us.

Buck held his bucket out to Collin. "Have a cigar, buddy. Let's light one up in Beckett's honor."

After Collin fished one out of the pail, Buck turned to Jimmy. "You too, man."

Not to make any sexist assumptions, Buck held his bucket out to me next. "Care to join us, cuz?"

"Ew," I replied. "No thanks. No one would want to kiss me if I smell like cigars."

A grin played about Collin's lips as he wet the tip of his cigar. "Don't be so sure about that." He wagged his brows at me.

I cocked my head. "Sure anyone will want to kiss *you*? This works both ways, you know."

T-Rex turned at the gate and glanced back at us. Had he overheard our flirty banter? I hoped he wasn't offended by it. We'd all been on edge since finding Beckett's body, and we needed to cut loose a little.

Once T-Rex continued out of earshot, I showed Collin the photos I'd snapped of the unknown man who'd attended the vigil, his belt buckle, and his license plate.

After taking them in, the detective looked up at Jimmy. "What do you think?"

Jimmy raised his shoulders. "Don't know. All I can tell you was the impression I got at the time was that the belt buckle was a bird foot. But whether I got a good look is debatable. Both me and the other guy were moving, it was dark outside, and my brain was foggy."

"Six whiskies will do that to you." Collin instructed me to text the photos to him so he could follow up. I forwarded them to his phone and they set off through cyberspace with a telltale *whoosh*.

Jimmy was the only one of the three men who seemed to know how to handle a cigar. He pulled a Swiss army knife from his pocket. "Hold up, boys. You've got to cut off the tip before you light it." He placed the cigar against the stucco and proceeded to saw at the end, releasing a cascade of tobacco. He looked down at the pile of dried leaves at his feet. "Shoot. That didn't go so well."

"My shop shears should do the trick." Buck went for his toolbox, retrieving the tool and holding it up proudly. "These babies are pure titanium."

After the men used the shears to snip the tips off the cigars, Buck flicked a butane lighter he used for various purposes on our jobs. The three men leaned in, one end of the cigar in their mouth, the other in the flame. Collin took one small puff and burst into a racking cough.

Jimmy chuckled. "Some tough cop you are." He proceeded to puff expertly on the cigar, releasing a dark cloud of smoke out his nose, as if he were a dragon. "See? That's how it's done. If you want to know how to smoke a hookah pipe, I can school you in that too. Smoked hookah several times on shore leave in the Persian Gulf."

Collin shook his head. It was all he could do with his lungs seized up by the smoke. I patted the poor guy on the back. While Buck didn't launch into an all-out coughing fit, he gagged a bit on the first few puffs before adjusting.

Jimmy popped the top on a can of warm beer. *Kshhh.* "Can't let my lungs have all the fun. Gotta get my liver in on the party too." He took a big swig before turning to Collin. "So? What did Mr. Hotshot have to tell you?"

"Rex Tomlinson, you mean?" Collin said. "You heard the best of it."

Jimmy sent a perfectly round smoke ring up over his head, like a smoky halo. "That Beckett might have stolen his hit song from this Shep guy?"

"Yeah." Collin gave Jimmy a sideways glance before gingerly holding the cigar to his lips and taking a tiny puff. He managed to keep breathing this time, but barely.

Buck held his cigar aloft. "Fame go to Beckett's head like this cigar is going to mine?" He crossed his eyes and let his head and tongue loll.

"Sounds like it," Collin said. "Tomlinson said he bought a customized passenger van for Beckett to tour in and the guy threw a fit, said it was no better than a daycare shuttle. He told T-Rex he'd only accept first-class flights or a fully outfitted tour bus."

Hmm. "His casual, country-boy shtick was just that? A shtick?"

"Looks that way," Collin said. "He said he saw a

side of Beckett others didn't, that he tried to help Beckett hide that side of himself because it wouldn't have earned him any friends in an industry where relationships are critical. He said Beckett was still a kid in many respects, so he cut him some slack, and he expected Beckett would eventually outgrow his childish behavior."

I was sad to hear it. Beckett had seemed humble and down-to-earth in his television interviews. But the expensive cigars and top-shelf bourbon he'd bought at the Poison Emporium were proof of his upscale tastes.

Collin rested a hand on his holster. "T-Rex said Beckett had dozens of girls on a string too. That he led them on, made each of them think they were special."

I finagled a large piece of 80-grit sandpaper out of Buck's open toolbox and used it to fan cigar smoke out of my face. "What about the women you talked to? Did they confirm what T-Rex said?"

"More or less," Collin said. "Each of them seemed to think she was something special to Beckett, despite the fact that they spent virtually no time together and weren't intimate. He told them it would be bad for his career if he settled down now. He had his image of a free and single partying cowboy to uphold. T-Rex said the image appealed both to a female fan base and a male base too. Men wanted to be him. Women wanted to be with him. That old cliché. None of the ladies' numbers were in Beckett's contacts list, though. I didn't have the heart to tell them that he hadn't bothered to add them. They'd all convinced themselves he'd call as soon as his tour was over and he was back in town for more than a few days at a time."

Jimmy's eyes narrowed. "Better to let them live with a lie?"

Collin met Jimmy's challenge with, "Better not to sully a murder victim's reputation."

Jimmy took another puff and spoke while attempting to hold the smoke in, his voice sounding odd and distorted and squeaky. "I bet one of those girls killed him. She found out she wasn't the only lady in Beckett's life and decided since he'd broken her heart, she'd stab him in his."

"Could be." Collin's nose twitched in response to the smoke and he bent down, grinding the butt out on the sidewalk. "That's enough for me. My respiratory system can't take anymore." He tossed the extinguished butt into a trash bin, turned to me, and pointed to the gate. "See me out?"

"Sure."

We walked together to the gate, where he stopped, cutting another sideways glance at Jimmy, who was teaching Buck how to blow a smoke ring. "I didn't want to discuss the phone records in front of Jimmy."

"I understand." The calls could be a major clue. If and when to disclose them to the public would be a tactical decision for a detective to make. J.C., whoever that was, was the last person Beckett had called on his phone. If J.C. was another musician, J.C. might have been in the SoBro area when they spoke, and it wouldn't have taken much time at all to walk over the bridge and meet up with Beckett at the motel. I fingered the petals of a red rose in my bucket. "Did you ask T-Rex about J.C.? If he knows who that is?"

"He offered two suggestions," Collin said. "Jesus Christ or Jose Cuervo. Barring either of them, he didn't know. Said he'd never heard Beckett mention anyone who went by J.C. I asked Wylie and Sawyer too. Neither of them recognized the nickname or initials."

"What about Beckett's late-night call to T-Rex?" I asked. "Did he tell you what that was about?"

"They talked about Gia Revello, the exec from the record company. Beckett was furious Gia had accosted him at the Ryman and embarrassed him in front of his fans and the other musicians. Tomlinson said Beckett's next contract is in negotiations, and that they made plans to discuss things over dinner on Saturday. Beckett never showed, of course. T-Rex said he sat in the bar area for over an hour, even showed me a receipt for a couple of bourbons he drank while waiting for Beckett."

That coincided with what Rex Tomlinson had told me, that he planned to meet Beckett over a glass of bourbon and a rib eye. It also explained the two calls T-Rex had made to Beckett's phone Saturday evening, and the final call on Sunday. No doubt he was wondering why his client had stood him up, had called Beckett for an explanation, maybe even an apology. T-Rex might consider himself a hotshot, like Jimmy said, but at least he'd been forthcoming. He'd given us information before we'd even asked for it.

I mused aloud. "If Beckett had actually stolen the song from another artist, he could have been exposed as a liar and a thief, and his career would have been ruined."

"True," Collin said, "only that would have given Beckett reason to kill Shep Sampson, not the other way around."

He had a point. "But if Shep Sampson really wrote the song and Beckett stole it, Sampson might have seen the success Beckett had with it, all the money it made him, and Sampson might have blown his top, killed Beckett out of rage. Maybe he trailed Beckett here Friday night after the show at the Ryman."

"That also could be true," he said. "Tomlinson told me that Beckett was incredibly talented, but that he was also one of the most big-headed and demanding artists he'd ever managed, called him a stubborn son of a gun. Could be Shep followed Beckett to the Poison Emporium and tried to reason with him face-to-face as they walked back toward the bridge. Maybe Shep asked him to share the credit and royalties like a decent person would, and Beckett blew him off. Who knows?"

"What's next?" I asked Collin.

"Right now? I'm going to have the lab locate J.C.'s phone again, track the person down and have a talk."

With that, he gave me a peck on the cheek and headed off. I heard him placing a call to the police forensics lab as he went.

Tuesday morning, I sat in front of the television eating a bowl of cereal and watching the morning news with Sawdust and Cleo on my lap. My roommates were still asleep, so I had the volume turned down low. A news crew had caught up with Lacy Spurlock at her hotel in Austin, Texas, where she was scheduled to perform tonight. They'd interviewed her in the lobby of the Four Seasons.

Her lips quivered and her eyes filled with tears as she said, "I could hardly believe it when I heard he was gone. Beckett didn't deserve what happened to him."

The reporter was relentless. "So you harbor no ill will against him after his refusal to kiss you at the Country Music Awards?"

Lacy's wet eyes flashed with lightning. It was a wonder she and the reporter didn't suffer electrocution and drop to the hotel's marble floor right then and there. But an instant later, her expression softened again.

"Of course not. I'm not that petty. I've let bygones be bygones."

Has she? Her since-released album, which was full of revenge songs, said otherwise. She seemed to be fixated on Beckett, unable to let him go. I might even think she was the seemingly obsessed blonde from the bridge if not for the fact that passersby didn't swamp the woman asking for autographs and selfies like they would have if she'd actually been Lacy.

She wiped her tears with her professionally manicured hand. "Beckett Morgan will always have a special place in my heart and, despite what happened, I know I had a special place in his heart too."

In his heart. That was precisely where the doorstop had been stabbed. A creepy feeling slithered through my stomach.

After finishing my cereal, I apologized to the cats for having to get up from the couch, and placed them gently on the floor. They accompanied me to the kitchen, where I rinsed my bowl and stuck it in the dishwasher. They continued to trail along with me as I went to the bathroom to get ready for work. One thing was for sure, cats never left you feeling lonely.

When I emerged from the bathroom freshly showered and blow-dried a half hour later, Emmalee rushed in after me. "Gotta go, gotta go, gotta go!" she called out before shutting the door.

Three women and one bathroom was not a great ratio. While it worked fine most days when we were on staggered schedules, on the days when all three of us had to get up early, at least one of us usually found herself dancing around with her legs crossed outside the bathroom door while she waited for her turn. The cats were lucky. Each of them had their own litter box.

Maybe I should spend some of the profits from the condos on adding another bathroom to this house. Colette's bedroom was the largest, around twelve by sixteen feet. A three-quarter bath with a sink, toilet, and shower stall would take up around thirty-five square feet. I was willing to bet she'd sacrifice the bedroom space to have her own private bath, and adding another bathroom would increase the property's value when it came time to sell the house later down the line. There would still be enough room in the master for a king-sized bed, which was a must for resale.

As I headed out to work half an hour later, Colette intercepted me when I went to fill my travel mug at the kitchen's coffeepot. She handed me a reusable grocery bag filled with three large thermoses. "I made jambalaya last night. I packed some for you, Buck, and Jimmy for lunch."

I gave her a hug. "You're the best roommate ever!" I turned to Emmalee, who was now drinking coffee at the breakfast bar, and cringed. "No offense, Em."

"None taken," she said. "I feel the same way. If I had to choose between a roommate who cooks for me or one who can repair wood rot, I'd take the cook any day."

I gave her a hug too. "You're a close second."

She laughed. "Right back at you."

I looked from one of them to the other. "What would y'all think about me adding a second bathroom to the house? I could turn Colette's room into a proper master bedroom. It means there'd be some noise and dust for a couple of weeks."

Their ensuing squeals of delight told me they were in full agreement.

"All right," I told them. "As soon as Buck and I finish with the Music City Motor Court, I'll get to work here."

After leaving the house, I ran by Home & Hearth to take Mrs. Hartley some of Beckett's flowers. She'd been a fan, said his "Warmest Kiss" duet with Lacy Spurlock reminded her of that long-ago time when she and Marv had been dating.

As I set the vase of red roses and white lilies on her desk, she leaned in and took a deep breath. "These smell lovely, Whitney. Thank you." She sat back and yanked a tissue from a box on her desk to dab her eyes. "That poor young man. It was so senseless."

Still sitting, Marv walked his feet to roll his chair over next to his wife. He draped an arm around her shoulders. "Whitney will help the detective get to the bottom of things. I have no doubt."

Mr. Hartley's confidence in me was both flattering and troubling. Many homicides went unsolved. If I couldn't help Collin nab Beckett's killer, I'd feel like a failure. Of course, there was a chance he'd already figured it all out last night, that the lab had pinged J.C.'s phone, provided the detective with its location, and he'd made an arrest. Maybe he'd been tied up long into the night with booking the suspect and had slept in late this morning. And maybe I was a little miffed that he hadn't texted me to let me know one way or another.

After showing an available duplex to a young woman looking for a yard for her rambunctious and adorable rescue dogs, I drove to the motel. A group of young women stood nearby, tears streaming down their faces, as a couple of workers from the fencing company wrangled a wide gate at the auto entrance, preparing to install it. I raised a hand in greeting to the fence crew as I drove through and, their hands full, they nodded in return. I noticed that Buck and Jimmy had knocked down what had remained of the crumbling brick wall around the pool too. *Darn.* I'd been hoping to take a few whacks at the wall myself. Nothing like smashing something with a sledgehammer to take the edge off your anxiety.

I climbed out of my car and went to the clubhouse. I retrieved one of the dusty boxes of facial tissue, blew the dust from it, and carried it out to the weeping women. "Here. Looks like you could use this."

One of the women took the box from me, bursting in fresh sobs as she did so. She tried to thank me, but her words came out garbled. I simply nodded and gave her a soft smile that said I understood her pain.

I went in search of Buck and Jimmy, finding them at work in Room 3, ripping the stained, worn carpet from the floor. Both wore masks and goggles to protect themselves from the dust the task inevitably stirred up.

I stopped in the doorway and waved my hand in front of my face. The dust was nearly as bad as the cigar smoke had been last night. "Colette packed us jambalaya for lunch."

Though I couldn't see Buck's mouth behind the mask, I could tell from the crinkles around his eyes that he was smiling. He turned to Jimmy. "Wait until you taste it. Best you'll ever have."

As they rolled the carpet up, I took a step back. "I'll get a broom and sweep up after you."

Buck's attention shifted from my face to the parking lot behind me. "Well, well, well. Look who's here."

I turned around to see Thad Gentry careening through the open gate in his midnight blue Infiniti Q70L sedan, acting as if he owned the place. His fast driving was a sign of how important he considered his time to be and how little he thought the rules of both traffic and decorum applied to him. He braked to a quick stop next to my SUV and slithered from his car. "Mornin', folks!" he called in a forced-friendly voice. He stepped over, spotted the bucket filled with the Nicaraguan Montecristo cigars, and clucked his tongue. "Those babies up for grabs?" He didn't wait for an answer before reaching down, snagging a handful of them, and stuffing them into his breast pocket.

"To what do we owe this visit?" I asked. No way would I call it a pleasure.

"It's your lucky day." He grinned. "Got a proposition for you."

"You always do." Gentry had offered to buy our first flip house from us at a nice markup before we'd started the renovations, but I'd turned him down. I'd been afraid it might put me at odds with the Home & Hearth client who'd sold me the place. Like Gentry, he'd been a real estate mogul. The two had been engaged in a ruthless rivalry, and I didn't want to end up in the middle of it.

Gentry gestured around the motel. "Heard you're turning this eyesore into condominiums."

Though we'd planned to publicize that fact once we were further along in our renovations, so far we'd shared our plans with only a limited group of people. Our families. The Hartleys. The subcontractors we'd hired. Our partner Presley, of course. "Where'd you hear that?"

Rather than reveal his source, he merely chuckled and said, "Word gets around."

More than likely, someone from the construction crew I'd hired had spilled the beans. Some of them did work for Gentry Real Estate Development. I suppose it didn't really matter that the news was out, though it nonetheless felt like Gentry had stolen our thunder.

He pointed to the roof. "I had my guys take a look up there. They say that roof's solid as bedrock."

My eyes narrowed of their own accord. "When, exactly, did your guys take a look at the roof?" Was it before Buck and I had won the bid on the place? Or was it afterward, meaning they'd trespassed? Could they have been the ones who'd pushed the fence back Friday evening while Jimmy was out at the bars on SoBro?

Gentry rocked back on his heels and chuckled again. "That doesn't matter. What matters is that the roof and foundation of this motel could support a second story. You'd double your money by adding another floor, six additional units. I'm here to offer you the seed money to do that. All I'd want in return is half the profits. It's a sweet deal. You'd be a fool not to jump on it. I know money's tight for you amateurs."

Amateurs?

Buck didn't cotton to the insult either. He stepped up next to me, a sharp utility knife in his hand, and muttered under his breath, "Call us amateurs again and there'll be another murder here."

"So," Gentry said, undeterred by our glares. "What's your plan for this place, design-wise?"

"Not that it's any of your business," I said, "but we're leaning in to the mid-century roadside motel look. We plan to use lots of colorful paint on the façade, restore the neon sign."

He snorted. "You're kidding, right? That's the tackiest thing I can imagine."

"Well, then," I countered. "You need to get a better imagination."

Buck cut me a look that said *Was that meant to be an insult? Because I'm not sure it was.* Heck, I wasn't even sure what I'd said made sense. But maybe if I kept talking, something I said would eventually shut him up.

"People love nostalgia," I said. "These units will sell in record time. Mark my words."

Gentry had the gall to roll his eyes. "You'd make more money if you went modern. People want the latest, greatest thing, not something that looks like a throwback to a tasteless time. My high-rise development in the Gulch had a waiting list before we even broke ground. I made money hand over fist."

"Good for you," I said. "But we're not just in this for the profit. These flip projects are works of art to us, our vision."

"I see," he replied. "They satisfy your creative spirit."

"Exactly."

He snickered. "You're not cut out to be a business-woman, Miss Whitaker. Real estate is not about fulfilling your soul, it's about filling your pocket."

"That, sir, is where we differ. It's also why we will never work with you." Ignoring him, I stepped over and grabbed the push broom that leaned against the stucco.

He stepped in front of me, blocking my path on the sidewalk. "I'll front you half a mil. We'll do these units up right."

He'd give us $500,000? That's a lot of cheddar. My fingers tightened around the broom handle as I mustered every ounce of my resolve. "No, thank you. Now please get out of my way."

Buck and Jimmy stepped up on either side of me. Buck cracked his knuckles. "You heard the lady. Scram."

Gentry glanced down at Buck's fisted hands and chuckled again before looking back at me. "You're missing out on a great opportunity. You're going to regret this decision."

"I sincerely doubt it."

Buck and Jimmy crossed their arms over their chests

and stared the man down until he climbed back into his car and drove off, but not before flooring his gas pedal and screeching out of the motel parking lot, leaving black tire marks on the asphalt and hollering out his window. "Amateurs!"

I might have hurled my broom at him like a spear if not for the fact that Collin pulled up in front of the motel at that moment. *Finally!*

As I sprinted out to his car, he rolled down the passenger window. I grabbed the ledge and stuck my head inside. "Did you find J.C.? Has the murder been solved?"

CHAPTER 15

SWAN SONG

WHITNEY

"No and no," Collin replied. "The techs pinged the phone's location to the pedestrian bridge, but when I questioned the few people up there, none were J.C."

"Are you sure? Did you ask to see their IDs?"

"I did. They all cooperated."

"Of course they did," I said. "This is Nashville." Though the city was on the cutting edge of the music industry, it was, in many ways, a place of old-fashioned values. People here still said "sir" and "ma'am," and generally respected their elders and authority. I eyed him closely, noting the dark circles under his eyes. No doubt he hadn't had much sleep since I'd discovered Beckett's body. Heck, I hadn't either. Nightmares of his face kept jerking me awake in the middle of the night, disturbing poor Sawdust, who would look at me, questioning and concerned. "Did you try calling the phone?"

"Several times. There was no answer."

Did J.C. purposely refuse the call, or had J.C. been otherwise occupied and not realized the Nashville P.D.

was trying to get in touch? "Were the lab techs able to follow the phone when J.C. left the bridge?"

"They tracked it," he said. "But the thing is, the phone moved downriver."

I gasped and jerked my head back reflexively, bumping the back of my skull on the top edge of the window frame. *Ow.* "J.C. jumped from the bridge?" Had J.C. killed Beckett, then found the guilt too much to bear? Or had J.C. confronted the true killer on the bridge, who then pushed J.C. from the precipice to prevent the truth from coming out? "Or did someone toss J.C. into the Cumberland River?" *Could a person survive a fall from that height?*

"No," Collin said. "Nobody jumped or was thrown in. The phone went down the river with the *General Jackson* and stopped dockside near the Gaylord."

The Gaylord Opryland Resort sat several miles downstream from downtown Nashville. The General Jackson Showboat docked there when the paddleboat wasn't taking tourists on an entertainment-filled cruise up the river.

"So J.C. left the motel after the vigil and somehow got on the boat near the bridge? How?" Short of leaping from the bridge onto the boat or dropping down by wire or rope like a live-action hero, there would have been no way to access the vessel. While the showboat made a slow turn just past downtown to return to its home base at the Gaylord, it didn't dock near downtown. It came reasonably close to the bank as it U-turned on the water, though. "Did J.C. go down the riverbank and swim out to the boat?"

"Nothing quite so adventurous," Collin said. "J.C. dropped the phone from the bridge as the boat was making its way underneath. We found the phone on top of the striped awning on the back. A few more feet, and it would've been ground up by the paddlewheel."

"Did J.C. ditch the phone on purpose?"

"Hard to say but, if so, it was an impulsive move. If J.C. thought the phone was being tracked, the smarter thing to do would have been to smash the battery, or drop it in the river, where it would have been difficult to retrieve. The phone hadn't even been turned off."

"Beckett's phone data showed he made an outgoing call to J.C. right before entering the Poison Emporium, right? Did he leave a voice mail?"

"He did. Unfortunately, he didn't say the name of the person he was calling. Listen." Collin had recorded the voice mail message with his phone, and he played it back to me, Beckett's voice eerie to hear now. *"Hey. It's me. Been a rough night. The show went good, but Gia Revello gave me an earful afterward, in front of God and everybody. Made me look like a fool to the fans. Sawyer and Wylie seemed to be eating it up, but they asked me out for a beer after, so maybe I just took them wrong. Anyways, I'm meetin' up with T-Rex tomorrow for dinner to sort things out. I'll let you know how it goes. Let's hook up on Sunday at our usual spot. 'kay? Love you."*

The voice mail seemed to implicate both Gia Revello and the musicians. "Were there any other voice mails on the phone? Maybe an associated e-mail account, or apps that would give you a clue as to J.C.'s identity?"

"No," Collin said. "If there had been any, they'd been deleted. So had any texts or photos. Whoever was using the phone wanted to keep it as clean as possible, figuratively speaking."

The phone might have been figuratively clean, but

was it literally clean? "Was the lab able to get finger-prints off the phone?"

"Plenty," he said. "Unfortunately, they didn't match anyone in the criminal databases."

In other words, J.C. had no criminal record. "So the phone provided no clues at all as to who J.C. is?"

"No. Beckett's did, though. The texts they sent each other were generally short and cryptic, but J.C. and Beckett were romantically involved. That much was clear. J.C. sent lots of heart and kissy-face emojis."

"So, J.C.'s a woman, then, right? At least we narrowed that down."

"Probably, but not necessarily." Collin cocked his head. "J.C. could be a woman, or he could be a guy. If it's the latter, that might be why the relationship wasn't made public. Maybe Beckett was afraid it would hurt his career."

While there were a handful of openly gay country singers, the genre was definitely more traditional and less diverse than other musical categories. It tended to be mostly white, straight, and male. In fact, in 2015, a scandal known as "Tomato-Gate" or "Salad-Gate" struck the country music industry after a radio consul-tant named Keith Hill advised stations not to play too many songs by female artists, and certainly not to play female artists back-to-back. He compared female per-formers to the tomatoes in salad, saying the male artists were the more substantial lettuce. *Grrr.*

I wasn't one to advocate violence, but perhaps some-one should have tossed Hill into the Cumberland, cool him off a bit. As for me, I enjoyed songs by female art-ists, and found them both clever and relatable. Colette, Emmalee, and I had attended several fantastic shows by the Song Suffragettes, which featured a rotating lineup of talented female singer-songwriters. All of us enjoyed Lacy Spurlock's hits too. She sang several powerful feminist anthems that made you want to burn your bra, raise your fist, and demand equal pay for equal work. Also a more comfortable bra.

I opened the passenger door and dropped into the seat. Collin's news had released a floodgate of questions in my mind. Might as well sit while I got some answers.

"Uh-oh." He cut me some suspicious side-eye. "You're making yourself comfortable."

Ignoring his wisecrack, I asked, "Beckett's call record showed three incoming calls from J.C. on Saturday morning, right? The first one went to voicemail. Did J.C. leave a message on Beckett's phone?"

"Unfortunately, no. There was just a second or two of silence and then a very faint man's voice in the background. He called out 'The biscuits are ready.' The caller sighed and hung up."

"J.C. might live with a man, then?"

"It's possible. Sounded like the guy was calling J.C. to breakfast. I got in touch with the phone company this morning. J.C.'s phone was on Beckett's account. He'd bought it with a credit card early last year, shortly after the release of 'The Warmest Kiss.'"

"When his career took off."

He nodded. "My guess is that the phone was used strictly for communications between Beckett and J.C., which tells me J.C. must have had another phone to communicate with people other than Beckett."

"A private phone?" I said. "Sounds like the two of them wanted to keep their relationship secret. Or J.C. did, at least."

"I can't think of another reason to delete everything

off the phone. I've put in a request for the phone records to verify whether my guess is right or not. I've also requested Beckett's credit card records. There might be something in them that could offer further clues. It'll take a day or two to get them."

"What about photos? Did Beckett have any pics on his phone that might indicate who J.C. is?"

"None that I could pinpoint. There were surprisingly few recent photos on his phone. Most were from before he hit it big. Pics of his high school sweetheart, friends from back home, a family photo or two. There was a funny video of his family's shaggy old mutt howling alongside Beckett while he played his guitar and sang 'you ain't nothin' but a hound dog.' Judging from his camera stream, it's almost as if his life ended when he left Kentucky."

"He's probably been too busy since he arrived in Nashville to take pictures himself," I pointed out. "More than likely, somebody else is always snapping photos of him."

"Could be," Collin agreed. "I get the impression that he didn't really have much of a personal life after he hit the charts. It's mostly been about his music career. Touring, shows, appearances at benefits. Other than whatever he had going on with J.C., that is. The fact that there appears to be no photos of him with anyone who could be J.C. tells me that, for one reason or another, he and J.C. didn't want photographic evidence of the two of them together."

His words sent dread slithering up my spine. "Maybe J.C. planned to kill Beckett and insisted there be no photos of the two of them together to avoid becoming a suspect. Maybe J.C. tossed the phone off the bridge without looking in the hopes it would sink to the bottom and never be found, but the showboat happened to be going under at just that moment."

"Could be," he said. "But without knowing who J.C. is, I can't establish a motive."

"Did you get in touch with Beckett's family?" I asked. "Do they know who J.C. is?"

"The answers to your questions are yes and no. Yes, I spoke with Beckett's parents and siblings. No, they didn't know who J.C. was. They said Beckett mentioned two musicians whose names started with J, a Jack and a Jasmine, but they didn't know their last names. I checked with T-Rex. He said he knew a Jack and a Jasmine that Beckett had worked with, but neither had a last name that started with C."

"You have any suspicions about him?"

"T-Rex?" Collin said. "Some. He was among the last to speak to Beckett, which could be a clue, and he admitted Beckett could be difficult. But T-Rex has been in the music management business a long time. I'm sure Beckett isn't the first oversized ego he's had to deal with. Killers sometimes tip their hand by saying their relationship with the victim was perfect, and that they had nothing but good feelings toward the deceased. The fact that he didn't paint his relationship with Beckett as all lollipops and rainbows makes me more inclined to believe him. Plus, I don't see a motive for Tomlinson to do away with Beckett."

"The guy was his golden goose."

Collin gave a nod of agreement. "Exactly. I was able to listen to the voice mails on Beckett's phone. T-Rex left two messages for Beckett Saturday evening, asking why he hadn't shown up for their dinner meeting at the steakhouse."

"That backs up what T-Rex said earlier, that he'd waited for Beckett at the restaurant."

"Right. T-Rex left another shorter message on Sunday, telling Beckett that if he was playing some sort of a game to please stop because he was starting to get worried since he hadn't heard back."

"What about the piano player and the drummer Sawyer mentioned?" I asked. "Have you talked to them yet?"

Collin exhaled sharply and scrubbed a hand over his face. "They're still on my list. There hasn't been enough time to talk to everyone yet, and I had to prioritize the persons of interest based on the information available."

"Was the man wearing the belt buckle with the crossed arrows a priority? Have you identified him yet?"

"Got a name and address," Collin said. "I've done some preliminary research. He doesn't have a criminal record. I plan to get in touch with him later."

"Later? What are you doing beforehand?"

"Speaking to Shep Sampson and Gia Revello."

I reached over my shoulder and grabbed the seat belt, pulling it down and fastening it with a *click*. "I'm going with you."

"Isn't that my decision to make?"

"Then make it."

He gave me a coy grin. "Convince me."

"Okay," I said. "You should take me with you because two heads are better than one. Maybe I'll pick up on something you don't. Also because Colette sent me to work with a thermos full of her delicious jambalaya. If you take me with you to interview Shep Sampson and Gia Revello, I'll share it with you when we get back."

He didn't look entirely convinced, but he didn't say

no. "Colette *is* a fantastic cook." He did a slow exhale. "All right. I suppose your presence could be justified. The murder happened on your property and you found the body."

When Collin started the car, Buck hollered, "Where do you think you're going, Whitney? We've got work to do!"

"The detective needs my help!" I called through the open window. "I'll be back soon!"

"If you're not," he warned, "I'm eating your jambalaya!"

Twenty minutes later, Collin's cruiser approached Music Row, a small district in Nashville that served as home to a number of both historic and new recording studios, as well as office space for music production companies. The parklike entrance to Music Row featured a bronze statue of Owen Bradley playing a piano, a tribute to the late producer who'd been the first to build a music business in the area. Bradley had produced many classic hits by Patsy Cline, Loretta Lynn, Kitty Wells, and Brenda Lee. Clearly, Bradley hadn't thought these women were tomatoes. *Keith Hill can kiss my asparagus.*

Collin pulled into the lot of a single-story studio. The mustard-yellow paint went nicely with the ketchup-red door and window trim.

As we climbed out of the car, I asked, "Does Shep know you're coming?"

"No," Collin said. "I didn't want to lose the element of surprise. When people are flustered, they sometimes accidentally reveal things they wouldn't otherwise."

We went inside and checked in with a receptionist in the foyer. She pointed down a hallway to our right. "Shep Sampson's in studio three."

"Is he alone?" Collin asked.

"No," she said. "There's two other musicians in there with him. Wait until the light goes off over the door before you knock, okay?"

We walked down the hall and waited in front of the door, both of us staring up at the round red light. I found myself involuntarily humming "Rudolph, the Red-Nosed Reindeer." Collin humored me until the light suddenly went off, then he stepped forward and knocked on the door. *Rap-rap-rap.* He pulled his badge from his pocket and held it at the ready, like a press member with a backstage pass.

A few seconds later, a fortyish woman with long auburn hair opened the door, a mandolin cradled in her arm. She took in Collin's badge and gun before her focus shifted to me. Her eyes ran from my face, down my coveralls to my scuffed work boots, and back up again. "Can I do something for you?"

"We need to speak with Shep Sampson," Collin said.

"All right." The woman waved us into the room, which incorporated two small sub-spaces, a control room filled with high-tech dials and screens and lights, the other with stools and microphones. The control room and the "live room" were separated by a half wall and a large pane of plate glass. Men sat on two of the stools in the live room, one holding a guitar, the other holding a banjo. In light of the fact that T-Rex told us Shep Sampson played the banjo, it was immediately clear which of the two was the man we were looking for. Shep even looked like a shepherd. The banjo picks he wore on his fingers and thumbs made it appear as though he had claws, like a dog. His shaggy hair had dark roots that blended into lighter brown at the ends, likely the result of sun and wind damage. He had big brown eyes, whiskers, and a rather large, protruding nose, not unlike a canine snout. He wore boots, jeans, and a cream-colored Western shirt with a bolo tie. The two black tie cords were held together by a round silver slide inlaid with a dog's paw print, complete with four round toe pads tipped with pointed claws. *Claws that look similar to bird talons.*

Alarm threw me off-kilter. Collin had told me before that eyewitness identifications were notoriously inaccurate. A witness's perception could be affected by light and distance, and the duration of time they had their eyes on a subject. The observer could be distracted by weapons, noises, or lights. Their observations could also be subject to personal bias or motivations. *Could Shep have a belt buckle with a similar paw print? And could Jimmy, in his six-whiskey state, have mistaken the four claws for three talons?* Maybe Jimmy even saw the tie, but wrongfully recalled it as a belt buckle.

A glance at Collin told me he wondered the same thing. His jaw flexed as he took in the tie.

As the two men stood from their stools, the woman said, "I suppose you'd like some privacy?"

"Yes, please," Collin replied.

The woman put her eyes on the guitarist and jerked her head toward the door. "C'mon. Let's grab a cup of coffee."

The man cast an anxious glance at Shep before leaving the room. With a *whup*, the heavy, soundproof door shut solidly behind them and seemed to take the air with it, the room feeling too still and suffocating. Just like the night before, I fanned my face, though this time I did it with my hand rather than a sheet of sandpaper.

Collin introduced himself and shook Shep's hand

before turning to me. "This is Whitney Whitaker. She owns the motel where Beckett Morgan was found."

Shep ducked his head. "Ma'am." He shook my hand and held out his arm, inviting us to sit. "Take a seat. I've been expecting you." As he lifted his banjo strap over his head and placed the instrument on a metal stand, he clarified, "Well, *you*, anyway, Detective." He cut his eyes to me. "Didn't know you'd be bringing company."

"We can talk alone," Collin said, "if you prefer."

"Nah." He waved a hand. "But if this conversation goes where I think it's going, it might get a little sensitive."

Collin reassured him. "If you become uncomfortable at any time, just say the word and I'll send Miss Whitaker out. I brought her along because she found Beckett, and I thought she might be able to help me better question his associates."

"Associate?" Shep snorted, not unlike that fake-sneeze sound dogs make when they're playing. "'Suspect' would be a more precise word now, wouldn't it?"

Collin didn't backpedal, instead meeting the man halfway. "How about 'person of interest.' That work for you?"

Shep shrugged and resumed his seat on his stool. "Call me whatever you want, but I didn't kill Beckett. Didn't like the guy one iota, but didn't put a bullet in him either."

A bullet? Beckett hadn't been shot. He'd died from either the blunt force trauma to his head, the doorstop stab wound, or a combination of the two. Was Shep trying to throw us off by pretending he thought Beckett had succumbed to a bullet wound? Or did he really not know how Beckett had been killed and simply assumed, wrongly, that a gun had been involved? While the location of Beckett's murder had been leaked, none of the news reports I'd seen had noted his cause of death, other than saying it was being investigated as a homicide. I cut a glance at Collin and again saw his jaw flex as he, too, processed Shep's statement.

Collin pulled one foot up, casually resting it on the crossbar of his stool. "What did you have against Beckett?"

Shep eyed Collin from under his shaggy brows. "You already know or you wouldn't be here."

"Fair enough," Collin said. "It's because of the song."

"Darn right, the song!" Shep barked. He jabbed his index finger, topped with the sharp metal pick, in the air, as if stabbing a ghost. "There are two things you don't steal from a country boy. His horse or his songs."

I might've guessed his gun, his girl, or his pickup truck, but I supposed a horse and a song mean a lot to a country boy too.

"Tell me about that," Collin said.

"Not sure how much I can." Shep crossed his arms over his chest, curling the metal claws back over his rib cage. "I'm legally sworn to secrecy."

"Are you talking about the nondisclosure agreement you signed with Rex Tomlinson?"

"He told you about that?"

"Yes. He said he paid you twenty grand after you accused Beckett of stealing 'Party in the Pasture.'"

"I suppose if he's already filled you in, I can't get in trouble for talking to you about it then, can I?"

"No," Collin said. "Besides, nondisclosure provisions in civil contracts don't apply to criminal investigations."

"Okay, then," Shep said. "Here's what happened. T-Rex hired me and some other session musicians to play on Beckett's last album. We'd practiced a bunch and were in the studio recording one day when T-Rex, the drummer, and Beckett got into a minor dispute with Gia Revello. She's with the record label, negotiates deals and oversees production, that kind of thing."

She was also the next person we planned to visit, but we wouldn't tell him that.

"You mentioned a drummer," Collin said. "What's the drummer's name?"

"Gabriel whozeewhatzit," Shep said.

Collin straightened slightly. I felt myself reflexively do the same. The drummer Shep mentioned had to be the same one Sawyer had told Collin about at the motel the night of the vigil, the one Sawyer had called Gabriel something-or-other. "You don't know the drummer's last name?"

"Nope," Shep said. "All I know it's got some Zs and a P in it, and that it's pronounced nothing like how it looks. Anyway, they couldn't agree on the drums in a certain part of one of the songs. The rest of us had already laid down our tracks, so they told us we could go on to lunch while they figured out which way they wanted to go. I walked down the street to get some barbecue and, while I was waiting in line, I looked at the mural they got painted on the wall in there. Bunch of cows grazing in a pasture. Took me back to my good old days, partying in horse pastures down in Tullahoma." A faraway look came to his eyes, as if he were looking back in time to when he was just a pup. "Anyway, I could feel inspiration coming on, so I got me a chopped beef sandwich and some tater salad to go, carried it back to the studio, and jotted down some notes on the napkins while I was eating."

I could relate. I got that same inspirational high when a piece of real estate set my creative juices flowing. I'd jotted down many a note on a napkin or the back of a receipt.

Collin asked, "Was anyone with you at the time?"

"No," Shep said. "Just me. I shacked up alone in one of the control rooms and came up with some of the best lines." He sang some of them for us. "Girl, I can't see past your eyes, Let's get pasture-ized, Baby, please just listen, It's not past your comprehension, It's a party in the pasture." He raised his hands as if praising the heavens. "It was like I was having some sort of divine inspiration, I tell you what. Wrote the whole darn song in under an hour." He lowered his hands. "Anyway, when T-Rex called us back into the studio I left the banjo case in the control room with the napkins sitting on top of it. When I came back later, they were gone. I figured someone must've thought they were trash and thrown them away, but I didn't find them in any of the garbage cans."

"Did you ask the others about the napkins at the time?"

"No, I didn't say nothing to nobody. I was the last to leave, so they were already gone. Figured if I thought hard enough I could remember most of what I'd wrote down. A few days later, Beckett's got us all back in for rehearsal and he starts picking out a song on his guitar, telling us it's this fun little ditty he came up with called 'Party in the Pasture.' Beckett had set my words to a different tune, but it was my words. Well, mostly my words, anyway. Close enough. Tell you what, I blew my top. T-Rex shooed everyone else out of the room, including Beckett, and we had ourselves what you might call a come-to-Jesus meeting."

"I can imagine," Collin said, empathizing. "That had to be upsetting to have someone steal your intellectual property."

"I was fit to be tied," Shep admitted. "T-Rex said that even though the idea was a good one, it wasn't exactly original. He agreed it was quite a coincidence that Beckett and I had come up with similar ideas, but he said that everyone from a small town had partied in a pasture at one time or another, or maybe a barn, swum in a stock tank, got lucky in a hayloft. Despite that, he said he didn't blame me for feeling upset about the situation. He had me wait in the room alone while he went to speak to Beckett. When he came back, he said Beckett would pay me twenty grand if I kept my mouth shut and walked away. I took it."

"Why?" Collin asked. "Why not hire a lawyer and fight for what was yours?"

"I don't know much," Shep said, "but I'm smart enough to know that the deep pocket always wins and the little guy gets screwed. The first thing a lawyer would ask me is what proof I had that I'd written the song and that Beckett had taken it. I didn't have any. The napkins was the only proof I had, and they was gone. It was either take the money Beckett offered me or walk away with nothing. Of course, I couldn't work for Beckett again after that. T-Rex said Beckett wouldn't have me, wouldn't stand for being called a thief when he wasn't."

"Twenty grand?" Collin said. "How much would you have earned if Beckett had given you songwriting credit?"

"Shoot," Shep said. "Somewhere in the neighborhood of a quarter million, I'd bet." He shook his head and muttered curses under his breath before picking up his banjo, plunking it down on his lap, and picking it, repeatedly playing a few notes as if to calm himself.

I pointed to his instrument. "Play us your version of the song."

His face brightened. "Really? You want to hear it? All righty, then." His fingers moved over the strings and frets as he belted out a version of "Party in the Pasture" that had less of a pop country vibe and much more of a bluegrass aesthetic. Heck, he even added a bit of yodeling after the chorus. I had to admit that, while the song was similar to the one that had made Beckett Morgan famous, it wasn't precisely a word-for-word imitation.

When he finished, he said, "What do you two think? Did he rip me off, or not?"

Collin raised his palms. "That's not for us to judge, Mr. Sampson. But you are certainly talented with that banjo."

"Thank you," Shep said. "Anything else you want to ask me?"

"Where were you last Friday night?"

"Same place Beckett was," Shep said. "At the Ryman for the Armadillo Uprising concert. Them boys sure know how to put on a show."

"Did you speak to Beckett that night?"

"No," Shep said. "Saw him backstage when I went to say hi to some of the other folks. He called out to me but I ignored him. He had some nerve smiling at me like nothing ever happened." He ground his teeth as if tasting Beckett's bones.

"What about after the concert?" Collin asked.

"I headed home," he said. "I'm not such a young buck anymore. Can't close down the bars like I used to."

"What time did you arrive home?"

Shep looked up in thought. "I suppose it was around midnight."

Collin rattled off an address in the Oak Hill area south of town. He must have looked up Shep's residence before we'd come here today. "You still living there?"

"Sure am."

Collin asked, "Anybody home with you that night who can vouch for you?"

"Just my dogs, Millie and Maggie." He pulled out his wallet and flipped to a photo of two fluffy mid-sized mutts.

I couldn't help myself. "They're adorable."

"They're a mess is what they are," he replied, smiling down at the picture.

Collin eyed the man. "Where was your wife Friday night?"

"She and her girlfriends were on a weekend trip to Memphis," he said, meeting Collin's gaze. "They go at least once a year, visit Graceland and hit the bars down on Beale Street."

"Is she a musician too?" I asked.

"Darn straight," he said. "Plays mandolin and the mountain dulcimer. She can work those strings better'n anyone I've ever known."

Collin stood to wrap things up. "Any chance you know someone that goes by 'J.C.'? Maybe someone with the initials J.C.?"

"Someone that would've known Beckett too?" Shep asked.

"Yes."

He stared at a spot on the floor as he seemed to be running through a list of contacts in his head. He looked up again. "Can't say that I do."

"If someone comes to mind, give me a call." Collin handed Shep his business card and thanked him for his time and cooperation. He turned back at the door. "You've got your pulse on the business. You have any idea who might have wanted to put an end to Beckett Morgan's life?"

"I do," Shep said. "Not sure I should say so. It could come back to bite me in the butt." Despite his admonishment to himself, he continued. "Take a look at Lacy Spurlock. Beckett made a fool of her at the CMAs, a total laughingstock. I was hanging out backstage while they performed. When they finished their song, she stormed into her dressing room and slammed the door so loud it shook our teeth. Beckett went in after her. Couple of seconds later there was a crash and Beckett came running out with his tail between his legs. He wouldn't tell anyone what happened in there, but rumor has it she hurled a vase of flowers at him and that, if he hadn't ducked, it would have hit him smack in the face. It's like they say. Hell hath no fury."

CHAPTER 16

FOR WHAT IT'S WORTH

WHITNEY

Shep's words left me wondering. Were Lacy Spurlock's tears during her television interview real? Or had they been mere crocodile tears, intended to mislead people into thinking she was actually sad about Beckett's demise when she had, in fact, caused his death? A glance at Collin, the repeated flex of his jaw, told me that he, too, was chewing over the idea.

As we exited the studio, we found the auburn-haired woman and the guitarist sitting on a bench out front, sipping coffee from paper cups.

"We're done," Collin said. "Thanks for giving us the room."

"No problem," the woman said.

Once we were back in his car, I turned to Collin. "So? What did you think? Is Shep a good boy or a bad boy?"

"He's not out of the doghouse yet. He doesn't have an ironclad alibi, and he's got one heck of a motive. He believes Beckett not only stole credit for his song, but also cost him hundreds of thousands of dollars. He could be our guy."

"Especially if he's the man Jimmy saw near the motel late Friday night." I whipped out my phone, typed with my thumbs to run an image search, and then scrolled down the screen, examining the photos. "Bingo."

I held up the phone so Collin could see it too. On the screen was an image of Shep Sampson wearing a belt buckle imprinted with a dog paw. Like the image on the slide of his bolo tie, the claws were visible. "Think this could be what Jimmy saw Friday night? A dog paw rather than a bird foot?"

Collin took my phone from my hand. It made a camera-shutter sound as he took a screen shot of the image. After texting the image to himself, he said, "We'll show this to Jimmy when we get back to the motel later."

He drove out of the studio's lot, only to turn into another parking lot a block down. This building was three stories high with lots of windows and, per the sign affixed to its façade, housed the offices of Cumberland River Records.

We walked inside, and Collin checked in with the receptionist. "I'm Detective Collin Flynn with Metro PD. Is Gia Revello in?"

The young woman's eyes grew wide. By now, everyone in town new about Beckett Morgan's murder. There'd probably been rumors flying about Gia Revello, too, how she'd confronted Beckett in front of his fellow musicians and fans outside the Ryman on the very night he'd later been found dead. The woman picked up her phone. "I'll let her assistant know you're here." She punched in a three-digit code and put the receiver to her ear. When someone picked up on the other end, she said, "There's a police detective here to see Ms. Revello." She paused a moment while she listened. "Okay. Thanks." She hung up the phone and pointed to a bank of elevators on our right. "She can see you now. Third floor."

We rode up to the third floor, exiting into another lobby that was lined with headshots of country-western recording stars. Waylon Jennings. Dolly Parton. Blake Shelton. Faith Hill. Even Beckett Morgan himself, wearing his signature gray felt cowboy hat and boy-next-door smile. Several people were seated in the foyer, all of them well-dressed and wearing slightly impatient expressions to go with their country-western finery. These were people who didn't like to be kept waiting.

A twentysomething hipster in a skinny-fit plaid suit and handlebar mustache intercepted us in the lobby. "Hello, there!" He raised a hand as he approached. "I'll escort you to Ms. Revello's office. Her time is precious. You'll be quick, won't you?"

Unfazed by the boy's brusque behavior, Collin said, "As quick as we can be."

Her assistant escorted us down a hall to a frosted glass door secured with a keycard entry, leaving a natural, woodsy scent in his wake. Was the aroma cigar smoke, or merely some type of hipster cologne?

I nudged Collin with my elbow, raised my nose, and twitched my nostrils. He got the message, stretching out his neck to take a discreet sniff of the young man. Collin's gaze moved downward, and I followed it with my own. Gia's assistant was wearing freshly shined boots with what appeared to be an N toe. Could his left boot be the one we'd seen in the security camera footage from the Poison Emporium?

After the assistant tapped his keycard on the pad, the door opened with a click. He led us through the glass door to a set of heavy wood double doors. The one on the right was cracked open. He peeked through. "We've arrived, Ms. Revello."

He pushed the door open and stepped aside, holding it for us as we walked through to enter her enormous corner office. Gia Revello stood from her desk in the back corner and circled around to the front, looking every bit the hard-hitting female executive she was known to be. She wore a black suit with a fitted pencil skirt, red patent-leather stilettos, and a red and white polka-dot scarf. Her dark hair was swept over her forehead in a shiny, shellacked wave. Behind her, floor-to-ceiling plate glass windows provided a view across Interstate 65 into downtown. I could even get a glimpse of the pedestrian bridge from here, though we were too far away for me to see if the blonde was standing on it. As she walked toward us, she waved the back of both hands, shooing her assistant from the room.

"As you wish, ma'am." He slunk out and closed the door behind him.

After introductions were exchanged, she stood her ground, not bothering to offer us a place to sit despite the fact that a six-seat conference table was situated directly to our right. Without preamble, she said, "I didn't kill Beckett Morgan. Had every reason to. Maybe even wanted to. But didn't."

"Wow." Collin offered her a smile. "You don't beat around the bush, do you?"

"Only trying to save us both some time," she said. "Well-behaved women might rarely make history, and they never make the kind of money I do. The direct approach has served me well over the years."

"Then I suppose I can be direct too," Collin said.

Gia gave a sharp nod. "Of course."

He tilted his head. "Tell me about those reasons you'd have for killing Beckett."

"He strung me along, the same way he did all those young women who chased after him. I took a big chance on him when he was an unknown, let him in on that duet with Lacy Spurlock after their mutual manager, Rex Tomlinson, suggested it. Gave him a generous contract for his first album. When he hit big, he forgot who helped him get there. I made him a good offer for a second album. Five times what we'd paid him for the first. Offered him more than he was worth, quite frankly. Other than 'Party in the Pasture,' the rest of the album wasn't much to speak of. He shot me down. Three times." Her eyes flashed as she thought back to Beckett's refusals. "I raised the initial offer by fifteen percent, then another five. Took him out for fancy dinners. Wined and dined him. Even sent him a box of his favorite cigars and a big bottle of bourbon. Those things don't come cheap. He wouldn't commit, kept pushing for more. He was talking to some other labels, too, doing them just like he was doing me. Wrong." She turned and pointed out her window toward downtown. "There are a dozen singers busking for tips on SoBro right now who are just as talented as Beckett. I could have replaced him in a heartbeat."

"Then why not do it?" Collin asked. "Why not find new talent? Why get so upset?"

She turned the finger on herself now, pointing at her chest. "Because I didn't get where I am by backing down from a fight. I'm a hot-blooded Italian woman."

"Hot blooded," Collin repeated. "Hot enough to—"

"No!" She tossed her hands in the air. "Not hot enough to kill someone. I already told you that. But I'd had enough of Beckett yanking my chain."

"I don't blame you." Collin leaned slightly toward her. "Is that why you confronted him outside the Ryman Friday night?"

"Yes," she admitted. "But it's not like I planned to cause a scene. I just happened to come across him outside signing autographs when I was leaving." She raised her palms. "It got a little uglier than I intended, I admit. But when he played dumb, it sent me over the edge."

"Played dumb?" Collin asked.

"I told him I needed an answer right then and then to my latest offer. He told me to talk to T-Rex, said it was a matter for his manager."

"But he was right, wasn't he?" Collin said. "That's what managers are for, aren't they? To plan tours and negotiate endorsements and record deals?"

"That's right," Gia said, "when their client is manageable. Beckett wasn't. He was a spoiled brat and T-Rex couldn't keep him in line." She shook her head. "Acting all innocent and naïve in front of his fans, playing the simple country boy. It was disgusting. Other people might buy the bumpkin act, but I knew better. Beckett hid behind T-Rex, had his manager do his dirty work for him. T-Rex never came right out and said so, but I sensed he was embarrassed by Beckett's behavior, by all the unreasonable demands. He only put up with the kid because he was a veritable gold mine."

"Did T-Rex tell you that?"

"Not in so many words," Gia said. "But I can't see any other reason for tolerating the twerp."

"You've told me why you'd want to put Beckett in his place," Collin said. "Now convince me you didn't do it."

"Same reason. The money. If I'd wrung the boy's neck, I stood to lose some serious bank. Besides, T-Rex talked me down from the ledge."

"Rex Tomlinson was at the Ryman too?"

"No," she said. "When I left the Ryman, I went straight to my car and texted him. He called me back a few minutes later. He was at a show down in that cave in McMinnville, listening to a band he'd had his eye on."

Ear on might have been a more appropriate term. The Volcano Room was a unique show venue located an hour and a half drive to the southeast of Nashville and in a cavern 333 feet underground. Over half a century ago, someone realized the cave system provided near-perfect acoustics, as well as an intriguing backdrop for shows. A concert series was launched, and bands had been playing underground there ever since.

Gia continued. "I told T-Rex what happened at the Ryman. He wasn't happy I'd made a spectacle, but he said he could understand my frustration with Beckett, that he'd speak with him, pin down what it would take to make him sign a new deal, and get back to me on Monday with his final offer."

"What time did you leave the Ryman?" Collin asked.

Her lips puckered as she thought back. "Must've been around midnight."

"Did you go straight home?"

"I did."

"To your residence in Brentwood?"

A sneer pulled up one side of her plump lips. "You've done your homework, haven't you, Detective?"

He echoed her earlier words. "I did."

"Yes," she said. "When I refer to 'home,' I'm talking about my home in Brentwood."

"What time did you arrive at the house?"

"I didn't check a clock," she said, "but I suppose it would have been around twelve thirty, maybe a little later."

"Can anyone vouch for that?"

"My husband," she said. "He was already in bed. He'd fallen asleep watching TV. But he woke up when I came into the bedroom. I had a glass of wine in the kitchen first, though."

It seemed awfully late to have a drink alone. Had she needed the wine to calm her nerves after committing a heinous act of murder?

Collin asked for her husband's name and phone number, and jotted them on his pad before looking up again. He pointed to the door with his pen. "Your assistant. Was he at the Ryman with you?"

"He was," she said. "I got tickets for my entire staff. It's one of the perks of working for a record label."

"Did you ride together?"

"No. Everyone got there on their own. Some took their own cars. Some took Ubers so they could hit the bars after the show."

"When did your assistant leave?"

"When the show ended, I suppose. Just like the rest of us. We didn't leave together, if that's what you're getting at."

"Was he outside the Ryman when you were interacting with Beckett?"

"Not to my knowledge. But there were still quite a few people about so it's possible he could have been among them."

"What's his name?"

"Jared—"

My heart skipped a beat. The guy's first name started with J. *Does his last name start with C?*

Gia finished with, "Vandervoort."

Darn. So her cigar-scented assistant wasn't J.C., then.

"If you had to hazard a guess about who killed Beckett, who comes to mind?"

She circled her finger to indicate herself, the detective, and me. "This stays between us?"

"Of course," Collin said.

I nodded in agreement.

"Sawyer Karnes and Wylie Pfluger," she said. "I saw their faces when I was chewing Beckett out. They were amused to see him finally getting what he'd had coming to him."

She could very well be right about those two. They'd admitted they'd been with Beckett shortly before his murder, and one of them could have been the person wearing the boot we'd seen in the security camera video at the Poison Emporium. They knew Beckett would be there. Wylie claimed he couldn't stomach cigars, but that could have been a ruse. So could Sawyer's claim that he couldn't afford the habit. I recalled what Collin had said earlier, that the guilty party often describes the victim and their relationship in glowing terms. When Collin had spoken with Sawyer and Wylie at the motel, Wylie had implied things had not been perfect between them and Beckett. Sawyer had been quick to cover, to shut Wylie up and say how grateful they were to have worked for the star.

"Those two are talented musicians," Gia continued, "who helped Beckett get where he is today. Not that Beckett appreciated it. I know Sawyer and Wylie asked Beckett about going full time with him, becoming permanent backup band members, but he wouldn't commit to them any more than he'd commit to me." She scoffed. "If ever there was a young man with commitment issues, it was Beckett Morgan."

"I see." Collin's head bobbed slowly as he absorbed

the information. "What about Lacy Spurlock? You think there's any chance she could've killed Beckett?"

Gia barked a laugh. "Lacy didn't need to murder Beckett to get back at him. You've heard her last album, right? That was her revenge. 'Kiss My Back Pocket' held at number three on the charts for over a month. 'I've Had Better, But I Haven't Had Worse' hit number eight. And 'Bless Your Itty-Bitty . . . Heart' hit number one. Stayed there for two full months. Lacy had no reason to end Beckett's life. She's already made a killing, thanks to his inspiration. Made a killing for me too. We produce her work."

"So her score was settled?"

"Sure seemed to be." Gia inhaled a long breath and her voice was softer when she spoke again. "That said, there were some rumors flying around after the CMAs. People hanging around backstage say they heard a crash come from her dressing room and saw broken glass and liquid on the floor when Beckett ran out. They say she hurled a bottle of champagne at him."

While her story didn't exactly mesh with Shep's, it confirmed that something had happened in Lacy's dressing room. The jury was still out on exactly what it was. Only two people knew for certain, and one of them was now dead.

I chimed in now. "Do you happen to know if your assistant smokes?"

"Why?" Gia asked, her eyes narrowing.

"I thought I smelled cigars on him. But it could have been his aftershave. Whatever the scent was, it was nice."

She shrugged. "I've never seen Jared with a cigar or cigarette in his hand. He makes coffee for the floor, though. It burned this morning. He's supposed to check and make sure nobody has left an empty pot on a hot burner, but sometimes he gets busy and forgets."

I'd smelled burnt coffee before. It was an unpleasant, acrid odor. Jared's scent wasn't.

"I assume we're done here?" she said, not bothering to wait for an answer before reaching for the door handle behind us.

Collin raised a palm to stop her from opening the door just yet. "One more question," he said. "Do you know anyone with the initials J.C.?"

Gia didn't miss a beat. "June Carter Cash. Or, I guess that would be J.C.C. if you include all her names."

"Someone still alive," Collin clarified. "Someone who would have been a friend of Beckett's."

"Hmm." She cocked her head and looked up at the ceiling for a beat, as if the answer might be written there, before returning her focus to Collin. "Can't say that I do."

"Okay. Thanks for your time."

When the woman opened the door for us, Collin held out a hand, inviting me to precede him through the door. As soon as Gia closed her door behind us, her hipster assistant escorted us to the elevators. Again, I smelled the cigar-like aroma on him. He took long strides as if to speed us up, jabbing the DOWN button and hanging around to make sure we got on. As the doors slid shut on us, he snapped, "Ciao!"

The elevator began to descend and I spoke to Collin's reflection in the shiny metal elevator door. "Gia's assistant seems oddly protective of her."

"I was thinking the same thing. Could be they're just insulted by my visit and the implication that Gia might have had something to do with Beckett's death."

I could understand that it would be an affront to be

wrongfully accused of a crime but, heck, Gia was the only one to blame. Had she behaved with more decorum at the Ryman Auditorium last Friday night, Collin might not have felt the need to stop by in person.

"Did Rex Tomlinson tell you the same thing Gia said, that he'd been down in McMinnville Friday night?"

"He did," Collin said. "He was scouting a band. Said they had promise but weren't quite up to snuff yet. He felt bad that he hadn't been at the Ryman to run interference when Gia confronted Beckett. He said he normally tries to attend as many of his artists' shows as he can, but that the Ryman is well run, a home base of sorts, and most locals are familiar with how things are done there. He felt less pressure to be on-site."

"Did he stay in McMinnville overnight, or drive back to Nashville?"

"He came home that night," Collin said. "He said the show wrapped a little before midnight, and that he'd stuck around for a few minutes afterward to talk to the stage manager. He wanted to find out what up-and-comers they had in the lineup the next few weeks, and whether there were any gaps in their schedule he could fill with the bands he manages. He was still a half hour out of Nashville when Beckett called him. He took the call in his car, made the arrangements to meet up with Beckett the following day at the steakhouse. He arrived home shortly after Beckett called him." As if anticipating my next question, he said, "There's nobody to verify what time he arrived home. Tomlinson's not currently married."

"Not currently? So he's been married before?"

"He's had three marriages, but none of them stuck. The longest lasted five years. Two of his wives were mu-

sicians in bands he managed, the third was a stage di-
rector at the Tennessee Performing Arts Center."

Looked like the third time had not been the charm
for T-Rex. Still, I had to admire that he had the optimism
to keep trying. "I've heard showbiz is hard on relationships. The travel, crazy hours, rarely seeing each other."
Long-lasting marriages were a rarity in Hollywood, and
the music industry was much the same.

Collin cut me a glance. We, too, worked odd hours,
and often had difficulty finding time to get together
despite our best efforts. He'd told me before that his
job had cost him a relationship. Even so, we seemed
to understand each other's situations, to cut each other
quite a bit of slack, and to make the most of the moments
we could find to spend together. Ironically, the current
murder investigation had given us the opportunity to see
each other more, though under less than ideal circumstances.

The elevator doors opened on the first floor, and we
walked out of the building. I stopped just outside the
doors, pulled out my phone, and ran a search for "men's
cologne that smells like cigars."

Realizing I was no longer beside him, Collin stopped
walking and glanced back at me. "What are you doing?"

"Trying to figure out if there's a men's cologne that
smells like cigars. If there is, maybe Gia's assistant is
wearing it."

His lip quirked. "Why would a man intentionally
want to smell like a cigar?"

"So women will think he's smokin'."

Collin groaned.

I defended my theory. "It could be true. I work with
wood in my carpentry projects, and I like soaps and

colognes that smell like pine or cedar. Must be some sort of scent association. A guy who smokes cigars could be partial to a cologne that smells like them."

"Wood smells are one thing," Collin said. "Cigars are another. Find anything?"

I looked down at my screen. "I did. Ha!" It was rude to be smug, but I couldn't help myself. I was proud to be proven right.

Collin turned sideways and eased up beside me so that he, too, could read the information on my phone. My search had brought up several scents. There was a fragrance called Cigar Cologne by Remy Latour that had notes of tobacco. Judging from its rating of 4.5 out of 5 stars, it must smell nice. Tom Ford also made one called Tobacco Oud. Another tobacco-infused fragrance was Angel Pure Havane. One reviewer described it as "addictive," just like the tobacco it was made from. Gucci men's cologne also incorporated the aroma of tobacco.

Collin grunted. "I stand corrected."

Had Gia Revello's assistant had been wearing one of these colognes or had he, in fact, smoked a cigar? *There's one way to find out.* "I'm going back inside," I told Collin. "I'll ask Jared about his scent. It'll seem less obvious coming from me than you. I'll tell him I liked his cologne and wanted to find out which one it was so I can get a bottle for my boyfriend."

Collin frowned, apparently not liking the idea of me directly interacting with a potential killer without him there to defend me. But he couldn't deny that my plan was a good one. He had no choice but to acquiesce. "Be careful."

I scurried back inside to the receptionist's desk. "Could you call Jared down here? I've got a quick question for him."

She nodded and picked up her phone, dialing Jared's extension. "Can you come down to the foyer? The woman who was with the police says she has something she needs to ask you right quick."

She gave me a nod to indicate he was on his way and hung up the phone. I stepped over by the elevator to wait. A moment later, the door opened and Jared stepped out.

Though he scowled, I gave him my best smile. "Sorry to bother you again," I said. "But I couldn't help but notice how good you smell, and I didn't want to leave without finding out what cologne you're wearing. I'd love to buy some for my boyfriend. His birthday is coming up."

The compliment softened his expression. "It's called Angel Pure Havane. They sell it at Macy's."

"Perfect!" I said. "Thanks so much. He'll love it."

I walked outside. Collin leaned back against the wall next to the door, waiting for me.

I stepped close to him and kept my voice low. "The cigar smell was his cologne. Angel Pure Havane." I realized that knowing he wore a cigar-scented cologne didn't necessarily eliminate him as a potential suspect, though. In fact, it could point more to his guilt. Maybe he wore the cologne as a cover-up.

As we walked back to his car, Collin pulled his phone from his pocket and dialed the number Gia Revello had given for her husband. He identified himself and said, "I'm investigating the death of Beckett Morgan. I just spoke with your wife. Do you recall what time she arrived home last Friday night?" He faltered in his step. "Two fifty-seven a.m.?" He cut his eyes to me. "You're certain about that?"

I stopped, too, every nerve on my back prickling. Gia

had said she'd arrived home at half past midnight, had a glass of wine in her kitchen, then gone to bed, rousing her sleeping husband. *Had she lied to the detective?*

Collin asked, "Will you be home for the next hour or so? I'd like to speak with you in person." A second or two lapsed, then he said, "I'm on my way." He thanked the man, ended the call, and slid the phone into his pocket.

"Wow," I said.

"Wow, indeed."

"You going back inside to arrest her first?"

"Not yet," he said. "I need to lock her husband down on the timing, see if their house has a security system and check the log to see when it was disarmed and re-armed Friday night. I'll also take a look at her clothing and car, see if I can get any physical evidence against her first. A defense attorney could easily discredit Gia's husband, say he was groggy and didn't remember the time accurately. I need something more concrete to nail her."

The fact that the murder investigation could be wrapped up so quickly was great news. In related events, Collin's plans to go to Gia Revello's house meant I wouldn't have to share my lunch with him. "This means the jambalaya is all mine, doesn't it?"

CHAPTER 17

A *TALON*TED
MUSICIAN

WHITNEY

By the time Collin and I arrived back at the Music City
Motor Court, a new group of mourners stood outside the
motel and the metal bin was overflowing with rolls of
old carpet. The fence guys had finished installing the
automated gate across the vehicle entry, as well as a
new fence around the pool area, complete with spring-
loaded safety gates that swung shut on their own. Collin pulled up to the closed auto gate and tapped his horn.
Honk.

Buck peeked his head out from one of the rooms and
I unrolled my window to holler to him. "What's the
code number?"

He turned his back to the mourners, lest they learn
the security code, and used his fingers to communicate
from the other side of the fence. He formed a zero by
touching the tips of his curled thumb and index finger
together. He held up eight fingers next, then one, then
four.

I recited the numbers softly to Collin. "Zero, eight, one, four."

Why does that number sound familiar? As Collin typed the digits into the keypad, I realized why the number had jogged something in my memory banks. It represented Colette's birthday, August 14th. Was it mere coincidence? Or had Buck chosen that number on purpose?

The gate slid back smoothly, no banging or clanging. The fence crew had done a good job, as always. They were a solid, dependable bunch. That's why I threw as much work as I could their way.

Collin drove through and pulled up in front of the room where Buck and Jimmy were working. I climbed out and called for Jimmy. "Come here a second. The detective needs to show you something."

Jimmy came out of the room and walked to Collin's window. Buck and I gathered around as Collin showed Jimmy the image on his screen, the photo of Shep Sampson wearing the paw-print belt buckle. "Could this have been the belt buckle you saw Friday night?"

Jimmy craned his neck to get a better look, before slowly shaking his head as if uncertain. "I can't swear to it, but I don't think so." He pointed to the screen. "This one is clearly a dog or a wolf, maybe a fox or coyote. Some kind of four-footed critter. My impression of the one I saw Friday was that it was a bird. But, like I said, I had a bit of whiskey in me and the lighting wasn't good so . . ." He let his words trail off, unsure.

"Thanks." Collin slipped his phone back into his breast pocket. "I'll be in touch," he said to me as he slid his gearshift into reverse.

Turning to Buck and Jimmy, I asked, "Who's hungry?"

"I'm nearly starved," Buck lamented, putting a hand on his belly.

Buck wasn't overweight, but by no stretch of the imagination could he be called thin. Still, I'd play along, "Good thing I got back when I did, then."

Buck picked up the piece of the spare plywood we'd used for the makeshift stage at the vigil the night before, and lay it over two sawhorses. Jimmy upended three large paint buckets and placed them around the improvised table for us to sit on. Our dining table in place, I passed out the thermoses, along with napkins and utensils. While some people ate jambalaya with a spoon, Colette's version of the dish was thick enough to eat with a fork. After grabbing drinks from the cooler, we took seats around the table and dug in.

One bite, and Jimmy moaned in bliss. "This is the best thing I've ever eaten. I have half a mind to propose to Colette."

Buck scowled. Jimmy and I laughed.

"Dude," Jimmy said. "You are so transparent."

Buck scooped up a forkful of food. "I don't know what you're talking about."

"I'm talking about Whitney's friend," he said. "You've got the hots for her."

Buck's scowl deepened. "I'm in love with her cooking. That's what I've got the hots for."

"Speaking of hots," I said, reaching into the bag Colette had packed for us, "here's your hot sauce." I retrieved the bottle and plunked it down on the table in front of Buck. "She knows how much you like the stuff."

Buck's cheeks turned pink, and his mouth quirked as he fought a smile. *So transparent.*

Jimmy belted out a laugh. "You're turning red, bro. You are crushing so hard."

"Am not!" Buck insisted. "It's the spicy food."

I gave him a pointed look. "Colette doesn't feed just anybody, you know." It was a ploy to further embarrass him. Buck hated to get mushy.

"Sure, she does," Buck countered. "She's a professional chef."

Jimmy and I shared a look and another laugh before I raised my palms. "All I'm going to say is that if you do have feelings for her, you better make a move. The sommelier at the restaurant has been really turning on the charm."

Alarm flitted across his face. "For real?"

"For real. She's been putting him off, but I don't think she'll keep doing that forever. He's like their fish of the day. A good catch."

As we finished up lunch, I asked Buck what he thought about Gentry's idea. "Should we consider adding another story to the motel?"

"Not if it means teaming up with that creep."

I felt the same way. Thad Gentry was a thorn in our side when he could have been a valuable partner if only he'd cede some control. It dawned on me then that my feelings must be similar to Gia Revello's feelings about Beckett, that if only the young singer would have set aside his ego and greed, they'd have both been better off. Beckett's behavior damaged important business relationships, just as Gentry's actions cost him opportunities. Still, while we wouldn't team up with Gentry under any circumstances, we didn't want to rely on the generosity of our families either. And while I'd been willing to let the Hartleys spot me some cash once, I wouldn't do it again. I needed to prove to myself that we could do this on our own, that we were legit.

"What if we could get a loan from a bank and do it

ourselves?" I asked. "I can put a proposal together for the loan officer, see if I can convince them to give us the money. You willing to sign?"

"Heck, yeah," Buck said. "In for a penny, in for a pound."

Buoyed by the idea of expanding our project, I stood and gathered the thermoses and silverware. "I'll arrange to get a structural engineer out here to write us a report. The bank will want to see one to make sure the plans are feasible. In the meantime, I'll work out a cost estimate for putting in the exterior of the second floor. We'll go with the same plan for financing the interior, using the buyers' down payments. That way, we won't have to ask for as much funding from the bank." The less we asked them for, the more likely we were to get it.

While the men continued their demolition work that afternoon, I made arrangements to have a structural engineer take a look at the place. I used a legal pad and pen to make notes regarding the materials we'd need. Because we'd be starting from scratch on the second-story units, we could put skylights in the ceiling and windows along the backside to let in more light. We could make them two-bedroom, two-bath deluxe units, with a bedroom on either side of a central living/dining area. We could maybe even divide the second bedroom into two smaller spaces, much like the studio I'd seen earlier today. The residents could use one as a guestroom and the other for a home office, hobby room, or storage. Already, my mind was spinning with ideas.

We wrapped up our work at half past five. As I slid my toolbox into the cargo bay of my SUV, my phone chimed with an incoming text. It was from my mother. *Come over for dinner tonight?*

So much had transpired in the last few days that I'd

barely had time to fill my parents in on the highlights. It would be nice to sit down with them for a meal and catch up. Besides, Sawdust would enjoy playing with Yin-Yang, my mother's black and white Boston terrier. I texted back. *Love to! I'll be there soon.*

After bidding goodbye to Jimmy and Buck, I drove home to shower, change, and round up my cat. Both Colette and Emmalee were at work at the restaurant, but I found Sawdust and Cleopatra spooning in his cat bed. Sawdust was sweetly licking the top of Cleo's head, giving his little charge a bath. Her head was tilted back and her eyes were closed. He'd made her feel loved and cared for. Unlike Buck, Sawdust wasn't afraid to openly show his affection.

"Hey, boy." I ruffled his ears and he turned his tongue on my hand, kissing me hello.

I took a quick shower, slid into a sundress, and slapped on enough makeup to avoid a lecture from my Southern belle mother, who thought venturing outside without a fully made-up face and freshly painted fingernails was a mortal sin. I'd tried teaching her the ways of modern feminism, but it was a losing battle. It was easier to just give in.

I grabbed my purse and opened the door to Sawdust's carrier. "Come on, boy! We're going to see Yin-Yang."

Sawdust stood from the bed and sashayed over, marching directly into the cage. *Such a good boy.* Cleo had followed him over, performing what appeared to be a modern-dance piece as she went up on her hind legs to grab at his swishing tail. When I closed the door to the carrier, she put her nose to the metal grate, wondering why her friend had been locked inside. She sat back on her tiny haunches, looked up at me, and issued a pathetic *mew*.

"All right." I opened the door for her. "You can come too."

She scampered inside, pouncing on Sawdust in the small space. He continued to patiently lie there, as if setting an example. She took the hint and settled in next to him. The sight made my heart melt, but I had to look away to text Em, letting her know where little Cleo would be.

A half hour later, we pulled into the driveway at my parents' house in the Green Hills neighborhood. I climbed out of my SUV and opened the back door to retrieve my feline cargo. Taking a shortcut, I walked to the picket fence and opened the gate that led to the back-yard, pool, and converted pool house that had served as a tiny home for Sawdust and me for several years while I saved up a down payment for a house of my own. While it had only been a matter of months since we'd moved out, it felt like eons ago now. So much had happened since. I'd made the decision not to pursue a real estate license, and had instead started a new house-flipping business that was better suited to my skills and interests. I'd moved into a house that I actually owned, subject to the mortgage lien, of course. And I'd proved to myself that I could play with the big boys and win. After all, I'd snagged the Music City Motor Court out of Thad Gentry's hands. Thank goodness too. He'd have razed the place or turned it into something unrecogniz-able. Buck and I, on the other hand, were working to preserve a piece of Nashville nostalgia.

Yellow roses and potted purple petunias graced the terrace around the swimming pool. An inflatable pink flamingo floated aimlessly on the water, adding another splash of color to the backyard. *I should get some pool toys for the motel's grand opening.* They would be a fun touch, add a bit of whimsy. I made a mental note to check online for an inflatable guitar.

Yin-Yang spotted me through the back window, perked up her head, and announced our arrival. *Arf-arf! Arf-arf-arf!*

My mother stepped up beside her dog, waving her arm as if she hadn't seen me in years. While I towered over my petite mother by several inches, we shared a similar smile and cut-pine hair color. Mine was natural. Hers now came from a bottle. Dad passed behind Mom and the dog, and opened the backdoor for me. "Hey, hon!"

I stepped in the door, set the carrier down, and gave both of my parents a hug. Dad closed the door behind me, and I bent down to release the cats. Yin-Yang tap-danced around the kitchen, thrilled to see her old buddy again. *Tap-tap-tap-tap.*

As Sawdust waltzed out of the cage, Cleo bolted past him. When she spotted the dog straight ahead, she put on the brakes, sliding to a stop on the tile floor, and issuing a terrified, spitting hiss. *Hisssss!* She did an about-face, and scrambled for purchase on the floor, her tiny claws unable to gain traction. When she finally got going, she ran pell-mell into the carrier, slamming into the back at full force. *Bam!*

I bent down to reassure her. "It's okay, baby." I reached in to stroke her back. "Yin-Yang's your friend. She won't hurt you."

Cleo refused to take my word for it. She cowered in the back of the carrier, hissing and spitting. Yin-Yang quickly lost interest, too excited to see her old pal. In seconds, she and Sawdust were playing tag, chasing each other around, over, and under my parents' sofa.

"What smells so good?" I asked my mother.

"Penne primavera," she said. "I made garlic bread and a salad too."

Just like that, I was twelve years old again. I clapped my hands and bounced on my heels. "Yummy!"

Minutes later, we were gathered around their kitchen table, chowing down. Mom's cooking skills could never match Colette's, but they surpassed my own. I could do all kinds of creative things with a cordless drill, but give me a food processor and I was clueless.

Over dinner, Cleo tentatively ventured out of the carrier to watch Yin-Yang and Sawdust wrestle on the rug. Meanwhile, I filled my parents in on the developments in the investigation.

My mother's face tightened into a pensive pucker. "So the killer could still be anyone at this point. Beckett's manager. The lady from the record label. Any of those studio musicians. One of Beckett's groupies. Lacy Spurlock." She gave me a dour look as she listed a final potential suspect. "Your new assistant."

"Jimmy is the only one we can definitively rule out."

"How can you be so sure?"

I knew she wouldn't be impressed if I told her it was my intuition that said Jimmy was innocent, or that such an upbeat, fun-loving guy was incapable of killing. I went with, "Because Detective Flynn would have arrested him by now."

"That's bad logic," she said. "Someone's guilty, and no one's been arrested. It could be Jimmy."

"I don't know how much I'm allowed to share," I told my parents, "but let's just say that Jimmy doesn't own a pair of the right kind of boots."

My mother's eyes widened. "I see. That gives me a little more comfort."

"Me too," my father said. "But only a little. It's not

hard to ditch a pair of boots. Your mother's been cleaning out her closet and she donated three pairs to charity."

She lifted her chin. "They no longer sparked joy in me."

"Even if Jimmy is guilty," I said, "we're supposed to keep our friends close and our enemies closer, right?"

"Not too close for comfort," Mom said. "That's more of your bad logic."

Fortunately, Cleo saved me from further grilling by deciding to join in the fray taking place on the rug. She hip-hopped over and batted the Boston terrier's earflap.

Mom put a hand to her heart. "That little thing is adorable!"

"Isn't she, though?" I stood and gathered the plates. "Coffee, anyone?"

CHAPTER 18

NEW FRIENDS

SAWDUST

What a wonderful night! He'd gotten to play with Yin-Yang, who'd been his best buddy when he and Whitney had lived in the pool house. It was fun to see her again.

He wasn't sure why Cleo had acted like such a fraidy-cat at first. The dog might growl and bark and run around, but it was all in play. He was glad when Cleo eventually came around. He'd like for his two best friends to be friends too.

But now, they were back home and both he and Cleo were pooped. They curled up with Whitney on the couch to catch up on their catnaps.

CHAPTER 19

RAISING THE ROOF AND RAISING SUSPICION

WHITNEY

Wednesday morning, I performed a walk-through at a townhouse I managed on behalf of Home & Hearth, comparing the condition of the place to the form the tenants had filled out when they'd moved in. Their cat had climbed the living room curtains, as evidenced by the pinholes letting the morning sun stream through. There were also a few new stains on the carpet. Wine. Coffee. Nail polish. But they'd been solid tenants, never late on their rent, and the curtains and carpet were due for replacement regardless.

"No worries," I told them. "We'll get your full deposit returned to you ASAP."

I drove to a new listing Mrs. Hartley had landed, and installed a lockbox on the door for the house key. Before leaving, I plopped an aluminum HOME & HEARTH sign in the yard near the curb so people could see that the place was for sale. With the real estate market picking up for summer, the place would likely be under contract very soon.

By the time I arrived at the motel, the sun was up and warming the city with uninterrupted rays, not a single cloud to be seen in the sky over Nashville. The day would be a scorcher, that's for sure. While we used fans in the rooms where we worked, there was no point in turning on the air conditioning. Many of the rooms still had the broken, patched windows, and we would be constantly going in and out of the doors carrying materials and supplies. Turning on the A/C would be a waste of money and we didn't have extra funds to burn.

Buck and Jimmy were removing bathtubs today, heavy work. I helped by removing the drains, overflow valve covers, and faucets before them, and by following after to chisel out what remained of the small square tiles in the shower stalls. In the spec unit, we'd install a new, taller tub with a pre-fab shower stall and frameless glass shower doors. Buyers could choose to duplicate the look in their units or, for an upgrade charge, they could opt for a contemporary walk-in shower. I planned to prepare several notebooks with pictures and information about the options buyers could choose, and have them ready for perusal at the grand opening.

As a sign of good faith, I snapped photos of the junk in the dumpster and a gutted bathroom, and texted them to Presley to show the progress we'd made on the rehab. She might be a silent partner, but she deserved some reassurance that her investment had been a good one, that she'd been right to trust us with this project, and that despite the setback with the murder, everything else was moving ahead.

A mid-afternoon *beep-beep* alerted me to the arrival

of our structural engineer. I scurried out of the motel room and activated the gate from the inside so he could drive his pickup through. A quarter of an hour later, the two of us were up on the roof, the sun beating down on us as we examined the area around the rooftop A/C. Heat radiated up from the surface below our feet. *Now I know how bacon feels.* I'd paused to wipe some sweat off my brow when a red Porsche Cayman pulled up to the gate below, and I admired the sports car from my new height. The model was one of Porsche's least expensive, but it still ran around sixty grand, much too rich for my blood. Rather than honk the horn, the driver parked in the short space between the street and the gate, and climbed out of the sports car. I stepped to the edge of the roof and looked down. It was Rex Tomlinson.

He spotted me on the roof and raised an arm to wave. "Afternoon, Whitney!" he called. "Got a minute?"

The structural engineer could proceed without me, so I told him I'd be right back and descended the extension ladder I'd leaned against the building to access the roof.

T-Rex entered through one of the smaller gates and pointed to the overflowing dumpster. "Looks like y'all have made a lot of progress since Monday evening. You certainly don't dillydally."

"We keep ourselves on a tight schedule." The sooner we had this place ready, the sooner we could enjoy our profits and start looking for another property to flip.

His face turned serious. "Any word on the investigation? I can hardly stand it, knowing Beckett's killer is still out there, getting away with his crime."

No way would I share details with this man and risk jeopardizing Collin's work. Besides, he could well be the very person who'd ended Beckett's life. I don't know why he might have done it in light of the fact that killing Beckett would cost him tens of thousands, if not hundreds of thousands, in management fees. But until Collin definitively eliminated him as a person of interest, I'd consider him as such. "Detective Flynn is doing his best," I said.

"I'm sure he is," T-Rex said. "Shep Sampson called me yesterday, said he discussed the song and the non-disclosure agreement with you two."

"That's right." I figured there was no point in denying it. After all, T-Rex had told us about the contract himself. I didn't see how my acknowledging that Shep Sampson had confirmed the terms could cause any harm.

Tomlinson dipped his head and looked up at me, speaking quietly. "Did Shep give you cause for concern?"

I hedged my bets. "At this point, Detective Flynn's still concerned with just about everyone who's been close to Beckett."

"Gia Revello told me the two of you had been by to see her too. She was pretty upset by it. Insulted, I guess you'd say. Couldn't believe anyone would consider her a killer. She still in the running too?"

"As far as I know." Actually, the last I'd heard, she'd given Collin cause for suspicion. She claimed she'd arrived home Friday night a good two hours before her husband said she had. Having not yet heard further from Collin, I didn't know how things had played out when he went to the Revello home to speak to Gia's husband in person.

T-Rex scratched his head. "Well, darn. I'd have thought Detective Flynn would have narrowed things down by now, be homing in on Beckett's killer so the poor boy can get justice."

Absent eyewitnesses, a smoking gun, clear fingerprints or DNA evidence, or an obvious motive, homicides were not easy or quick to solve. I didn't like this
man's implication that Collin should be further along in
the investigation. He was working hard, putting in long
hours. An unintentional edge slipped into my voice.
"He'll get there."

T-Rex nodded. "I'm sure he will. He seems like a
very smart guy."

"We haven't spoken today," I said. "There could have
been some recent developments I'm not aware of. You
could try calling him."

He raised his palms. "No, no, no. I don't want to in-
terrupt his work, cause any delay. In fact, that's why I
came to talk to you instead of bothering him. I got the
impression there was something going on between the
two of you, that you were close, so I thought you might
be able to give me an update without me having to take
up the detective's time."

It wasn't really any of this man's business whether
Collin and I were involved, and I didn't want to say
anything that could discredit Collin or his work, so I
evaded his question. "When an arrest is made," I said,
"I'm sure you'll be among the first to be informed. Collin knows Beckett's family and business colleagues are
very concerned."

"We sure are."

Recalling that T-Rex managed both Beckett and
Lacy Spurlock, I said, "I'm one of Lacy Spurlock's biggest fans. Does she have any shows coming up here in
town?" It was a ploy to find out when she'd be around in
case Collin wanted to speak with her.

He chuckled. "You looking to score some tickets?"

"No." I raised my palms in innocence. "Not fishing

for freebies. Honest. I'd just love to see her live, that's all. Haven't had a chance to check her tour schedule online."

"She's out on tour right now," he said. "Flew out Saturday afternoon. I drove her to the airport myself so we could tie up some loose ends during the drive."

Lacy had flown out the very day Beckett had been found dead? *Hmm*. If not for the fact that the tour must have been scheduled months in advance, it might seem like she was evading arrest or at least hoping that, if she was out of sight, she'd also be out of mind. "Is it a long tour?"

"No," he said. "Not this leg of it, anyway. She'll be back in a couple of weeks. She's doing a special one-woman acoustic show at the Country Music Hall of Fame when she returns. I'd suggested it to her a while back. I'd heard Bruce Springsteen and Rick Springfield had done them, shared some inside information about their lives and songs, and I thought she might find it fun to do a show like that too. It's a totally different experience from the large, loud venues. Much more intimate. Fans eat it up."

"Sounds like a great idea."

He reached into his back pocket, pulled out his wallet, and fished around in it for a few seconds before pulling out two tickets and holding them out to me. "There you go. Center stage, fifth row. Take a friend."

I raised my palms again. "I can't. I'd feel like a mooch."

"Quit being so stubborn." He smiled and extended them a couple of inches farther. "I'd be happy for you to have them. I've already given away dozens of tickets to media sources. I'd hate to see these two go to waste. Even more, I'd hate for Lacy to see two empty seats when she looks out at her audience. Really, you'd be doing me a favor."

Now I was smiling too. I took the tickets from him. "You're very persuasive."

He chuckled again. "It's an acquired skill, forged through decades of contract negotiations." He glanced around, his smile melting away. "I'm glad the motel won't be torn down. Razing this place would be like erasing Beckett's memory, you know? Like taking away a part of his story."

I could understand how he felt. A big part of why I liked flipping houses was to preserve the property's history, to let it live on in refurbished form, to see better days again.

"These units will be unique homes," I said, hoping I didn't sound insensitive by promoting the condominiums with Beckett's death less than a week behind us. "You wouldn't happen to know anyone who's looking to buy a place, would you? They would be perfect for musicians. This location is convenient to the performing venues on SoBro and the studios on Music Row. We'll have one-bedroom units on the ground floor, and we're looking into adding a second story with two-bedroom, two-bath units with a bonus room."

"I'll put the word out."

"Thanks. We'll hold a grand opening once the spec unit and common areas are complete. I'll be sure you get an invitation."

"Wonderful." He took a step back. "I'll let you get back to your business. You have a good day, now. And be careful going back up that ladder. Climbing up on a roof can be dangerous."

So could standing next to an empty swimming pool,

or sitting on the edge of the deep end. Beckett was proof of that.

"Before you go," I said, causing him to turn back, "can you tell me something in confidence?"

He lifted his shoulders. "What do you want to know?"

"Your thoughts on Sawyer and Wylie."

"Whether they might have killed Beckett, you mean?"

"Yeah."

He looked off toward the skyline and took a shuddering breath before returning his gaze to me. "I don't like to cast aspersions, but I don't think it's out of the question. They were with Beckett shortly before he was killed, and they resented the guy. His relatively easy success. His talent. His fame. The women who were always throwing themselves at him. The kid had it all and they wanted it, too, been trying to get it for years. They felt like Beckett wasn't giving them a fair shot, that he was holding them back by not letting them be part of a permanent backup band. I can't see them planning beforehand to do away with the guy, but could they have lost their tempers and done something stupid Friday night? Pulled a pocketknife or punched him or something? I don't think they're above it, especially after they'd got a few drinks in them. Wylie can overdo it sometimes. I believe it's gotten him into trouble before."

"Thanks, Rex. I appreciate your candor."

As he exited through the walking gate, I headed back up the ladder to finish discussing the roof with the structural engineer. When the man finished his assessment, we made our way back down the ladder so that he could issue his opinion to me and Buck together.

My cousin pulled a bandana from the pocket of his coveralls to wipe sweat from his brow. "How's it look?"

"Good," the engineer said. "A second story is totally doable. The roof and walls can easily bear the additional load, no problem."

I pumped my fist. "Yes!"

The engineer smiled. "It'll take me a day or two to write up my report. But you'll have it by the end of the workweek."

We thanked him and saw him to his car. As soon as his bumper passed the gate, I was on the phone with our bank, making an appointment with a loan officer for first thing Monday morning.

As I turned to head into one of the rooms, my eyes spotted the blonde woman on the near side of the bridge again. She was dressed in black today, too. *Could she be the killer, returning to the scene of the crime?* It seemed plausible. After all, she'd been on the bridge the morning we'd found Beckett in Room 10. She seemed to know something was up at the motel before we did. Then again, it might not even be the same woman, or she might be up on the bridge for other reasons. Either way, it was time to find out. "I'll be right back!" I called to the men, setting off at a jog.

"Where are you going?" Buck yelled after me.

"The bridge!"

"Why?"

I raised a hand to signal that I'd explain when I got back. I had neither the time nor the breath at the moment to holler back to him.

As I ran toward the bridge, the woman on it turned and began to walk over it toward downtown. *Nooo!* I sped up, my jog now an all-out sprint. *Did she see me headed her way? Is she intentionally avoiding me?*

As I approached the last cross street before the final stretch to the bridge, a red light, a DON'T WALK signal, and three oncoming cars forced me to a stop. I put my hands on my knees and took advantage of the moment to catch my breath. Once the cars had passed, leaving the smell of exhaust in their wake, I looked both directions and decided to jaywalk—or jayrun—across the street. I barely made it across before another vehicle came barreling up the street. If I'd been a couple of seconds slower, it would have clipped me.

I'd lost precious time at the light. Up ahead, the woman grew smaller and smaller as she neared the opposite end of the bridge. I had to get to her before she reached the end. Once she took the elevator or staircase down to street level, she could go in several directions, and I might not ever find her.

I skirted a fire hydrant and rushed forward, reaching the steps. I took them at double time, my work boots stomping a fast beat as I made my way up. *Clop-clop-clop-clop.* As I reached the bridge platform, the blonde woman's head disappeared as she descended the other end.

I cupped my hands around my mouth and shouted, "Wait!" All I succeeded in doing was catching the attention of people standing at the bridge rail, admiring the river and the view of the skyline. Several heads snapped my way, expressions of concern and curiosity on their faces. I ran past them, running out of steam halfway across the bridge and having to slow to a fast walk. While my work kept me in decent shape, I'd already spent time in the heat on the motel's roof, and my energy was zapped. I could feel sweat running down my back, my coveralls sticking to my spine.

When I reached the far end of the bridge, I skipped down the staircase as fast as I could, stopping at the bottom to look in all directions. The woman was nowhere to be seen. Had she blended into the teeming crowd of tourists on Broadway? Had she turned left to continue to Riverfront Park? Or had she gone straight down the pathway that led past the Schermerhorn Symphony Center to the Music City Walk of Fame?

I ran a few steps to my left, saw nothing, and turned to run in the other direction. Had she gone into one of the buildings? I jogged down to Broadway and looked up the street. There were dozens of blonde women up and down the sidewalks. Was one of them her?

I hurried up the block, having a hard time weaving among the groups of tourists stopped on or meandering down the sidewalks. I crossed the street and circled back. I still didn't see her. I stopped and let out a loud sigh. *Who is she? Why does she seem to be so interested in the motel? Could she have had something to do with Beckett Morgan's death?*

CHAPTER 20

FILL ME UP AND FILL ME IN

WHITNEY

As I headed back down Broadway, I came upon one of the smaller bars, tucked between a pizza place and candy store. The bar hosted a nonstop lineup of acts on its small stage, their colorful flyers posted in the window to generate interest. A bright yellow one was of particular interest to me. It featured professional headshots of Sawyer Karnes with his guitar, Wylie Pfluger with his bass, and a man named Gabriel Przybyszewski sitting behind a drum set. *A-ha! That's one mystery solved. No wonder they just call him Gabriel something-or-other.* The flyer read:

COME HEAR THE BARNYARD BOYS!
FORMER MEMBERS OF BECKETT MORGAN'S BAND
PERFORM BECKETT'S HITS AND ORIGINAL
    MATERIAL.
8:00 SATURDAY. NO COVER CHARGE.

Wow. It had taken Sawyer and Wylie no time to re-group and capitalize off Beckett's fame and music. Even the name they'd chosen, the Barnyard Boys, had the same folksy tone as "Party in the Pasture." But perhaps I was being too harsh. They could consider their act to be a form of tribute and, despite Beckett's traumatic death, they still had to make a living. Besides, how could I fault them when I'd been promoting the condos to Rex Tomlinson only an hour earlier?

I'd left my phone back at the motel, so I couldn't snap a pic of the flyer. Instead, I went inside to see if they might have extra copies on hand. Luck was with me. Atop the bar were copies of the various flyers spread out like a rainbow. An inverted lowball glass sat atop each stack to prevent the papers from going airborne when patrons opened the door and let in the breeze. I lifted the glass, snagged a copy of the yellow flyer for the Barnyard Boys, and folded it up to stick in my pocket.

The bartender came over. "Can I get you something?"

"No, thanks," I said. "I don't have my wallet with me."

He eyed my red face and sweat-soaked coveralls. "At least let me get you some water. You look like you could use it."

"I'd appreciate that." I might not have any cash on me to tip the guy now, but I made a mental note to come back and make up for my breach of etiquette.

He set a glass of ice water in front of me. I downed it in five gulps, thanked the guy, and walked back to the motel.

As I stepped into the room where Buck and Jimmy were working, Buck asked, "What was so important you had to run off to the bridge?"

"The blonde," I said. "She was back."

"You sure you're even seeing the same woman each time? Lots of people go up on that bridge."

He had a point. I'd only seen her from afar and couldn't be certain. But she did seem to hold herself the same way each time. Her head down, arms close to her sides. My gut told me that it was the same woman, and that she could be an important clue. "She's always alone," I said. "Most people up there are in groups, or at least couples. She's always dressed in black too."

"Like a black widow," Buck said.

Jimmy added, "Or like she's in mourning."

"Huh," I said. "I hadn't thought of that."

Having left my phone behind when I'd taken off after the blonde, I rounded it up now and took a look at the screen to make sure I hadn't missed any calls or texts while I'd been gone. *Nope. Nothing.* A thought niggled at me then. I'd just solved the mystery of Gabriel's last name, maybe I could solve the mystery of J.C. too. We'd been assuming the initials represented a first and last name, but what if the C stood for a middle name?

I typed the name Jared Vandervoort into the browser and ran a search. He popped up on every social media site in existence. Facebook. Twitter. Instagram. Pinterest. Snapchat. TikTok. Some I hadn't even heard of. He seemed to be the most active on Instagram, so I focused my efforts there. I scrolled through his posts and comments, looking for anything that might indicate whether his middle name started with a C. *Nope. Nope. Nope.* As I scrolled further back in time, the handlebar mustache disappeared from his photos, and he grew younger, like a Benjamin Button. It took nearly three minutes of cyber-snooping, but then *bingo!* I hit pay dirt. Years

back, he'd been designated Cumberland River Records'
employee of the month. His award was printed on a
certificate made to look like a record album. His full
name appeared on the certificate—Jared Cole Vandervoort. *He just might be J.C., after all.*

Though I was excited by this find, I slid my phone
back into my pocket. Collin hadn't been in touch to update me on Gia Revello, so he must be swamped. For
all I knew, he had her in custody and was working with
the district attorney's office to cement their case. I'd wait
until I heard from him and share my find then.

Buck, Jimmy, and I continued the demolition work
until well after six, during which several groups of
Beckett's fans came by and left more flowers along the
fence. I'd begun to wonder whether I'd hear from Collin today, when he pulled up to the gate while I was rolling a wheelbarrow filled with broken shower tiles to the
dumpster.

He unrolled his window and jerked his head in a
come-here gesture. "Why don't you pack it up and
let's grab some food? I'll fill you in on the case over
dinner."

I looked down at myself. Dust clung to my hair, and
my coveralls were stained with sweat and dirt. I spread
my arms wide. "You really want to be seen in public
with me looking like this?"

"Gosh, no." He grimaced in jest. "I need to run by
the station, anyway. How about I pick you up at your
place in an hour? That enough time for you to freshen
up?"

I couldn't be pretty by then, but I could be present-
able. Besides, any man who was going to be with me
would have to accept that he would often see me at my
worst.

Buck made a shooing motion with his gloved hand. "Go on, Whitney. One of us should have a personal life."

"Thanks, cuz."

An hour later, Collin was at my door. He came inside briefly to say hello to Sawdust and Cleopatra, and to give them a friendly scratch under the chin. Cleo used her paw to grab at his hand, turning her head to chew softly on his finger once she'd captured it.

"Ouch!" Collin cried in jest. "This vicious tiger is attacking me!"

Cleo stopped chewing and looked up at him in concern, as if wondering whether she might have crossed a line she hadn't yet learned about in her tender kitty years. Collin chuckled and rubbed her under the chin. "It's okay, girl. You're exonerated on the grounds of cuteness."

We headed out to Collin's car, and in minutes were seated in a quiet booth at the back of one of Nashville's many cafés that served Southern cooking. The smells of cornbread baking and okra frying filled the air. After glasses of iced tea were set in front of us and we'd placed our order with the server, I said, "So? What's happened since I last saw you? Did you arrest Gia Revello?"

He flicked a sugar packet between his fingers to loosen the crystals. "No. Turns out the reason why her husband thought she arrived home at 2:57 was because those were the only numbers he saw when she came into the bedroom. I took a look for myself. The remote control for their television was lying in front of the DVR he consulted. It could have blocked the first digit of the time." In other words, the remote might have obscured the 1 in 12:57, making the time appear to be 2:57, instead. "Her husband also didn't know she'd spent some time in the kitchen drinking wine before she came to the bedroom. All he can say for sure is that he woke up when she came into their bedroom, and that it was at either 12:57 or 2:57 that night."

"So she might have been telling the truth, that she arrived home at half past midnight."

"Exactly," Collin said. "If she'd killed Beckett just after two o'clock, rushed home, and skipped the wine, there's a chance she could have been in her bedroom by 2:57. But I can't make an arrest on such flimsy evidence."

"Did he say whether she seemed upset or agitated?"

"He said she mentioned getting into a little tiff with Beckett at the Ryman earlier that night, but she didn't elaborate. Other than that, her behavior was normal."

"What about their alarm system? Do they have one?"

"They do," Collin said, "but her husband hadn't armed it before he went to bed, so Gia didn't have to disarm it when she returned home. In fact, it was never armed at all that night. The records showed that they use it only sporadically. Seems like it's something they rely on more when they're out of town rather than on a regular daily basis."

"You didn't find anything else? Maybe some of Beckett's blood on her clothing?"

"No. Her husband said their housekeeper normally handles their laundry and dry cleaning, but by the time I stopped by Gia had already washed the dress she'd worn to the Ryman Friday night. I went back to Cumberland River Records in the late afternoon to ask her about it, and she claimed she'd gotten some oily salad dressing on the sleeve when she'd gone out to eat with another of the label's executives before the show. She was afraid if she let it sit too long, it would cause a permanent grease stain."

"Do you believe her?"

"I'm not sure what to think. She had a response locked and loaded, so either it was the honest truth or she'd known she better come up with a good excuse in case she was asked about her clothing."

"Did she wear boots that night?"

"Yes, but they had round toes. She voluntarily gave me the keys to her Lexus and let me search it. I didn't find anything."

My nerves began to tingle at the news I had for him. "I might have something."

"Oh, yeah?"

"You remember Gia's assistant?"

"Jared Vandervoort? Sure."

"I looked him up on social media. Guess what letter his middle name starts with."

He cocked his head. "Is it C?"

I nodded. "C for Cole. He could be the J.C. we've been looking for."

The server stepped up from behind me with our blue-plate specials.

"Hope you two are hungry!" She sat a plate down in front of me, then another in front of Collin. Both were piled high with enough fried okra, sweet corn, and mashed potatoes and gravy to feed an army. As if that wasn't enough, she left us a basket filled with corn muffins and butter.

We thanked her and she walked off to take care of other customers.

Collin leaned forward over the table. "I've discovered another J.C."

I leaned forward too. "Who?"

"Remember the guy from the vigil that you followed?"

"The one wearing the belt buckle with the feathered arrows and driving the Dodge Challenger?"

"Yeah. His name is Cameron Caravelli. He's from out of town. Chattanooga, to be exact. He said he and his wife attended the vigil together after she learned about it on Facebook. Her name's Josselyn."

Josselyn Caravelli. J.C.

"But she couldn't be J.C., could she?" I said. "I saw Cameron and Josselyn drive off together, but you tracked J.C.'s phone to the bridge not long after the vigil was over. She couldn't be two places at once."

"Or could she?" He took a sip of his tea and raised his brows.

"So, what?" I said, impatient for details. "She had an evil twin? A clone? She could teleport?" I waved my hand, urging him to hurry up and fill me in.

"Cameron said they rented a room at the Omni Hotel when the vigil was over. He stayed in the room to watch the tail end of a West Coast baseball game, but Josselyn went out for a run along the riverfront. He said it wasn't unusual for her. She's very into fitness. She's a flight attendant, based out of Atlanta. She spends a lot of time cooped up on planes, so exercise is her release."

While the drive from Chattanooga to Atlanta's Hartsfield-Jackson airport would take a couple of hours, I'd heard that it wasn't unusual for flight crews to live a farther distance from their home airports than most people lived from their workplaces, especially if they had a spouse with a job elsewhere. Attendants generally flew only a few days a month, with several days off between shifts, so a short commute was less of a concern.

Collin scooped up a blob of mashed potatoes and

gravy. "Her job would have given her flight benefits. She could've been flying out to rendezvous with Beckett while he was on tour."

I speared a piece of fried okra with my fork. "If she went for a jog, she could have been up on the bridge and dropped her secret phone."

"It's a plausible theory," Collin said. "She and Beckett could have been involved. I checked out her social media. There's a photo of Cameron and Josselyn with Beckett taken six months ago when he played a gig in Chattanooga." He retrieved his phone from his pocket and logged into Facebook, pulling the picture up onto his screen. Beckett stood to Josselyn's left, his lip curled up just so in what appeared to be a well-practiced smile, his right arm encircling her waist. She, likewise, had an arm around his back. Her head was tilted toward him as if she was trying to put as much of herself in close contact with the star as possible. A broad smile spanned her face, and her eyes gleamed, starstruck. Her husband stood on her other side. Rather than facing the camera, his head was turned to look at his wife and Beckett. No broad smile for him. Though he wasn't frowning either. His expression was neutral, difficult to read.

Collin pointed to Josselyn. "Why don't you look at me like that?"

"How's this?" I clasped my hands under my chin, angled my head, and batted my eyes my eyes at him.

"That's downright terrifying."

"Sorry. I'll practice my look of adoration." My gaze shifted from Collin back to his phone screen. "Is there just the one photo?"

"Yes, but it's enough to show Beckett and Josselyn met at some point. She could've slipped her contact information into his back pocket that night, or maybe she attended to him on a plane another time and he asked for her number. Who knows? I'm going to check with Sawyer and Wylie, see if she's the blonde they mentioned, the one who often hung around the fringe at Beckett's performances."

"If Beckett was involved with Josselyn that would explain why he had no photos of her on his phone. It would have hurt is career if the news got out that he was involved with a married woman. Blake Shelton took a lot of heat for cheating on Miranda Lambert."

"I thought it was the other way around," Collin said. "That Miranda cheated on Blake."

"Who knows?" I said. "Either way, there was a lot of mudslinging." I took a sip of my tea. "Do you think Cameron could have found out that his wife was cheating and killed Beckett in a jealous rage? It wouldn't have been too hard to follow Beckett after he left the Ryman. Cameron could have seen him go into Tootsie's, and waited nearby until he came out. He could have followed Beckett, Sawyer, and Wylie over the bridge, and then kept on following Beckett once he split off from the pack."

"It's possible. If that's what happened, my guess is Josselyn is in the dark, has no idea her husband learned of any indiscretion or acted on it. Cameron claims he was at their house Friday night, but it's unverified. Josselyn was working a red-eye from Atlanta to Los Angeles. She didn't arrive home until Sunday. This is all speculation and what-ifs at this point, and I could be way off base. They both seemed surprised I contacted them. Maybe even a little outraged. They claimed they were simply fans who wanted to pay their respects. They wanted to know why they'd been targeted."

"What did you tell them?"

"I fibbed and said we were desperate for leads, so we'd collected license plates numbers from the night of the vigil. I said we were following up with everyone who'd had any personal interaction with Beckett, no matter how brief, and that they were merely two of hundreds of people we were questioning."

"Did they buy it?"

"Hard to say. I'm going to get a list of the hotels where Beckett has stayed while on tour the past few months and see if a Josselyn Caravelli booked a room at any of them. My guess is he wouldn't have brought her into his room where he was more likely to be caught with her and cause a scandal. He probably would've taken the stairs or service elevator and sneaked into her room."

I bit into the fried okra, burning my tongue. "Hot, hot, hot!" I cried, grabbing my iced tea and taking a gulp to cool my sizzled taste buds. While the steaming food cooled, I unzipped my purse, pulled out the folded yellow flyer, and handed it across the table to Collin. "Check this out."

He unfolded the paper and perused it, a series of emotions crossing his face. He pointed at the photo of Gabriel Przybyszewski with his raised drumsticks. "Can't say that I blame anyone for calling him Gabriel something-or-other. Can't say that I blame Sawyer and Wylie for promoting their connection to Beckett either. With so many wannabe stars in this town, they have to use any advantage they've got to get ahead." He looked up at me. "That said, I looked into these two. Wylie's name came up in a police report. He and some other guy got into a shoving match outside a bar a couple of years ago. He threw a punch at the responding officer before he realized the guy was a cop."

"Whoa. Looks like Wylie might have a temper." The

incident must have been what T-Rex was referring to earlier when he told me Wylie's drinking had gotten him in trouble.

Collin held up the Barnyard Boys' flyer. "Why don't we go to this show? It'll give me another excuse to talk to Sawyer and Wylie. We could bring Buck and Colette with us, if she's not working. Make a night of it. We haven't been out in a while."

"Tell me about it." I sent him a smile to let him know there were no hard feelings. "I'll check with them."

He eyed the flyer a final time before asking, "How did you come across this anyway?"

I told him about the woman on the bridge. "It could be nothing, but she seems to turn up every couple of days—assuming it's even the same woman. Buck says there's no way I can be sure from so far away. He's probably right. But she seems to always be wearing black and looking in the direction of the motel, which seems odd."

"When was the first time you saw her?"

"Saturday. Before we found Beckett at the motel."

"If you see her again, call me right away. Okay?"

"Sure."

He refolded the flyer and tucked it into his breast pocket. "By the way, the lab was finally able to extract DNA from the second cigar butt."

"The one that was in the muck at the bottom of the pool?"

"Yeah."

"And?"

"The DNA didn't match Beckett."

"Someone else smoked that cigar, then." *Someone who had very likely killed the singer.*

"Right. Whoever it was, their DNA isn't on record

with law enforcement. In other words, they were never convicted of a crime. Tennessee law also allows a cheek swab to be taken from anyone who's been arrested for a violent felony, regardless of whether they're convicted."

"Wylie's shoving match at the bar," I said, "when he swung at the cop—" I swung my fist, miming a right hook.

"Wylie wasn't arrested," Collin interjected. "The report said he apologized to the officer, and that he and the other guy shook hands and smoothed things over. Nobody was injured, so the officer let it go."

"Meaning Wylie's DNA isn't on file."

"No such luck."

"Can you ask Sawyer and Wylie for saliva samples?"

"I could, but they'd be within their rights to refuse. There's not enough evidence against them for me to get a warrant forcing them to provide a sample. I'm also not sure I want to tip my hand, let anyone know that the case at this point is resting on DNA evidence. I can always grab their garbage and see where that gets me."

As he'd informed me before, trash put out at the curb or in a public refuse bin was considered abandoned property and was not protected from search and seizure. Several cold cases had recently been solved with DNA collected from trash a suspect had tossed in a public can.

My food had cooled enough to eat now, and I dug in. For the rest of the meal, we discussed more pleasant matters than murder. The rapid progress Buck and I were making at the motel, with Jimmy's help, of course. Cleo's first introduction to the canine species at my parents' house the evening before. The great view Collin had through his telescope that morning of the globular star cluster Messier 75.

"It was right between Jupiter and Saturn." He raised

his hands, making fists to represent the planets. "Really cool."

"How early did you have to get up to see it, Ziggy Stardust?"

"Four thirty."

"Four thirty? Sheesh. Even the roosters are still fast asleep then."

"It was worth it. When I solve this case, I'm going to treat myself to a new telescope with a built-in camera so I can share the images."

"That's probably the only way I'll ever see them. I won't get out of bed at four in the morning for anything." It wasn't true. I'd get up early for a good reason, and supporting Collin's hobby was a good one. I let him know with a soft smile that I was merely teasing. I buttered a corn muffin. "T-Rex came by to see me today."

"He did? Why?"

"Seemed like he was curious about how the investigation was coming along. He said he didn't want to bother you because he knew you were busy working the case and he didn't want to do anything to slow you down."

"Why did he think you'd know anything?"

"He seemed to realize we're involved. I'm pretty sure he overheard us after the vigil when we were joking about whether we'd kiss the other after smoking a cigar."

Collin sat back in his seat, contrite. "Guess we should've been more discreet."

"You think it means anything? Him coming around and asking questions?"

"It means he wants information," Collin said. "I suppose that's obvious. But why he wants it is anyone's guess. As Beckett's manager, he's probably fielding a lot of questions from the media, fans, venues where Beckett was supposed to play. I know better than anyone how frustrating it can be to have to tell people you don't have answers. But I'm sure there's a personal element to it too. Beckett might not have been the ideal client, but I got the sense that T-Rex considered himself a sort of father figure to Beckett. The death must have taken an emotional toll. Plus, he said he felt bad that he hadn't been with Beckett that night to protect him. Maybe he's hoping an arrest will relieve his guilt."

"You know what always makes me feel better?" I picked up the dessert menu and pointed to an entry. "Blueberry pie."

CHAPTER 21

WALK THIS WAY

SAWDUST

On Thursday morning, Whitney sat up, stretched, and climbed out of bed. Sawdust hopped down to the floor too. He wasn't sure where she was headed first—the bathroom or the kitchen—but he'd found that if he ran ahead of her, sometimes she'd follow him where he wanted to go.

His tactic worked this morning. He skittered along in front of her, glancing back over his shoulder to make sure she was still coming along. *She was. Good.* In the kitchen, he sat down in front of his empty food bowl and looked up at her.

As he'd hoped, she reached down and ruffled his ears. "Want some breakfast, boy?"

Did he ever!

He rubbed along Whitney's ankles as she filled one bowl with dry kibble, and another with canned salmon. When she finished, he looked up at her, offered her a *mew* of gratitude, and dug in. *Yum! Was there anything better than fish for breakfast?*

CHAPTER 22

GETTING HITCHED

WHITNEY

On Thursday morning, I walked through a new property Home & Hearth had been hired to manage, making sure it complied with all state and city codes. I installed smoke alarms and carbon monoxide detectors, turned the water heater down to a lower temperature to prevent scalding, and changed the locks on the exterior doors. *Done, done, and done.*

My duties to the real estate company complete, I drove to the motel. Today would be all about repairing the stucco and installing new windows in the units. While we planned to finish out the interiors after the units sold, we'd have better luck selling those units if the exterior looked inviting.

While Buck and Jimmy removed the plywood and old windows, I made my way around the building with a trowel, a chisel, and a bucket of premixed patching plaster to fill in the pockmarks. Fortunately, the repetitive motions required little in the way of concentration, leaving me to ponder Beckett Morgan's murder.

Many people remained suspects at that point and, just as movie credits sometimes listed a cast in order of appearance, I considered them in the order in which they'd appeared to me.

First, of course, was Jimmy. He'd been at the motel the night Beckett was killed, and had the opportunity to do the singer in. But while Collin initially thought Jimmy might have been motivated to hurt Beckett if he thought the guy was on site to steal his motorcycle, it seemed pretty clear now that Collin considered him a weak suspect at best.

Next were Sawyer Karnes and Wylie Pfluger, both of whom had a motive for offing Beckett. The star had refused to help them advance their music careers as they'd hoped. Gia Revello said they'd seemed amused when she'd chewed Beckett out at the Ryman Auditorium the night he'd been killed. The voice mail Beckett had left J.C. later that night corroborated her story. Beckett, too, had noticed their apparent amusement at his expense. Though they'd invited him out for beers after the show, the two seemed more interested in the attention they'd garner by being seen with a celebrity than they did in smoothing things over with him. No, there appeared to be little love lost between them and Beckett.

What's more, not only did the two musicians have a motive for murdering Beckett, they had the opportunity. They'd been with him shortly before he was last seen alive, and they could have easily followed him to the Poison Emporium and attacked him afterward in the motel parking lot. Wylie had been involved in at least one violent incident in which the police had been called. What's more, the night of the vigil, they seemed to realize they'd said too much and attempted to backtrack on their statements and paint a rosier picture of their relationship with Beckett than was really the case. They'd both admitted to smoking cigars with Beckett in the past, maybe because they knew others had seen them do it and could attest to it. One of them might have had a cigar on them. They very well could have lit up to smoke with Beckett again as he left the Poison Emporium, then dropped or tossed the butt into the motel pool when they'd gotten into a physical confrontation with him.

Another possibility that had yet to be explored involved another musician, the drummer Gabriel Przybyszewski. He'd played with Beckett the night of the murder, and he'd evidently tangled with Beckett, Gia Revello, and T-Rex over the drums in one of their recordings the day Shep claimed to have written "Party in the Pasture." If Collin didn't get a chance to talk to Gabriel before Saturday, maybe he could corner him at the bar when we went to see the Barnyard Boys play.

T-Rex seemed to consider his client a minor thorn in his side, but any motive to kill Beckett for being demanding seemed to be offset by his far greater motive to keep Beckett alive and reap the financial rewards the young man brought him. Though Collin had confirmed with the staff in McMinnville that T-Rex had indeed stayed after the show to discuss business matters as he had claimed, T-Rex had no rock-solid alibi for the time afterward. He claimed to have arrived home shortly after Beckett called him, which might very well be true. But had he gone home directly from the show in McMinnville, or might he have hunted Beckett down to hash things out? The latter seemed unlikely given the late hour, but it wasn't out of the question. Even so, T-Rex seemed to be a straightforward person. He'd described

Beckett as neither a sinner nor a saint, which seemed honest and realistic. The jury was still out on him too.

Gia Revello was also still in the running, though I had my doubts where she was concerned. She'd been seen arguing with Beckett at the Ryman. Would a woman smart enough to rise to the executive level at a large record label be stupid and impulsive enough to later hunt Beckett down for another round of argumentation, one that ended with her shoving him into an empty swimming pool and stabbing him in the heart with a loose doorstop? It seemed doubtful, especially given that she had called T-Rex and seemed to have accepted that the two of them would later be settling the matter of the outstanding contract. Like T-Rex, she seemed honest, though brutally so. She didn't seem to adhere to the old adage that it wasn't nice to speak ill of the dead. If she'd been guilty, wouldn't she have attempted to temper her comments to reduce suspicion? Or maybe, being the shrewd businesswoman she was, she realized that by being unapologetically blunt about what she thought of Beckett, it would make her seem more sincere, less like she was hiding something or pretending to have warm, fuzzy feelings she didn't truly have. I also wondered whether she'd be strong enough to drag Beckett's body up out of the pool. She was a spitfire, but she wasn't a big woman. Then again, adrenaline enabled people to do all sorts of things that didn't seem possible.

Gia's assistant, Jared Cole Vandervoort, could be the elusive J.C. that Beckett had contacted shortly before his death and who had left the sigh on Beckett's voice mail. As Gia's assistant, he'd surely had repeated contact with Beckett. He'd smelled like cigars when we'd followed him down the hall at the record company's offices earlier in the week. The scent could have been solely his cologne, but it might also have been from actual cigar smoke. If he was J.C., though, what reason would he have to hurt Beckett? J.C. and Beckett seemed to be on good terms. If he wasn't J.C., maybe he'd killed Beckett because he wanted to avenge his boss, knew she'd been upset by Beckett's behavior. Still, even if he was a dedicated employee, it seemed a stretch to think he'd kill for his boss—on purpose at least. Maybe Beckett had been argumentative with him and things had simply gotten out of hand.

Cameron and Josselyn Caravelli were also still on the list of possible suspects. The photo from Facebook proved they'd met Beckett, and Josselyn's initials meant she could be J.C. Cameron had worn a belt buckle that Jimmy could have mistaken for a bird's foot. While Josselyn had been out of town at the time of the murder, if she'd been having an affair with Beckett and her husband found out, Cameron might have been the one to kill the superstar.

Then there were the women. Not only the young ladies who seemed to think they had some sort of unspoken romantic connection to Beckett, but also Lacy Spurlock, the singer he'd spurned in front of not only a packed live audience in a theater, but also hundreds of thousands more people watching on television or streaming on their devices.

If J.C. wasn't Jared or Josselyn, then, whoever J.C. was, he or she was still a person of interest too. So was the blonde I'd seen multiple times on the bridge. My gut told me she had something to do with Beckett.

An hour later, I was spackling the backside of the motel and listening to an audiobook through my headphones when a finger tapped on my shoulder. On reflex, I tossed the trowel into the air and slapped my hand to my chest to still my exploding heart. Luckily for me, the person who'd tapped my shoulder was Collin. Also luckily for me, the trowel turned three flips in the air and landed handle-up in the tub of stucco.

While I tried to catch my breath, Collin gently tugged the ear buds from my ears. "I called your name three times." He gave me a disapproving look as he held up the cord, the earpieces hanging from it. "You shouldn't wear these things. Anyone could sneak up on you."

"You nearly gave me a heart attack." I snatched the earphones out of his hand. "You could have waved your arms or something to get my attention."

"You think a killer is going to wave his arms?" he demanded. "Let you know he's coming?"

He had a point. Realizing his concern was a sign of affection, I met him halfway. "I'll put only one in next time."

He raised his other hand, which held a stack of paper. I took the papers from him. They were copies of Beckett's credit card statements for the last few months. My eyes made their way down the statement on top. A large purchase at an electronics store. Several high-dollar charges at Western outfitters. Expensive meals at fancy local restaurants. "Anything helpful in here?"

"Beckett bought some high-end clothing, the usual tech gadgets guys can't seem to live without, a big-screen television, and the like. Saw them when I went through his condo in the Gulch. But there was a transaction last month that caught my eye."

"What was it?"

He pointed to an entry of $1,892.57 from late April.

I looked from up from the page. "He spent nearly two grand at a jewelry store. What for?"

"Don't know yet," Collin said. "Could be he bought

himself a nice watch or could be he bought a gift for J.C. or someone else. Maybe he bought his mom something nice for Mother's Day. I'll find out when I swing by the store later."

"You think it could be an important clue, then?"

Collin shrugged. "It's not every day a guy drops that much coin at a jewelry store. Not even a wealthy guy like Beckett. Besides, nothing else has panned out. I called the hotels where Beckett stayed while on tour. None had any reservations under the name Josselyn Caravelli. I even tried other hotels within walking distance. I thought maybe he'd had her stay somewhere nearby instead of at the same hotel to reduce the chance of them being spotted together. No luck."

"Maybe she made reservations under an alias or used her maiden name."

"Could be," he said. "But hotels generally ask for identification. It would be difficult for her to use an alias unless she had a fake ID, which seems like a stretch." He wagged a finger at me. "A maiden name could be a different story, though. If nothing else pans out, I'll try that."

I rolled up on my toes, proud I'd thought of something helpful. "Have you showed her picture to Sawyer and Wylie yet?"

"I did," he said. "Both said she wasn't the blonde they'd seen hanging around the shows. Josselyn is older and her hair is more golden. They said the woman at the shows has long, pale blonde hair."

"Like the woman on the bridge."

"They could be one and the same. Unfortunately, we still don't know who she is."

"Have you tried to contact the drummer?"

"Left him a voice mail this morning, as a matter of fact. He hasn't called me back yet. His outgoing message said he'd be tied up with a recording session the next couple of days, so I don't know when I might hear from him. If he doesn't get in touch with me before Saturday, I'll corner him at the show."

Realizing Collin was frustrated and discouraged, I said, "Well, if none of these other leads pan out, maybe when Lacy Spurlock comes back to town, she'll confess right off the bat and you can put this to rest."

"A murder confession?" he said. "That's rare. You've either watched way too many crime shows on TV or huffed too much paint on the jobsite."

"We haven't started painting yet," I countered. "But I have inhaled quite a bit of window sealant."

A smile played about his mouth. "That explains it."

He gave me a peck on the cheek and headed off to the jewelry store.

Emmalee, Colette, and I were sitting at the breakfast bar sharing coffee and gossip when there was a knock on the front door of the house around eight o'clock Friday morning. The three of us exchanged glances.

"Either of you expecting someone?" I asked. "Maybe a delivery?"

"Nope," Emmalee said.

Colette, who had a mouthful of coffee, shook her head.

Because my roommates generally worked later in the day, they were both still in their pajamas. I, on the other hand, had already donned a pair of coveralls. As the only one properly dressed, I deemed it my duty to see who was on our porch. Cleo deemed it her duty to skitter after me, attacking my ankles all the way to the front of the living room.

Sawdust stood on his cat tree by the front window,

looking out. I stepped up beside him to take a quick glance outside. Buck's van sat at the curb. Attached to the hitch was a colorful food trailer. Painted on the side was a dancing cartoon taco wearing a sombrero and shaking maracas, along with the words TACOS TA-GO! There was a huge dent where the taco's tummy would be, as if someone had sucker-punched him. *What in the world. . . . ?* I opened the door to find Buck on the other side of it, beaming.

He hiked a thumb over his shoulder. "Look what I just took in trade."

"In trade for what?" I asked. "Your sanity?"

"Shoot, no," he said. "I lost my sanity years ago. I traded some carpentry work for it. I went to the trailer place to get a new tire for my flatbed after I picked up a nail on the interstate, and I saw this baby for sale on the lot. I thought maybe Colette could use it."

"Did someone say my name?" Colette eased up next to me, a throw blanket wrapped around her shoulders in an attempt to cover her pajamas.

Buck grinned anew and stepped aside, sweeping his arm. "Look what I brought you."

"Tacos?"

"No. A food trailer. I thought you could use it for cooking at our grand opening. After, too, for festivals and whatnot. You've been talking for a while about wanting to start your own catering business, maybe a food truck."

Her mouth gaped and she looked up at him with starry eyes. "I *have* been talking about it. I just didn't know you'd actually been listening."

"Of course I was. I've got a proposal for you." He went down on one knee and took her hand in his. "Colette Chevalier. Will you marinade for me?"

"I will!"

She giggled and her mouth spread in a wide smile. In response, a red flush rushed up Buck's neck to inflame his cheeks. He looked away, glancing back at the trailer. "Don't worry about the unsightly dent. Won't take any time for me to hammer it out."

"What happened?" I asked.

"Minor collision with a funnel cake vendor at a street fair."

Colette walked past me and out the door, moving as if she were floating on air.

I rounded up Sawdust from his cat tree and called back to Emmalee in the kitchen. "Hey, Em! Come see this!"

Buck, Emmalee, Sawdust, and I followed Colette out to the trailer. She stood on the lawn in her slippers, ogling the thing, shaking her head in disbelief.

"I can repaint it," Buck said. "Put a name on it too. Whatever you want."

Colette raised her hands as if envisioning words on a marquee. "Voodoo Vittles."

It was the perfect name. It tied in with her New Orleans heritage and was catchy enough that people would remember it.

"Let's paint it purple," she murmured, still staring. "With gold lettering outlined in green."

"Mardi Gras colors," Emmalee said. "Sounds right."

Buck opened a door on the back, and we all stepped inside to take a closer look. The space was tight, but well designed to enable several people to maneuver around. I sat Sawdust down on the stainless-steel prep table so he could sniff around and satisfy his cat's curiosity.

"It's eight by sixteen feet," Buck said. "One of

the smaller food trailers, but looks to be pretty well equipped. 'Course, I can change things out if needed."

Still in awe, Colette ran her hand over the shiny countertop, calling out the features as she took them in. "Double-sided sink, flat-top grill, convection oven, two basket fryers, broiler, steam table, four burners on the range. Looks like it's got everything I could possibly need."

Buck gestured toward the front. "Fridge and freezer too."

She turned around to face him, happy tears welling up in her eyes. "Buck, I could kiss you for this!"

He raised his palms. "What's stopping you?"

She raised up on her toes and gave him a noisy smooch on the cheek. *Smoooooch!* Back on flat feet, she said, "How can I ever repay you?"

"With free food," he said. "In unlimited quantities."

"As far as I'm concerned," she said, "you can eat until you burst."

Emmalee and I exchanged a look. She quirked a lip and leaned in to whisper, "Was that supposed to be romantic? Because now all I can see in my mind is Buck exploding."

I rounded up Sawdust from the sink where he'd wandered and we exited the trailer. Buck turned to close it up.

"One problem," Colette said. "My car can't pull something this big."

She was right. Her Chevy Cruze wasn't made for heavy-duty work. Fortunately, my SUV could handle it. "You can borrow my car or Buck's van when you take the trailer to gigs."

She stepped forward and enveloped me in a tight hug. "You Whitakers are the best."

When she released me, I asked, "Do I get all the food I want too?"

"Of course." She turned to Emmalee. "You too."

"Yum!" Emmalee said. "And if you ever need help—"

"Oh, trust me," Colette said. "I'll be counting on you."

CHAPTER 23

SHOWDOWN LOWDOWN

WHITNEY

Luckily, Buck's brother Owen, my younger cousin, had wrapped up a carpentry job earlier than expected and was available to help out at the motel on Friday. Owen was a slightly leaner, clean-shaven version of Buck. Unlike his older brother, Owen was married with three little girls at home, each of whom I utterly adored. To my delight, the sentiment seemed mutual. Show up with new toys every time you babysit, and children will think you're the best aunt ever.

With Owen's help, Buck and Jimmy finished installing the new windows in no time. While my two cousins started on the flooring for the spec unit, Jimmy grabbed a roller and a pan and helped me begin painting the outside. I'd chosen complementary shades of blue and orange. It felt fun to be bold for a change. When Buck and I rehabbed our first two flip houses, we'd taken the safe route and stuck with neutral tones. This project allowed us far more latitude. I hoped the next project would too.

I wondered what our next project might be. After working on this motel, I wasn't sure just any old house would excite me anymore. It would have to be something unusual, something special.

In the middle of the afternoon, my phone vibrated with an incoming text. I set my paint roller down in the pan and pulled my phone from the pocket of my coveralls. The text was from Collin. Though the moving dotted line told me he was typing a message to me, all that had come through so far was an image of an unpretentious, yet nonetheless beautiful, ladies' ring. The ring had a thin platinum band topped with a petite pear-shaped diamond. The gem sparkled nearly as much as Colette's eyes had this morning when Buck made his grand gesture. Or would giving someone a taco trailer be a *grande* gesture? Like this colorful paint, it had been a bold move. Maybe the two of them would finally move past this perpetual flirtation, this relational impasse that both seemed too chicken to break.

My romantic life wasn't at an impasse, but it was still far too early in my relationship with Collin to even think about exchanging rings. Even so, I quickly texted Collin back. *Proposing?* I added the winking face emoji to let him know I was joking.

A few seconds later, his text came through, telling me what the pic had been all about. *That's what Beckett bought at the jewelry store.*

My mind reeled. *Beckett had bought an engagement ring? For whom?* It had to be J.C., didn't it? After all, their communications documented on Beckett's phone proved they shared a romantic connection. But who was J.C.? Could it be Josselyn Caravelli? Had she planned to leave her husband for Beckett? Could be. Maybe the reason Beckett's family didn't know he had been seriously involved with someone was because he hadn't told them about her. A good reason for keeping things under wraps would be if the woman was currently married, right?

The only thing that seemed clear was that whomever he'd bought the ring for, it was now in her possession. After all, if Beckett had retained the ring, Collin would have found it in Beckett's condominium when he'd searched it shortly after the singer's death.

Though nearly two grand was certainly nothing to sneeze at, convention said a man should spend two months' wages on an engagement ring. I wasn't sure if people still adhered to that notion. It seemed unnecessarily extravagant to me. If a man ever proposed to me, he could win me over with a tiny quarter-carat ring and a 3100 PSI power washer. What's more, two grand would be merely a drop in the bucket to Beckett, nowhere near two months of his earnings. Heck, he probably earned that much in two *days*. What did it say that he'd spent so little? Did it mean he was a cheapskate when it came to the woman in his life? Or did it mean that, despite his fame, he hadn't forgotten his simple country roots? That whomever he'd bought the ring for would love it more for what it stood for than for its market value?

These questions would remain unanswered until Collin figured out who Beckett had given the ring to—*if* he could figure it out. J.C. had proven to be frustratingly elusive so far.

Owen came around again on Saturday to assist us with the flooring. After retrieving his rubber flooring mallet from his toolbox, he turned to me. "Can I ask you a favor?"

I scoffed in jest. "You're kidding right? I'll never be able to repay all the help you've given us. Ask away."

"Could you watch the girls tomorrow afternoon? If I don't take my wife on a date, she just might file for divorce."

He wasn't serious, of course. His wife was a wonderful, patient woman who loved him with all her heart. She wasn't going anywhere. Even so, with three young children at home, she did deserve some time off now and then.

"Dude," Buck interjected. "It's supposed to be date *night*, not date *afternoon*."

"Last time we went out at night," he said, "we both fell asleep at the movies."

"I remember," I said. I'd been the one to babysit for them that night too. "Is that really the last time y'all went out? That was weeks ago."

"I'm ashamed to say it was," he said.

Buck donned his kneepads. "You know Mom and Dad would keep the girls anytime."

"I know," Owen said. "But we already hit them up a lot for when we need to run errands and stuff."

My uncle Roger and aunt Nancy weren't only a fabulous aunt and uncle to me, they were the best of grandparents to their three granddaughters. Even so, I could understand Owen's concern. "I'd be happy to watch them," I said. "In fact, I'll take them to the Adventure Science Center. They always love that."

Owen's jaw went slack. "You mean we'll actually have time alone *at home*?"

Buck chuckled. "Use it wisely, bro."

We scrounged up a spare pair of kneepads for Jimmy, as well as another flooring mallet and mask. While he and I worked in the living room and kitchen area, Buck tackled the bedroom. Owen used the jigsaw to cut the wood planks so that they fit precisely against the wall. The air was filled with dust, the fresh scent of hardwood, and the *bang-bang* and *buzz* from our mallets and saw.

By late afternoon, we'd installed the wood flooring, as well as the quarter-round trim, in the entire unit. To make sure the moisture content in the wood matched that in the air, we'd have to give the floors at least three days to acclimate before we could stain them. But that wouldn't slow us down. There was plenty of work to be done outside, and we could easily fill the time.

As we packed up our tools, I asked Jimmy whether he had any interest in joining Collin, me, Buck, and Colette for the evening. "We're going to see Sawyer and Wylie and Gabriel something-or-other play on SoBro."

He snorted. "Keeping an eye on the suspects, huh?"

I gave him a coy smile. "I'll never admit to it."

"I'm game," he said. "I'll meet you there."

"First whiskey is on us," I said. The guy had proven to be a workhorse. We were getting our money's worth out of him and then some.

Buck, Owen, and I headed out. At home, I cleaned myself up, put some makeup on my face, some curl in my hair, and dressed in a long red maxi dress that was not only super comfortable, but also flattering for my height. After a day sweating on my hands and knees, it felt good to look girlie. Ready for the night, I spent some time playing with Sawdust and Cleo while Colette took her turn in the bathroom. I grabbed the fishing pole toy and dangled the fuzzy caterpillar in front of the cats, making it dance on the string to their feline delight. Cleo pounced again and again, missing the bug every time, but Sawdust expertly used his teeth to grab it and bring it into submission. I rolled jingle-bell balls for them and watched them chase them across the floor. When one ricocheted of the wall and came back at her, Cleo scrabbled to back up and ended up doing a reverse somersault. I fed them Sawdust's favorite treats and gave them scratches under their chins.

Buck arrived a few minutes early.

Colette twirled in front of him, her full, knee-length skirt floating out around her, showing off her shapely legs. "How do I look?"

"You cleaned up okay." Buck's grin said he thought she looked much better than just *okay*.

I twirled too. "How about me?"

Buck quirked his nose. "Looks like I'll to have to keep paying Collin to give you some attention."

I treated him to a raspberry. *Pfffft.*

While I waited for Collin inside, the two of them wandered out back to take a look at the raised garden Buck had installed a while back so Colette could have fresh vegetables, fruits, and herbs to cook with. I watched them from the kitchen window. They stood side by side, their shoulders almost, but not quite, touching. Buck said something and Colette laughed, reaching out to touch his forearm. *What are they waiting for?*

Rap-rap. Collin had arrived. I called out the backdoor to my best friend and cousin. "Time to head out!"

We piled into Collin's car and drove to the free lot down the street from the motel. As we walked across the bridge into SoBro, I glanced back at the motel. The bright blue and orange paint was impossible to miss. The place looked distinctive, fun, and cheerful, if admittedly a little kitschy. I wondered what the blonde woman I'd seen on the bridge thought of the place. In one week, she'd watched it go from a sleazy, garbage and graffiti-covered murder scene to a gated, freshly repaired and repainted residence. Once we finished installing landscaping, a deck, and the pergola around the pool, it would look even better.

As we walked along, I thought about J.C. being up on this bridge the night of Beckett's memorial, of her dropping the phone over the side onto an awning on the General Jackson Showboat. Could she have been the one to kill Beckett? It certainly seemed possible, though again I had to wonder if a woman would have been strong enough to drag his body up and out of the pool. Besides, the footprints I'd seen in the bottom of the pool seemed too big to belong to a woman. Then again, I was tall and had large feet myself. Besides, as Collin had mentioned, they were smeared and elongated from the person sliding their feet along. He'd said it had been impossible to determine the boot size. We couldn't rule out a female attacker. Still, J.C. seemed to lack a motive. Besides, J.C. had attempted to contact Beckett Saturday morning, after he was already dead. Didn't that indicate that J.C. was innocent?

We entered the bar, finding it already packed to the rafters despite the relatively early hour. New York might be the city that never sleeps, but SoBro was hopping most hours of the day, as well. As my eyes scanned the crowd, I spotted an arm waving in the air and a face popping up over the others' heads. Jimmy hopped up and down, and motioned to get our attention. I waved back to let him know we'd seen him. We maneuvered our way through the tight throng of bodes until we reached the back wall. Luckily for us, Jimmy had snagged a table at the far end of the stage. It was right next to a speaker, which would leave our ears ringing by the end of the night, but at least we'd have somewhere to sit. The table was also close to the bar, which was a plus.

Soon after we plunked ourselves down in our seats, a female server came by to take our order. While Jimmy ordered his usual whiskey straight, Colette and I opted for Lynchburg lemonade, a spiked drink made with Lynchburg, Tennessee's, own Jack Daniel's classic whiskey. Buck and Collin requested draft beers. The bartender moved like a man on fire as he fixed our drinks, and our server returned in under a minute with her loaded tray. I paid for Jimmy's first whiskey as promised, and raised my glass in toast. "To good friends and fun times!"

We clinked our glasses and bottles together and each took a sip. We made small talk for several minutes until Sawyer, Wylie, and Gabriel stepped up onto the stage. A look of unwelcome surprise skittered over Wylie's face when he spotted Collin at our table. Collin stood and gave him a friendly smile before easing over a few steps to speak to the musician. "Whitney saw your flyer and suggested we come out tonight. Can't wait to hear what you've got in store for us. I'd also like to thank you and Sawyer for your help on the case. How 'bout I buy the band a round?"

The look on Wylie's face shifted now to one of *welcome* surprise. "We'd be fools not to take you up on that." He quickly checked with Gabriel and Sawyer, and came back with their orders. "Jack and Seven for Gabe. Beers for me and Sawyer."

"You got it." Collin walked back past the table and headed directly to the bar to buy their drinks. When he returned, they took the drinks, raising their bottles and glass in thanks.

After taking a generous slug of beer, Sawyer set his bottle down on the stage at his feet, propped himself on the edge of his tall stool, and performed a mic check. "Testing one, two, three." He followed up his words by strumming a few chords, then looked to the far end of the room where a technician worked a soundboard. The tech gave Sawyer a thumbs-up, letting him know the sound was good.

Sawyer replied with a nod and looked out at the audience. "We appreciate all you folks coming out tonight. This is our first appearance as the Barnyard Boys, and we hope you'll enjoy our music as much as we're going to enjoy playing it for you. As y'all know, we lost a musical great this week. Beckett Morgan was taken from us much too soon, and our hearts are heavy. We'd like to kick things off by honoring him the best way we know how, with a song. This is one of our originals, and it's called 'An Angel's Voice.'"

They began to play a slow, sad song. The lyrics told of a young singer who'd been called home to heaven, only to delight the angels with his beautiful voice. The song was sentimental and sweet, even if slightly sappy. Could Sawyer and Wylie have written the song out of guilt or an attempt to defray suspicion? Or were they simply doing their best to pay homage to Beckett, a star they'd seemed to have both admired and resented? It was impossible to tell.

When they finished, the crowd applauded to offer their respects. Wylie spoke into his mic now. "Beckett was a guy who not only knew how to write a hit song, but how to have a good time too. We know he'd want all of you to have a good time tonight. Let's keep his party going, shall we?" With that, the three launched into "Party in the Pasture," earning them whoops, whistles, and applause from the crowd, many of whom sang along. Everyone whooped it up and shouted, "Let's get pasture-ized!"

As the three played, I occasionally turned my attention to Collin. Though he was hiding it well, he was keeping a discreet eye on their drinks. He seemed to grow rigid, like Sawdust did just prior to a pounce, as he watched Wylie finish off the last of his beer. Collin had begun to rise out of his chair when Wylie plunked his empty bottle on the tray of a passing server. Collin shifted in his seat, trying to look casual, but I knew better. Something was going on.

Over the next few songs, Collin continued to eye Gabe's lowball glass and Sawyer's beer bottle. As soon as both were empty and they'd finished their next song, a server reached out to snag them from the stage, adding them to her tray. While there were other bottles and glasses on the tray already, Gabe's glass was the only whiskey glass and Sawyer's beer bottle was the only one of his particular brand. Collin stood and followed the young woman as she made her way to the bar. He took a quick glance back at the stage, but the Barnyard Boys had already started playing the next song and weren't paying any attention to what Collin was doing. I was, though. When the waitress set the tray down on the bar, he leaned forward to tuck a bill into the bartender's tip jar and surreptitiously swiped the glass and bottle. Turning his back to the stage, he slipped off down the hallway that led to the restrooms. A few seconds later, he peeked around the corner, caught my eye, and jerked his head in a *come-here* gesture.

"I'll be right back," I told the others. I slung my purse over my shoulder and headed toward the hallway as if going to the ladies' room.

As soon as I was in the hall, Collin said something, but my ears were buzzing too much from sitting next to the speaker for me to hear him.

"What?" I asked, locking my eyes on his lips in an attempt to read them.

He leaned close and repeated "Open your purse," while also pointing to the zipper and miming the act of unzipping it.

I did as he'd asked, and he slipped two clear plastic evidence bags inside. One contained the beer bottle, the other held the whiskey glass. He didn't have to tell me what he was doing. I figured it out on my own. He was collecting their DNA to compare to the sample the lab techs had drawn from the second cigar butt found at the crime scene.

I zipped up my purse to hide the beer bottle and the whiskey glass he'd appropriated. "Did you just made me an accessory to petty theft?"

"No." He cupped a hand around my ear so I could hear him better. "I made you part of my chain of custody. But if you ever did get arrested for a crime, you'd have one of the prettiest mug shots the precinct has ever taken."

Aww. A warm, light feeling spread through me. I was a sucker for flattery. "What about Wylie?" I asked. "You want his DNA, too, right?"

"Yes." Collin raised a shoulder. "But I missed my chance to grab his bottle, and if I offer to buy them another round, they might get suspicious. One round is generous, two would seem like a scheme. Besides, maybe I'll get a hit with Gabe or Sawyer."

If either of them matched the DNA the lab extracted

from the cigar butt in the muck, they'd be sunk. The case would be closed, and Collin could reward himself with that new telescope with the built-in camera he'd been wanting.

Collin told me to count to twenty before returning to the table, and headed back himself. I counted—*one, Mississippi, two, Mississippi*—until I reached twenty. I returned to the table too.

The Barnyard Boys went on with their show. As they did, I cast glances at Gabe, wondering if he had anything to do with Beckett's death. He'd played with Beckett both at the studio the day Shep claimed to have scribbled his notes on the napkins, composing the lyrics for "Party in the Pasture." He'd also played with Beckett at the Ryman the night Beckett lost his life. Could Gabe have been the one to steal Shep's song and give it to Beckett? Might he have had second thoughts and gotten into an altercation with Beckett about it? There was no evidence that he'd been anywhere near Beckett after the star had left the Ryman the night he was killed. Even so, a glance at his tapping toe told me his boots had what looked to be a D toe or N toe. Maybe he was the person whose toe appeared on the security camera footage from the Poison Emporium.

Sawyer chatted up the crowd as Wylie returned his dobro to its case. He rounded up his mandolin case but, before opening it and removing the instrument, he pulled a plastic mandolin pick from his breast pocket and clamped it between his teeth. As he crouched down to open the case, the speaker issued a horrible electronic squelch. *BRRZZZT!* Everyone reflexively clapped their hands over their ears. Wylie grimaced and shook his head, as if to shake the horrible sound out of his ears.

The pick tumbled from his mouth, bouncing off the stage to land on the floor near my foot. Seizing this unexpected opportunity, I lifted my toes just slightly and moved my foot over to cover the pick. Wylie peered over the edge of the stage. All of us looked down, too, as if trying to locate the missing pick. Rather than keep the audience waiting while he scoured the floor, he pulled a spare pick from his pocket and retrieved his mandolin from the case. The band launched into their next song.

When they took a break three songs later, I discreetly nudged Collin's foot with my toe and flicked my eyes downward. He took the hint. While some men hid a flask of liquor in their boot, Collin had used his boots to stash his detective gear tonight. With his back, the table, and the tight crowd obscuring anyone's view but mine, he reached down and tugged another evidence bag from his left boot, along with a small pair of tweezers. He used the tweezers to retrieve the pick and slide it into the small evidence bag. He slid everything back down into his boot and sat up.

Minutes later, the Barnyard Boys returned and played another five songs before wrapping up their show. Although those who played string instruments brought their own gear to performances, most venues provided a drum set for the use of any bands who played the house. After all, drum sets weren't exactly portable. While Sawyer and Wylie packed up their instruments, Gabriel was otherwise unoccupied.

Collin stood and waved the drummer over. "Hello, Mr. Przybyszewski," Collin said, pronouncing the name easily: *sheb-eh-shev-ski*. "I'm Detective Flynn."

Gabriel's brows lifted. "I'm impressed, Detective.

Most folks butcher my name. Heck, most people don't even try. They just call me Gabriel Something-or-other." He shrugged, seemingly unbothered by the nickname, taking it in stride.

"Could we speak privately somewhere?" Collin asked.

Gabriel glanced over at Sawyer and Wylie, who were still packing up but both clearly watching the exchange out of the corner of their eyes. "Don't see why not," Gabriel said. "We're all done here."

While I waited with Colette, Buck, and Jimmy at the table, Collin and Gabriel went outside to talk. When Sawyer and Wylie descended from the stage with their various instrument cases in their hands, I called out, "Great show! We enjoyed it."

They both dipped their heads in thanks and chuckled.

"What?" I asked.

"You don't realize it," Wylie said, "but you're hollering. That's the hazard of sitting by a speaker."

I offered a laugh myself. "Oops!" I said, lowering my voice to what I hoped was a reasonable level but which sounded like a whisper to my decibel-damaged ears. "Sorry!"

They thanked us for coming and walked out the door.

When Collin returned, I said, "Get any new information?"

He gave a quick, almost imperceptible shake of his head. *Darn*.

The rest of us gathered up our things and headed back toward the walking bridge, enjoying the cool evening air along the way. I repeatedly plugged and unplugged my ears with my fingers and forced a series of yawns. But while yawning might work for clearing plugged ears on an airplane, it did nothing to repair noise damage.

Jimmy issued a positive critique of the Barnyard Boys' inaugural performance. "They weren't half bad."

"I'm inclined to agree," I said. "Gabriel's a solid drummer."

"Even so," chimed in Buck, who was a big country music fan, "he's no W.S. Holland."

Jimmy asked, "Who's that?"

"Johnny Cash's drummer," Buck clarified. "I learned all about him when I toured Johnny's museum. His train-beat snare is what gave Cash's songs their iconic rhythm. He played for some other big names too. Elvis. Bob Dylan. Carl Perkins. But he spent forty years working for the man in black."

I was dying to ask Collin if he'd learned anything from the Barnyard Boys' drummer, but I knew better than to ask in front of the others. I'd have to wait until we got back home. Even so, I didn't have to wait to ask, "How did you figure out how to pronounce Gabriel's last name?"

"Internet," Collin said. "I'd have never figured it out on my own."

When we were halfway across the bridge, I said, "Let's stop here a minute."

The others concurred and we stepped to the rail. To our left were the colorful lights of the SoBro honky-tonks and the white lights of the taller buildings downtown, all towered over by the signature AT&T Building, the tallest in Tennessee, a structure we locals referred to as the "Batman Building" because of the tall spikes at either end of its roof that resembled Batman's ears. To our right was the mammoth Tennessee Titans' football stadium, a virtual black hole with no illumination at the moment. On game nights, though, the place lit up the sky on the east side of the river. With the stadium currently dark, the guitar-shaped neon sign at the Music City Motor Court captured the eye. We very well might have stumbled upon what would become an iconic property.

Shush-shush-shush-shush. The sound of water churning below pulled our attention downward. The huge paddlewheel on the General Jackson Showboat carried it slowly past us, sending up the scent of fresh water, until it eased over to begin its laborious U-turn in the tight space. Like SoBro, the boat was lit up, passengers lining its rails to get a glimpse of downtown. As it turned, some of the people at the rail waved up at us. We waved back. Buck even cupped his hands around his mouth and called out, "Hello, down there!"

The boat finished its course correction and disappeared underneath us as it headed back to its dock. We, too, decided it was time to move on, backing away from the railing en masse. As we neared the end of the bridge, lights far off to the right caught my eye now. The pyramid atop the Adventure Science Center was lit up day-glow green.

"You busy tomorrow?" I asked Collin.

"No," he said. "Why?"

I pointed to the science center. "I promised Owen I'd take his girls there tomorrow. Want to come along?"

"Absolutely," he said. "The center's planetarium was my favorite place when I was a kid."

Buck faked a sneeze as he said, "Nerd."

I elbowed my cousin in the ribs.

Unfazed, Collin said, "Guilty as charged. Collin is my name and astronomy is my game."

The rest of us groaned and I found myself now the one fake-sneezing "Nerd."

Collin slid me some side-eye and a smile. "You wouldn't have me any other way."

Darn it! He was right.

CHAPTER 24

SNUGGLE TIME!

SAWDUST

He woke to sound of rain pitter-pattering on the roof. He opened his eyes only a small slit to look at Whitney. She was still fast asleep, her arm draped over him. He loved mornings like this, when Whitney didn't have to rush off but instead could lie in bed and snuggle him. Yep, these times were the best. As far as he was concerned, it could rain forever.

CHAPTER 25

HANDS ON

WHITNEY

Sunday dawned dark and drizzly, the perfect day to sleep in. I took advantage of my day off to do just that, curling myself around Sawdust, whose purr created a pleasant vibration, not unlike the vibrating beds the Music City Motor Court had featured back in the day.

At one that afternoon, Collin and I arrived at Owen's house to pick up his girls. Rather than go through the hassle of moving all of their car seats into my SUV, he suggested we drive his wife's minivan to the Adventure Science Center. As we made our way, I settled back in my cushy seat and said, "These minivans might be the least sexy cars made today, but they certainly are comfortable."

"What's sexy mean?" the oldest girl, who'd just recently turned five, asked.

Uh-oh. I'd forgotten to censor myself. Not a good thing when the little queen of questions was sitting directly behind me with her curious and inquisitive brain. "It means attractive," I said, meeting her gaze in the rearview mirror. Anticipating her next question, I said, "And something that's attractive is something that people like."

"Okay," she said.

Phew.

Knowing the girls might have a difficult time sitting still for the planetarium show, we decided to wear them out first by visiting the hands-on exhibits. We went through the BodyQuest exhibit, where they learned all about the human body, from the inside out. We climbed up the Adventure Tower, which was essentially an indoor playground. We visited the beekeeping exhibit, which included a clear tube through which bees could enter from outside to come to an indoor hive. The exhibit unleashed a litany of smart questions from Owen's oldest daughter that I was ill-prepared to answer.

"Is that the queen bee?" She pointed to one of the bees that looked slightly larger than the others.

"Maybe," I told her. "I'm not sure."

"Why do bees buzz?"

"That's the sound of their wings moving when they fly," I told her.

She pointed through the glass to the hive. "But those ones are buzzing, and they aren't flying."

Collin issued an impressed "*Hm*. You're an observant little girl. Maybe you should be a detective when you grow up."

"Like you?" she asked.

"Yes," he said. "Like me. Detectives find out the answers to questions."

Her face scrunched, befuddled. "Can't you just ask somebody?"

A grin played around Collin's mouth. "I wish it was that easy."

She turned her expectant face on me and repeated her question. "So how come some of them are buzzing when they're not flying?" She seemed to assume I had all the answers. I only wished I was half as smart as she thought I was.

"I don't know, sweetie," I told her. "I'll have to look it up on my phone."

Before I could even type the question into my browser, she had moved on. "How far away do they fly before they come back? How come they don't get lost? Do they not eat until the honey is all ready? How come they don't starve before they're done?"

I glanced at the clock on the wall and managed to stop her bombardment of inquiries. "Look at the time. We better get down to the planetarium so we can get good seats."

She threw her little fists in the air. "Yay!"

Now it was Collin who faked a sneeze. "Nerd."

I gave him a soft elbow to the ribs. "Takes one to know one."

Fifteen minutes later, we were seated in reclining chairs, looking up at the dome ceiling as a simple, family-friendly astronomy lesson played out over our heads. The show covered the fundamentals of astronomy, including the planets in our solar system, suns and moons, orbits, and the different types of stars, including dwarf stars, giant stars, and pulsars, among others. The show ended with a short piece on the dinosaurs, how they were wiped out by a big meteor from outer space.

When the show was over, the girls clamored to visit

the dinosaur exhibit in the room next door. The youngest was getting tired, so I picked her up and carried her on my hip as we made our way in.

I stopped in my tracks and my heart skipped a beat when I saw a dinosaur with its arms raised. The beast's hands had three thick fingers with claws, not unlike a bird's foot. *Could the belt buckle Jimmy had seen been imprinted not with a bird's footprint as he'd thought, but instead with the print of a Tyrannosaurus rex? Was T-Rex the one who'd killed Beckett?* I was just about to say something to Collin when my unceasingly inquisitive little cousin asked, "What kind of dinosaur is this?"

My eyes moved to the informational plaque that arose out of the plastic ferns obscuring the creature's feet. The enormous lizard was not a T-Rex, as I'd thought. Rather it was an allosaurus. "It's an allosaurus," I told her.

She slowly repeated the word. "All-o-saur-us."

She pointed to the next one in the display. "What's that one?"

I took a few steps and read its placard. "This one's a Tyrannosaurus rex."

I took a closer look. To my surprise, while the allosaurus had three fingers on its hands, all with sharp claws, the Tyrannosaurus rex posed among the fake foliage had only *two* claw-tipped fingers. Two fingers didn't seem like they'd be of much use. They'd only allow the tyrannosaurus to pinch something or make a peace sign. Still, relief flooded me. I'd been wrong, thank goodness. A T-Rex print wouldn't have three prongs like a bird foot. It would have only two.

Although the exhibit was geared toward children, I learned some other interesting things too. The displays discussed the fact that birds evolved from a type of dinosaurs called theropods. They noted that some of the biggest were plant eaters, including the triceratops, stegosaurus, and diplodocus. "That's why you should eat a lot of spinach," I told the girls. "So you can grow big and strong too."

"Ew!" cried the oldest.

Following her lead, the two younger ones squealed "Ew!" too.

I ruffled their heads, just like I did with Sawdust. "If spinach doesn't sound good, how about we go and get pizza for dinner?"

The oldest threw her tiny fists in the air. "Pizza! Yay!"

Once again, the two younger ones followed suit. "Pizza! Yay!"

Collin did the same, pumping his much larger fists. "Pizza! Yay!"

Monday morning, after arranging for a roofer to take a look at a Home & Hearth rental property that had sprung a leak during yesterday's rain, I drove to the bank for my appointment with the loan officer. I'd prepared a detailed proposal, complete with cost projections, a marketing plan for selling the units, and the structural engineer's report. I'd included photos of the motel's transformation thus far, hoping it would prove to the loan officer that Buck and I knew what we were doing and performed high-quality work. I'd also prepared myself, practicing my spiel in the bathroom mirror. I couldn't have been more ready. Even so, every nerve in my body was on edge. This was all on me. If I didn't impress the woman, she could say no and I would have cost both Buck and myself an impressive profit.

I'd worn a blazer and slacks rather than my usual coveralls. As I waited, I picked stray Sawdust fur from my pants. No matter how many times I ran a lint roller over my clothing, I always managed to take some of his hair with me.

"Ms. Whitaker?"

Darn, I'd been caught mid-act. I stood, stepped over to the fiftyish woman in the doorway, and extended my hand. "Nice to meet you."

She shook my hand and motioned for me to follow her down the corridor. "Cat or dog?" she asked over her shoulder as we made our way.

"Excuse me?"

"The fur you were picking off your pants," she said. "Was it from a cat or a dog?"

I panicked, wondering if this were some type of test and if I picked the wrong species I'd fail and be denied the loan. "Cat?" I said tentatively.

She grinned. "Right answer." She stopped and extended her arm to indicate her office. On the bureau behind her desk were umpteen photographs of a solid gray, long-haired cat. The cat lying on a windowsill, gazing out of the glass. The cat curled up on an easy chair, its fluffy tailed wrapped around itself. The cat sprawled on its back in what resembled a centerfold pose. She saw me eyeing the photos. "That's Stormy."

"He's gorgeous," I said. I took the seat she offered me and pulled out my wallet to show her a photo of my own adorable fur baby. "This is Sawdust."

"Ah!" she exclaimed. "What a cutie."

"Thanks." I beamed like a proud mother. Silly, since I hadn't given birth to the sweet little beast. I couldn't take any credit for his delightfully lovable personality either. He'd been born with it.

"Is that your business plan there?" She reached out a hand. "Let me see what you've got."

I handed her the document and spent the next few minutes walking her through it. "The structural engineer's report shows that the current structure could easily support a second story." As she turned the page, I said, "That's a mock-up of what a fully finished unit will look like. Of course, we're offering buyers a variety of mid-century style options so they can customize their condominium to their tastes."

She turned to the list of appetizers Colette planned to make for the grand opening. "What's this?"

"My roommate is a professional chef. She's going to serve appetizers that were popular back in the fifties and sixties at our grand opening celebration."

"Stuffed cherry tomatoes," the woman said, reading aloud. "My mother used to make those when I was little. Hated them then, but I bet I'd love them now."

"You're welcome to come to the grand opening and try them," I said. "Bring your mother too." Okay, so I was sucking up. Short of selling my soul, I was willing to do whatever it took to get this loan.

When she finished looking over the documents and moved on to the most recent photos, her gaze locked on a picture of the neon sign lit up. "Wait. This place you're renovating is the Music City Motor Court? Where Beckett Morgan was murdered?"

I fought the urge to grimace. "Yes," I said. "We don't believe the incident will significantly impact the value of the condominiums." Guilt twisted my gut as I reduced a man's murder to an *incident*. But what choice did I have? Besides, I'd done what I could to assist in the investigation, to see that the singer got justice. "We've changed the look of the exterior, and all of the interiors have been gutted for a complete rehab."

The woman frowned. "It doesn't matter how much

you change the appearance, the fact remains that the motel was the site of a violent crime. Against a popular celebrity, no less. That's sure to turn off potential buyers."

I felt this opportunity slipping away, and I made a desperate grab to hang on to it. "Buck and I have excellent credit scores. We've never defaulted on a debt in our lives. Never even been late."

"Be that as it may," she said, closing the notebook I'd fastidiously prepared, "you're asking for a quarter million dollars. If these condos don't sell, how could you afford to pay the money back? Both of you have sunk nearly your entire net worth into the place."

She wasn't wrong about that. The only other asset we had was my house on Sweetbriar Avenue, and we hadn't owned it long enough to amass much equity. "If we couldn't come up with the money to repay the loan," I said, "my parents would help out. My father's a doctor with a successful medical practice."

"Great," she said. "Let's get him in here to cosign."

"No!"

She looked taken aback by my outburst. I couldn't blame her. Even I was surprised by it.

I softened my voice. "I'm thirty," I told her. "Buck's thirty-one. It would be humiliating to have to ask our parents to cosign a loan for us at this age."

"I understand," she said, "but imagine the humiliation I'd feel if I gave you this loan and you defaulted. I could lose my job for not getting proper security."

"I understand." I took my notebook from her and stood. "I appreciate your time. I guess if we decide to proceed with the second story, we can rethink Thad Gentry's offer."

She threw up a hand to stop me and stood too. "Wait. Thad Gentry's involved in this?"

"He offered us the money for the second story," I explained, "but he wanted a big piece of the action in return. We want to maintain control, so we turned him down."

"Did he make his offer before or after Beckett Morgan was murdered at the motel?"

"After."

"So he didn't think the murder would jinx the place," she said, clearly thinking out loud. "Huh." The woman motioned for me to sit back down. "That man has an eye for real estate. Other than the record label execs and top-tier recording artists, he moves more money around this town than anyone. If he thought this motel was a good investment, it probably is."

I gilded the lily. "He knows exactly what we'd already determined too. Downtown and the Gulch are built out. The east side of the river is going to be the next place to pop. The land the motel sits on will be worth a fortune in a few years."

"All right," the woman said. "I'm convinced." She handed me a loan document and a pen.

Although I was miffed it took Thad Gentry's stamp of approval to seal the deal, I wasn't going to let my pride stand in the way of taking the funds. I tried to think of it another way: That Gentry had just unintentionally helped us out—*ha!* I filled in the date and signed my name at the bottom of the page with a determined flourish.

After I handed the loan agreement back to her, she said, "The funds will be in your account by the end of the day."

"Perfect. Thanks." I extended my hand and gave hers a firm shake.

Twenty minutes later, I typed the code into the keypad, waited for the automobile gate to slide open, and drove into the motel's parking lot, tapping my horn all the while. *Beep-beep-beep!*

Buck's and Jimmy's heads popped up from inside the pool, where they were patching cracks in the concrete. As soon as I climbed out of my car, Buck called, "Did we get the loan?"

I made a fist, blew on it, and shined it on my blazer. "Of course!" I proceeded to perform Snoopy's classic happy dance in the parking lot.

Buck raised a fist in victory. "Booyah! I knew you could do it!"

I didn't tell him it took me threatening to take my business to Thad Gentry to close the deal. No sense raining on my own parade.

Buck climbed out of the pool and performed his own happy dance next to me. Though he had no skin in the game, Jimmy climbed out and did the same as an act of support. *See? He's a nice guy.* There was no way he killed Beckett Morgan. It was ridiculous that Collin still hadn't affirmatively crossed the guy off his list of potential suspects.

I pointed to Room 9. "Mind if I change in your room?" I asked Jimmy.

"Be my guest."

I went into his room and changed out of the blazer and slacks and into my coveralls and work boots. I placed a quick call to Presley to let her know the loan had been approved.

"That was quick," she said. "There's no grass growing under your feet."

"There will be soon," I said. "We're putting in the
landscaping this week."

"Send me pics," she said.

"Will do."

I stepped out of the room to see that T-Rex had swung
by the motel again. He was talking with Buck through
the fence. I walked over to say hello.

"Hey, Whitney," he said in greeting. "Sawyer told
me y'all attended their debut show Saturday. Buck and
I were just talking about it. What did you think of the
Barnyard Boys? Should I sign them?"

I supposed Beckett's passing had opened up space
on Rex's roster for a new band, maybe even several
smaller bands. "We liked them," I said. "The rest of the
crowd seemed to feel the same. They got quite a bit of
applause."

"I'll take that under advisement," he said. "I'm going
to give things a few weeks to settle down before I make
a decision. Hard to know how much of the audience's
response was liking the Barnyard Boys, and how much
was a reaction to them playing Beckett's songs. They've
got several more gigs planned around town. If they can
still draw a sizable crowd two months from now, that'll
tell me something."

"So you were there?" I asked. I hadn't seen him in
the bar, but it wasn't necessarily a surprise. The place
was so packed it was difficult to see beyond a few feet
in any direction.

"I was," he said. "Way at the back, by the guy running
the sound board. Sound's more pure back there. Besides,
I've lost so much hearing going to concerts all these

years, I don't dare sit up front near the speakers. Got to protect what hearing I have left."

"I don't blame you," I said. "My ears are still buzzing."

He gestured to the motel. "How are things coming along?"

"Couldn't be better," I said. "We haven't run into any snags"—other than finding Beckett's body, which went without saying—"and we just got approved for a loan to fund a second story."

"You're going to put in another floor?"

"That's the plan. They'll be bigger units. Two-bedroom, two-bath with a bonus room for storage or a home office."

"Can't wait to see them when they're done." He glanced around before saying, "Any updates on the investigation? Sawyer said the detective was with you at the concert. Was he there strictly for fun, or was he mixing business with pleasure?"

I hedged my bets. "If he was mixing things up," I said, "it was news to me." Okay, so it was an outright lie. I couldn't blame T-Rex for being curious, but I wasn't about to share any details of the investigation without explicit authorization from Collin.

T-Rex took a small step closer to the bars of the fence. His facial features seemed to tighten. "Between you and me, the big reason I want to wait before signing the Barnyard Boys is to make sure they're cleared first. The last thing I need is to be representing anyone who might get caught up in a murder case, especially when the victim was one of my top clients."

Buck concurred. "Don't blame you. Your name could end up dragged through the mud too."

T-Rex backed away from the fence, raising a hand in goodbye. "You folks enjoy the rest of your day. And be sure to invite me over for a swim when you finish that pool."

CHAPTER 26

SHATTERING ASSUMPTIONS

WHITNEY

On Monday morning, Collin phoned me with the results of the police lab's DNA tests. "None of the Barnyard Boys matched the DNA on the cigar butt found in the swimming pool."

"Well, shoot." I'd hoped the test results would match one of them and put an end to Collin's angst and frustration. No such luck. "What now?" I asked.

"I've exhausted all my leads except the woman on the bridge, the one from your security camera who stopped in front of the motel and stared at it. I've scoured the feeds and it doesn't look like she's been back. Chances are she's just another fan. The only thing I can do now is wait until Lacy Spurlock is back in town."

"You'll solve this, Collin," I said, trying to encourage him. "You always do."

"But there will come a time when I won't," he said. "When I can't figure a case out. All of the seasoned homicide detectives have told mc that. They've all got a cold case. They've told me to buy Tums in bulk, because it eats at you. I'm beginning to think I should make a run to Costco."

"Not yet," I said. "Wait until after you speak with Lacy." If interviewing her didn't lead to a break in the case, I'd buy him the antacids myself.

Over the following two weeks, neither Collin nor I made any further progress on Beckett Morgan's murder case, but the time was busy and backbreaking for Buck, Jimmy, and me.

We finished patching the pool and installed lime-green tile around the edges. We surrounded the pool with wood decking, which would be less hard and hot than concrete, and thus kinder to the bare feet of residents when they came out to swim or sunbathe. We painted the deck a vivid pink, adding sand to the paint to give it texture and make the surface slip resistant. With occasional help from Owen, we installed a pergola at the far end of the pool to provide dappled shade, as well as a place for residents to cook out or simply enjoy the company of others. We also put in flowerbeds around the pool, and filled them with pink crepe myrtles, blue hydrangeas, white impatiens, and forsythia bushes. We filled the spaces between the plants with cedar mulch. The orange hue of the wood chips tied in well with the paint on the building, and the bark provided a pleasant, woodsy scent, as well.

Once the wood floors had acclimated, we sanded, stained, and sealed them. With the flooring finished, we were able to move ahead on the interior. By the time Lacy Spurlock returned to town, we were down to a much shorter list of remaining tasks. Countertops. Light fixtures. Interior paint. Crown molding. The clubhouse and laundry rooms were also nearly complete.

We'd scheduled the grand opening for the following Saturday. I'd sent invitations to every high-end real estate agency in town, to the loan officer from the bank, and to family and friends, including the Hartleys. I'd sent invitations to T-Rex and Gia Revello too. Gia might not take me up on the invitation, given that our only interaction had been less than pleasant, but it was worth a shot. She was likely to know people who would be our target market for the units, singles or couples with solid incomes who'd pay a premium for the motel's extraordinary view and prime location.

The night of Lacy's concert, Collin picked me up at five and took me to a nice dinner at an Italian restaurant within walking distance of the Hall of Fame. We arrived at the music venue before they'd opened the doors. Collin led me past the long line waiting outside. The line was at least eighty percent women, with only a few men in the mix. The scattered males looked sheepish, as if their wives or girlfriends had forced them to come.

When we reached the entrance, the beefcake working security didn't even wait for Collin to speak before crossing his arms over his chest and spreading his legs wider as if to form a physical barrier. "No one gets in until seven thirty."

Collin showed the man his badge. "I'm a detective with metro PD. I need to speak with Ms. Spurlock."

The man frowned, said, "Just a sec," and pulled a shortwave radio from a clip on his belt. "Got a detective says he's here to talk to Lacy."

A woman's voice came back. "I'll be right there."

A moment later, a dark-haired fortyish woman unlocked the glass door behind the security guard and waved Collin and me inside. As soon as we were in the foyer, she asked to see Collin's badge, business card, and driver's license. "I'm sure you understand," she said. "We get all kinds of fans pulling odd stunts to try to get close to the performers. We have to ensure their safety."

"No problem." He showed her everything she'd asked for.

Still not fully convinced, she placed a quick call to his station to verify that a Collin Flynn was indeed a detective for the agency. His credentials now verified, she relocked the door and turned a serious face on us. "What's this about?"

Collin was vague. "Police business, ma'am."

"Oh, for goodness sake," she spat. "It's about Beckett Morgan, isn't it?"

Collin didn't deny it.

The woman huffed an indignant breath. "Any chance this can wait until after the show? If you arrest Lacy and I have to cancel tonight's performance, we'll be out a pretty penny in refunds."

Sheesh. Would she rather have a killer crooning on her stage?

Collin cocked his head. "Do you have some reason to believe she's guilty?"

The woman chuckled mirthlessly. "Only if you believe the rumors. I heard that on the night of the Country Music Awards, after Beckett backed away from her onstage, she attacked him in her dressing room. Broke one of the mirrors. There was glass everywhere." She sighed. "I'd hate to see a repeat of that performance happen here."

"I'll do my best not to rile her up," he said. "But I'll subdue her if necessary."

"I suppose I don't have a choice, do I?" the woman said finally. "Follow me."

She led us down a long, wide hallway before turning down a shorter, narrower one at the back guarded by not just one, but two pieces of beefcake. When Collin caught me ogling their biceps, he cut me a sour look. I mouthed *Sorry*. But really, a woman couldn't help herself.

She led us through a door that took us to the backstage area. We walked behind a high, burgundy-colored velvet curtain until we reached a door marked DRESSING ROOM 1. She knocked on the door and called, "Lacy? You decent? The police are here to see you."

There was a pause of several seconds, during which I wondered if she might be climbing out a window, before the singer's recognizable voice came back. "Send them in."

The woman held out a hand, inviting us to enter.

We opened the door to find a large dressing room with three salon-style chairs set up in front of a mirror. Lacy sat in the center of the three wearing a shiny satin floral-print robe that barely covered her cleavage or thighs. I'm ashamed to say that Collin did a much better job of refraining from ogling Lacy than I had with the beefcakes. Her blonde hair was pulled up in oversized hot rollers, and her back was to us. A woman flitted about her, using an airbrush to apply foundation to her face. I supposed your complexion had to look flawless when your face would be magnified a hundred times on a jumbotron screen. Another woman sat on a low stool, coating Lacy's fingernails with sparkly purple polish.

To the right was a rolling clothes rack. Three simi-

larly spectacular outfits hung from it, all trimmed in
her signature lace. I wondered which of the three Lacy
would choose to wear tonight. Whichever one she chose
would be paired with the plum-colored boots that stood
below. Their toes appeared to be a D or an N toe, like
the ones we'd seen in the video from the Poison Emporium. Still, a country-western sensation like Lacy
probably owned twenty pairs of boots, if not more, and
could be expected to own several different styles.

Collin eyed the other women before meeting Lacy's
gaze in the mirror. "Could we speak to you alone,
please?"

"I'm so sorry," she said, her voice dripping with
Southern sweetness, "but there's simply no time to
spare. I don't want to keep my fans waiting, and my
makeup and wardrobe crew are behind as it is. Besides,
these ladies already know everything about me. Don't
you?"

The women murmured noncommittally.

Collin acquiesced. "Okay." He pointed to the empty
chairs on her right and left. "Mind if we sit?"

"Of course," Lacy said. "Make yourselves comfortable."

While Collin took the chair on her right, I slid back
into the one on the left. It was nice and cushy. It felt good
to put my feet up too. It had been a physically demanding
day. My body had earned a break.

After introducing both himself and me, Collin said,
"Your time is important, so I'll cut right to the chase.
Your name came up several times during my investigation of Beckett Morgan's murder. It's no secret that
he embarrassed you on stage at the awards show when
he refused to kiss you after you two performed 'The

Warmest Kiss.' I was told things got physical in your
dressing room afterward, that glass was broken."

Lacy rolled her big blue eyes, much to the chagrin
of the makeup artist who was now attempting to apply false eyelashes to Lacy's lids. "You've got it mostly
right. Yes, he embarrassed me and, yes, a glass of water
fell to the floor in my dressing room and shattered after
our performance. But there were lots of singers performing that night, and my dressing room was itty-bitty.
I knocked the glass over accidentally with the neck of
my guitar when I turned around to talk to Beckett." She
pointed her freshly manicured index finger at Collin.
"You should know better than anyone, Detective Flynn,
that you can't believe most of what you hear. People are
always looking for a scandal. Rumors fly."

"That's exactly why I'm here," he replied. "To separate fact from fiction."

"I'll give you the facts, straight." Lacy hesitated a moment while her nail tech finished her right hand and
circled her stool to the other side to begin work on the
left. Once the woman had set back to work, Lacy said,
"Beckett and I argued. That's probably no surprise. I told
him that I didn't appreciate him making me look like a
lovelorn loser on stage after I'd lifted him out of obscu-
rity and let him ride my coattails to fame. He apologized. *Profusely.* All but kissed my backside, truth be
told. He said he was in love with someone else and that
it was just an instinctive reaction for him to shy away. He
said if the woman saw him kiss me, she'd be upset, and
that the last thing he wanted to do was hurt her. Blah,
blah, blah."

Collin and I exchanged a glance. The woman Beckett had been referring to must be J.C. *But why hasn't J.C.
surfaced?*

"To be perfectly honest," Lacy continued, "I understood. I only wished he'd told me beforehand that he was involved with someone. I never would have tried to kiss him otherwise, but I had no idea. I never saw him with anyone or heard him mention a girlfriend, so I thought he was single. He asked me to keep that information between the two of us. I told him I forgave him and that I'd keep his secret. As far as I was concerned, that was that."

"You forgave him?" Collin said. "Why didn't you make your feelings public?"

"Because I was mentioned in more Tweets and Instagram and Facebook posts in the hour after the awards show aired than in the entire year prior. I gained thousands of new followers and trended for weeks after. Hashtag Lacy Didn't Deserve That. You know how many women out there have been done wrong by men? Nearly all of us at one time or another." She scoffed. "Women make up almost my entire fan base. The media ate it up. I've never gotten so much free publicity. My face was on the cover of five national magazines at once. Can you believe it? I'd have been a fool not to capitalize on the moment. It gave me some great fodder for my next album too. Besides, the publicity didn't really hurt Beckett. Some less-evolved guys worshipped him even more. After all, he was 'the man who turned down Lacy Spurlock.'" She made air quotes with her fingers. "That made him some kind of hero to the knuckle-draggers."

"This woman Beckett mentioned," Collin said, "the one he was purportedly in love with. Did he give you a name? Maybe some details about her?"

"No, and I didn't ask. It didn't really matter to me who she was. At that point, I was still a little ticked off and licking my wounds."

Collin seemed to mull things over for a moment. "If I were to call the venue where the CMAs were held and ask about damage in your dressing room—"

"They'd tell you they found none," she said. "My mama raised me right. I cleaned up after myself. I used a makeup wipe to clean up the mess I'd made and tossed the shards of glass and the wipe in the waste bin. Unless their janitors take stock of what's in every can they empty, they probably can't verify what I've just told you. But they could verify that the room was not damaged in any way, shape, or form."

Collin scrubbed a hand over his face.

Lacy's brow furrowed. "Are you okay, Detective?"

"Not really," he admitted. "It feels like I'm going in circles." He sat back in the chair. "If you had to hazard a guess about who killed Beckett—"

"I'd say a crazed fan," Lacy said.

"Any one in particular?"

She shrugged. "He never mentioned anyone to me, but you wouldn't believe the kind of weird stuff that happens to you when you're famous. I'd bet some deranged fan accosted him on the street, that Beckett somehow upset the person, and the person attacked him. People think they know celebrities much better than they really do. They listen to our music and feel like they've got some sort of bond with us, when we have no idea who they are. I've had a couple of stalkers myself. It's terrifying."

Collin slid off his seat and thanked her for her time. "We're looking forward to your show."

"You've got tickets?"

I pulled them from my purse and held them up. "Fifth row, center. Rex Tomlinson gave them to me when I told him I was a fan of yours."

"That man. He's always building bridges." She gave us the thousand-watt smile she was known for. "Enjoy the show!"

CHAPTER 27

ANOTHER SHAKESPEAREAN TRAGEDY

WHITNEY

Lacy's show was a load of fun, especially for me. She was nothing short of a feminist folk hero. I stood and danced alongside the other women in the audience, even going so far as to pull Collin to his feet and force him to join in even when I knew he'd rather sit down and contemplate the case.

I bought myself a concert T-shirt on the way out. You know, so I could prove how cool I was to the kids in homeroom.

As we drove back to my house, I asked Collin what he thought of Lacy's stalker theory.

"She could very well be right," he said. "You've seen that woman on the bridge repeatedly, and your security camera video picked up a woman who could be her staring at the motel. The type of stalker Lacy mentioned? They suffer from a condition called erotomania. It's when a person thinks a celebrity is in love with them and that they have some sort of relationship even when they don't. The groupies I interviewed seemed to suffer a bit of it, though none struck me as excessively irrational and they'd at least had some real interactions with Beckett. I didn't see anything strange or threatening in Beckett's personal e-mails or texts, and no one else so far has brought up the idea of an unstable fan, but maybe they just didn't know about it. I'll check back with T-Rex, the other musicians, and Beckett's family to see what I can find out, whether he'd ever expressed concern about a fan." He cast me a look. "But if that doesn't pan out, I'm heading to Costco for that barrel of Tums."

Two days before the grand opening, the blonde woman was back on the bridge, dressed again in black and staring our way.

"Don't look now," I called out to Jimmy and Buck, "but the blonde is back on the bridge."

Naturally, the two did exactly the opposite of what I'd told them and turned their heads to look at the bridge. The woman immediately turned and headed in the opposite direction. *Had she realized we'd spotted her? Is that why she's leaving?* I couldn't let her get away again, but there was no way I could catch her on foot. She already had a quarter mile head start.

"Jimmy!" I cried. "Get your motorcycle. Now! We have to intercept her!"

He darted into his room and rolled his motorcycle out onto the parking lot. He held his helmet out to me. "Put this on."

"But that's not fair to you."

"I know how to ride," he said. "You don't know squat about motorcycles. You're more likely to fall off the back."

"Well, when you put it *that* way." I took the helmet from him, slid it over my head, and snapped the clasp under my chin. I handed him my hardhat in return. It wasn't as protective as the helmet would be, but it was better than nothing.

We couldn't ride his bike on the pedestrian bridge. It would be both illegal and dangerous. We'd have to take a circuitous route to intercept the blonde. I only hoped we could get there before she disappeared into the crowd again. *Who is she? Could she be one of those crazy stalkers Lacy talked about?*

I wrapped my arms tightly around Jimmy's waist and, with a *vroom-vroom* of his engine, off we went. As we rode along, my entire body vibrated, and I wondered if this was how Sawdust felt when he purred.

Jimmy had learned his way around the immediate area fairly well in the time he'd been in Nashville. He raced down Shelby Avenue to Korean Veterans Boulevard. Leaning into the curve, we turned onto 2nd Avenue South, where the stairs and elevator from the pedestrian bridge took walkers up and down between the bridge and street level.

I spotted her black dress from a block away. "There she is!" I hollered, removing one hand from around Jimmy's belly to point.

He cranked his wrist back. *Vroom!* In seconds, we were on her. Jimmy pulled to the curb a few steps ahead of her. I climbed off the bike as she reached us.

"Stop!" I hollered, stepping in front of her and raising my palms. "We need to talk to you."

The woman in front of me looked both bewildered and young, in her early twenties. She had dark brown eyes that were more common on people with brown hair than blondes. A glance at her roots told me why. She wasn't a natural blonde. The part that bisected her hair showed a half inch of roots in a chestnut shade. She stammered when she spoke. "What . . . why . . . what's happening?"

"I'm Whitney." I motioned to Jimmy. "That's Jimmy." He raised a hand in greeting. "We're remodeling the motel. We noticed you've been watching us."

She didn't deny it, as I thought she might. She simply bit her lip.

"What's your name?" I asked.

"Bess Martindale."

The name rang no bells for me. "Why have you had an eye on the motel? Does it have something to do with Beckett Morgan?"

She nodded. "Beckett and I were high school sweethearts."

Ah-ha! That explains it.

Tears welled up in her eyes as she lifted her left hand to show off a small, pear-shaped diamond mounted on a platinum band. "I was also his fiancée."

So that's where the engagement ring went! I realized this woman must be the one Beckett had mentioned to Lacy Spurlock, the reason he'd backed away from her kiss at the awards show.

She looked down at the ring. "I know it doesn't look like much, but Beckett knows"—she corrected herself— "*knew* better than to spend a lot of money on a ring for me. I don't need fancy things. All I wanted was him."

It was a sweet sentiment, and one I could understand. I wasn't into material things either. The things that meant the most to me were the people in my life, my cat, my home, my work. "I hadn't heard about your engagement. I'm surprised the media didn't report it."

"We kept it quiet on purpose," she said. "Beckett said

it would be better for his image if people didn't know. His fans liked to imagine him as a fun-loving single guy who partied all the time. I didn't much like that, but I wanted to be supportive, so I went along."

I gave her a soft smile. "You put his needs first, before your own."

"That's what you do when you love someone, right?"

It was a rhetorical question, so I didn't bother to answer.

"I figured we'd work through it somehow," she continued, "that maybe things would settle down after a while. Nothing changed for a long time, but lately I'd been able to drive down for more of his shows. I never spoke to Beckett at his performances. We were afraid someone would figure things out. But at least we got to see each other even if we didn't get to talk."

Bess must be the shy blonde that Sawyer and Wylie had seen hanging around the fringes. "The police will want to talk to you," I said.

She lifted her thin shoulders. "I don't have anything to tell them. I don't know anything. If I did, I would've gone to them myself. I want Beckett's killer caught and put away for life."

"Talk to the police anyway. You might know more than you think." Before she could argue with me, I whipped out my phone and placed a call to Collin. "I caught up with the blonde," I said when he answered. "Her name is Bess Martindale."

Though the name had meant nothing to me when she'd mentioned it, Collin was clearly familiar with it. A rustling sound came through the phone, as if he was already on the move. "Where are you?"

I gave him our location.

"I'll be right there."

I kept Bess talking while we waited. I asked her about life in Bowling Green, what Beckett had been like as a teenager, how the two of them had met and become a couple. From what I could tell, her heartbreak seemed sincere, her happy memories of Beckett both sustaining her and cutting her to the core. I could be wrong, but she certainly didn't seem like a killer to me.

A few short minutes later, Officer Hogarty's squad car came up from behind Bess, its lights flashing. Hogarty sat at the wheel, while Collin rode shotgun. Hogarty's usual partner had been relegated to the back seat. As soon as the cruiser pulled to the curb, Collin and the uniformed officers climbed out and stepped over.

Hogarty addressed Bess. "Mind if I pat you down? Search your purse?"

"Okay," Bess said. "But may I ask why?" She looked confused, too naïve to realize she could be a suspect in her fiancé's murder. But a moment later, a look of horror crossed her face as realization sunk in. "You don't think I hurt Beckett, do you?"

"Just routine procedure." Hogarty handed the purse off to her partner and began to pat Bess up and down, feeling for a weapon. Apparently she'd felt none, because she stepped back and gave Collin a nod. The result would have been entirely different if she'd patted me down. I had my big wrench in my pocket, as usual.

Hogarty's partner set the purse on the hood of the cruiser and riffled through it, unzipping the inside pockets for a thorough examination. Satisfied there was no weapon inside, she said, "It's clean," and handed it back to Bess.

After I'd filled Collin in on what Bess had told me so far, he locked his gaze on her and launched into his interrogation. "I'm confused about your engagement. It was my understanding that you and Beckett had broken up for good."

"We hit a rough patch a while back," Bess confessed. "Right after Beckett released that duet with Lacy Spurlock. We broke up for a few weeks then. I'm in nursing school at Western Kentucky University. We're between semesters right now so I've got some free time, but when school was in session I didn't have much time to drive down to Nashville to see Beckett. He didn't have time to come home to see me either. We each thought the other should be making more effort. Things got ugly." She looked off into the distance for a moment as if picturing how ugly things had been. The pain on her face said it had not been a pretty picture. "We were both stressed out and everything was . . . *different*. We used to spend time together every day. Once he moved to Nashville, we were lucky if we saw each other once a week, if even that, and it was usually only for a short time. Sometimes we'd meet halfway, in the parking lot of a golf course just over the Kentucky border off the interstate. It was the only way we could talk and have any privacy. Every time Beckett went out in public, people would recognize him and ask for autographs. The paparazzi followed him sometimes too. He said he felt like he was living under a microscope."

Collin gave her an empathetic nod. "I could see how that would get old."

Bess went on to say that when Beckett hit it big, he no longer seemed to be himself. "I hate to say it, especially now, but the money and fame changed him. He used to be happy with cheap beer from a can, but he started drinking expensive bourbon and smoking cigars. I hardly recognized him anymore. Then his parents got involved. They'd liked me before, but they knew I was pressuring Beckett to come home more often, and they thought I would hold him back in his music career. My parents seemed glad we'd broken up too. They said Beckett wasn't the sweet, simple boy who sang in the church choir anymore, that he'd gotten too big for his britches and thought he was better than the folks he'd grown up with. They didn't think he was treating me right."

"Is that when you went blonde?" I asked. "After your breakup?"

Collin cut me a look that said *Is that really relevant?*, but Bess offered a soft laugh. "Yeah. That's what we do when men break our hearts, right? Change our hair?"

The difference in hair color explained why Collin had been unable to identify the unknown blonde as Beckett's former, and formerly brown-haired, girlfriend.

She went on to tell us that, when she and Beckett had reconciled, they knew it would still be hard to spend much time together, and they didn't want to debate the matter with their parents, so they'd decided it would be their little secret for the time being.

Rather than continue to stand out here on the street with passersby gawking, Collin asked if Bess would be up to going for a coffee or a glass of iced tea. When she agreed, he dismissed Officer Hogarty and her partner. "I'll have Whitney give me a ride back to the station."

Jimmy asked, "Does this mean I'm free to go too?"

I nodded and exchanged his helmet for my hard hat. "We'll see you back at the motel. Thanks for driving me over."

"No problem." He donned the helmet, started his motor, and vroomed off.

Five minutes later, Collin, Bess, and I were seated on

the patio of at a small café along the riverfront, glasses of iced tea on the table in front of us.

Collin readied his paper and pen before launching further into his interrogation. "When and where was the last time you saw Beckett?"

"About five weeks ago, at the golf course." She choked up. "He called me late the night he was killed, but I was asleep and didn't realize he was trying to reach me. I always kept the phone in my purse and turned to silent mode when I was at my parents' house. I didn't want them to figure out that Beckett and I were together again."

"You were at your parents' house that night?"

"Yes."

"Would they be willing to verify that fact?"

"I'm sure they would."

"All right." Collin redirected the conversation back. "Beckett called you late at night. Then what happened?"

"He left me a voice mail. He said something about it being a rough night and that Gia Revello had caused a scene after his show at the Ryman. She's the lady he deals with at his record company. Beckett said he was going to meet with his manager for dinner the next day and sort things out." She swallowed hard. "That's the last I heard from him."

Collin's eyes narrowed. "What's your phone number?"

"For my regular phone, or the one Beckett gave me?"

"You have more than one phone?"

"Not now," Bess said, "but I did then. Beckett had gotten me a phone on his plan so my parents wouldn't know we were staying in touch. My regular cell phone is on my parents' family account."

"What was the number for the phone Beckett gave you?"

She rattled it off.

His eyes went wide. "You're J.C.?"

She offered a small, sad smile. "I am. It stands for Juliet Capulet. It was a joke between the two of us. We said that with our parents trying to keep us apart, we were like Romeo and Juliet."

Collin had been right. J.C.'s phone was a secret device used solely for communicating with Beckett.

Bess went on. "When Beckett didn't answer my calls Saturday morning, I got worried. I used the locator app to see where his phone was. The app showed that his phone was at the motel. I couldn't understand why. I drove down to find him, but the place looked abandoned. I watched the motel from the bridge and saw people working there, but I didn't see Beckett. I figured maybe he'd accidentally dropped his phone somewhere around the motel, or that maybe his battery had died or the app wasn't working right because it seemed frozen in place. I had no idea he'd been killed at the motel until I saw the police cars and ambulance arrive."

The realization that the man she'd intended to marry had died at the motel must have been horrifying for her. My heart squirmed with emotion.

"I came to the vigil at the motel," she added. "There was such a big crowd I figured I could blend in. I walked up onto the bridge after. I was shaking and crying so hard my phone got wet and slipped from my hands and fell over the side. I was very upset. That phone had Beckett's voice-mail message on it." She choked up once more, her voice a mere squeak when she spoke again. "That was the last time I heard his voice."

Collin's tone was gentle when he asked, "Why didn't you contact the police, Bess?"

She shrugged. "I figured if the police thought I could help, they would come to me. Besides, I had nothing to offer. I had no idea why anybody might want to kill him. I figured it was just a random mugging, that he might have gone to that store by the motel for some liquor or a cigar and maybe someone followed him from there."

For all we knew, she could be right. Beckett's murder might have been the result of a random crime. None of the other leads had panned out so far.

"I wasn't a part of Beckett's life in Nashville," Bess said. "He didn't tell me much about it, to be honest. Just the big things, not the details. I think his time with me was sort of his escape from all that craziness, you know? He was tired. That much I know. *Overwhelmed* might be a better word. It was too much for him, all the long hours and travel. He was getting burned out on the fast pace of the music business. He wanted to take things slower, but the record label already wanted another album from him."

The image Bess painted of Beckett was very different from the one Beckett's Nashville crowd had provided. Bess seemed to see Beckett as a small-town boy whose dreams of stardom had come true, only to learn he should have been careful what he wished for. To his local crew, he was a demanding artist who thought very highly of himself, didn't give others credit where credit was due, and climbed over people on his way to the top. *The truth may very well lie somewhere in between.* People could be complex, complicated, and inconsistent.

Collin said, "We didn't contact you because we had

no idea who you were and no way to reach you after you dropped your phone. Beckett's parents had mentioned you, but they told me you were no longer in their son's life. We didn't realize you were the J.C. from the phone."

"I'm sorry," she said. "If I'd known you were trying to figure out who J.C. was, I would've gotten in touch."

Collin took a sip of his drink before asking, "Any idea who got Beckett started on the cigars?"

She shook her head. "Probably another one of the musicians. He knew I didn't like it, so he didn't smoke around me, and he promised he'd never smoke more than one at a time. I'm not sure he could have anyway. He said they made him lightheaded."

I interjected here. "Had y'all set a wedding date yet?"

"No," she said. "We were waiting to find out about his new contract, when his album would be due and what his tour schedule would be."

Sounded to me like Beckett might have been stringing her along, just like Gia Revello had accused him of stringing *her* along. Sawyer and Wylie said that Beckett had wanted to keep his options open as far as the musicians he worked with. He'd strung them along too. He'd had more strings than a twelve-string guitar. Maybe he wanted to keep his options open as far as his record label and future wife too. Maybe he had no real intention of marrying Bess, but had given her a shiny, but relatively inexpensive bauble to appease her until he figured out what he wanted. Or maybe I was entirely off base. But it would make his murder seem slightly less horrifying if he were a selfish, self-centered jerk than if he were simply a country boy who'd had a hard time dealing with his meteoric rise to stardom.

"Beckett's hit, 'Party in the Pasture,'" Collin said. "You know anything about that? His writing process? Where he got the idea for the song?"

"I don't know much," Bess said. "He mentioned that his manager had once said something about going to parties in barns and fields when he was younger and asked Beckett if he'd done the same. We had, of course. That's country life, you know? I think the question might have planted the seed in Beckett's mind. We always had fun at the pasture parties. Everyone just hanging out, being themselves, no pressure. The part of Beckett that missed that easy, unpretentious life? That's the part of him that wrote the song."

Collin fingered his napkin, perhaps an unconscious action as he thought back to Shep Sampson and his claim that he'd scribbled the song down on napkins during his lunch break at the studio. "Did Beckett ever tell you that another songwriter accused him of stealing the song?"

Bess had slumped lower and lower as the interview had progressed, as if Collin's questions were sucking the life out of her. But now she sat bolt upright. "What? What are you talking about?"

"There's a musician by the name of Shep Sampson who claims he wrote 'Party in the Pasture.' That Beckett stole the song from him."

"No!" she insisted. "Beckett would never do that. I mean, he had high hopes and lots of ambition, at first anyway, but he'd never stoop to stealing a song from someone else. He wasn't like that."

Or was he? She'd admitted only minutes earlier that Beckett had changed with his fame, that she'd hardly recognized him as the boy she'd fallen for in high school. Odds were, she was still sorting through her thoughts and feelings, trying to come to terms with what had really happened. *Who was the real Beckett Morgan?*

CHAPTER 28

OPEN AND CLOSED

WHITNEY

When Collin ran out of questions for Bess, he asked for her current contact information and jotted down her number as she rattled it off.

She used her napkin to dab at her wet eyes. "You'll call me once you know something?"

"I will," Collin said. "And if anything comes to mind in the meantime, I want you to let me know too." He handed her his business card and left a twenty-dollar bill on the table, more than enough to cover our drinks, as well as a very generous tip.

We parted ways with Bess outside the restaurant. My heart wrenched as I watched her walk away. She looked not only heartbroken, but also just broken in general. If for nothing else than her sake alone, I hoped that Collin could bring Beckett's killer to justice.

As he and I walked back over the bridge to the motel, I said, "At least you can cross Josselyn Caravelli off your list of suspects. She's not the J.C. you were looking for. That's some progress."

Collin issued a derisive snort and waved jazz hands. "Woo-hoo!" he shouted sarcastically, garnering the attention of others on the bridge.

"I'm only trying to help."

"I know," he said with a sigh. "That wasn't directed at you. I just need a break, some little hint that will tell me what I'm missing."

"Maybe you haven't missed anything," I said. "Maybe the clue you need to solve the case hasn't turned up yet."

"I wish it would," he said. "There's a comet that will be close to Earth next week. I'd really love to get some pictures of it."

"You know you can buy a new telescope without solving the case, don't you?"

"I know," he said. "But I won't let myself. It's my incentive to keep my nose to the grindstone."

I could relate. I had told myself I wouldn't swim in the motel pool until we'd sold at least half the units. Summer was rapidly approaching, and a dip in a cool swimming pool was starting to sound like heaven. I hoped the units would go quick before the temperatures soared.

The day of the grand opening, while Sawdust watched from the window of Jimmy's room, Buck, Jimmy, and I ran around like crazed chickens, taking care of last-minute details. We moved the bedroom furniture from Jimmy's room to the spec unit. We set up the living and dining room furniture as well. Jimmy power-washed the parking lot and pool deck. Buck strung festive lights along the perimeter fence and the pergola. I vacuumed and dusted the spec unit, fluffed up the pillows on the couch and bed, and used glass cleaner to shine the appliances, faucets, and wall mirrors to perfection. I placed notebooks featuring the design alternatives on the dinette, the coffee table, and the bathroom counter-top, where prospective purchasers could peruse the information and photos and see the choices available to them.

Beckett's fans were still leaving flowers at the motel and, after arranging a fragrant vase of flowers on the credenza in the living room, I carried the cleaning supplies to the clubhouse and laundry, giving those rooms a thorough cleaning too. I placed another vase of sweet-smelling flowers on the counter that had once served as the motel's registration desk, and which now served as a bar the residents could use for parties. No sense letting the bouquets go to waste, right? Beside the vase, I laid another notebook with pictures of the various décor options buyers could choose for their units. I placed a final binder on the coffee table.

When I was done in the spec unit and clubhouse, I went to Jimmy's room and gave my cat a quick peck on the cheek and an under-chin scratch. I'd brought Sawdust along because I knew he'd enjoy watching the festivities from the window. Besides, a cat in the window would make the place seem homey. After loving on my cat for a bit, I grabbed the small electric air pump I'd bought to inflate the nylon guitar-shaped pool toy. I carried the pump out to an outdoor electric socket in the pool area, plugged it in, and stuck the tubing into the flaccid toy. As I switched it on, the motor kicked in with a *whirr* and the pump began to breathe life into the float.

I'd just finished filling the inflatable guitar with air when Colette pulled up in my SUV, pulling her food trailer. Buck had painted it purple, green, and gold, as she'd requested, and used a stylish stencil to embellish

it with the name VOODOO VITTLES. Emmalee had come
along to help, and was sitting in the passenger seat. I
used my foot to nudge the air pump under a hydrangea
bush. I'd come back and round it up later. Right now, I
needed to let my friends through the gate.

As I hustled out of the pool enclosure, the spring-
loaded gate swung shut behind me with a resounding
clang. I hurried over to the exterior fence and grabbed
two adjacent bars with my hands, putting my face up to
it. "The code is your birthday!" I called to Colette.

She smiled. "Aw. You make me feel special."

"You are special to me," I said. "But Buck's the one
who chose the code."

Her smile broadened, though she ducked her head,
trying not to let it show. *So obvious.* She punched in
the code and the gate slid back. With my guidance, she
eased the SUV and the trailer through without scratching any of the vehicles or fencing.

"I did it!" she cried. "I should join the Teamsters.
Where should I park the trailer?"

"Over there." I pointed to a space at the opposite end
of the motel from the spec unit. Situating the food there
would help spread out the crowd—assuming we'd have
one—and hopefully lessen the chances that someone
would spill food in the spec unit.

Just as we'd done before when Jimmy, Buck, and I
had sat down to eat jambalaya out of thermoses, we fash-
ioned a table out of sawhorses and plywood. Once we
covered it with a tablecloth, no one would be the wiser.
We placed the improvised table next to the food trailer
to serve as a drink station. Buck hooked up an electrical
cord to supply power to the trailer. The propane tank
mounted on the back would provide heat for the grill and

oven, while the water tank would provide enough water for washing produce, hands, and dishes.

While Colette and Emmalee began the food preparation, I returned to the pool area, where I attached thick, comfy cushions to the chaise lounges and turned the cranks to open the brightly colored patio umbrellas that would provide shade for the two round, wrought-iron tables.

Lastly, I freshened up in Jimmy's unit and slipped into a sleeveless turquoise sheath dress. My outfit not only complemented the colors of the motel's paint, but was tailored enough to look professional yet bright enough to be festive—just the right balance for tonight's event. I slid my feet into a pair of low-heeled pumps, applied my makeup, and fixed my hair.

When I was finished, I took a step back to admire myself in the mirror. I looked every bit the confident real estate professional I'd worked so hard to become. *Yay, me!* I only hoped this real estate professional could move some units tonight.

I helped Emmalee set up stacks of plastic cups and several large glass dispensers on the drink table. One had sweet tea, another unsweetened. A third dispenser contained Lynchburg lemonade. Our final task was filling a metal horse trough with ice and bottled beer.

Collin arrived a half hour before the grand opening. Following Jimmy's lead, he wore a festive Aloha shirt with ukuleles printed on it, along with jeans and boat shoes. Despite the cheerful attire and party atmosphere, his face looked tired and tense. Who could blame him? He'd be seeing lots of people from the country music scene here tonight, and those who knew him were likely to ask how the investigation was going. No doubt he'd hoped to have solved the crime by now.

I'd hoped so too. The outstanding murder investigation had the potential to cast a pall over the event. I could only hope that wouldn't happen.

Collin glanced around. "Wow. You and Buck have really transformed this place."

"We have, haven't we?" I waved him over to the club-house, where I pointed to the switch that would turn on the neon sign out front. "Would you like the honors tonight?"

"Really?"

I reached out and gave his arm a squeeze. "I know how hard you've worked on the investigation. No one could have done better."

"Thanks, Whitney," he said with a sigh. "I needed to hear that."

He reached out and flipped the switch. The parking lot lit up like a Las Vegas casino. Out in the lot, Jimmy and Buck whooped and raised bottles of beer in salute, tapping them together in toast. *Clink.*

"That reminds me," I said. "I need to put out the bottle openers by the beer." I scurried outside, rounded up the guitar-shaped promotional bottle openers I'd ordered as party favors, and fanned them out on the drink table for partygoers to use and take home.

Presley arrived, and I took her on a quick tour. "Wow," she said when we were done. "Y'all did this place up right." She smiled and scrunched her shoulders, giddy. "I think we're going to make a fortune!"

At promptly six o'clock, we opened all of the gates. Buck walked over to the exterior fence and unfurled the banner. MUSIC CITY MOTOR COURT GRAND OPENING! Below that, we'd listed my phone number and the project's website so people would know where to go for more information. I set out a sandwich board on which I'd drawn an arrow pointing down the street, along with instructions telling attendees to park at the free lot.

Drinks in hand, we all walked to stand at the open auto gate. I'd say all we heard was crickets, but apparently even crickets had no interest in attending our grand opening. Our ears met nothing but silence.

We stood in hushed despair for a long moment before Jimmy broke the awkwardness with, "Uh-oh. This isn't good, is it?"

Colette tried to remain optimistic. "Don't start worrying yet. You know how people like to be fashionably late."

Buck sighed. "It's too quiet out here. I'll put on some music." He went to the clubhouse and plugged his phone into the speaker system he'd installed, launching his favorite country playlist.

My parents walked up a few minutes later. When Mom saw that no guests were here, her smile faltered. "Oh. I must have been mistaken. I thought you said the party started at six."

"It did," I said sourly.

"Oh. Well." She forced a fresh smile. "What smells so delicious?"

"Follow me," Colette said, motioning with her hand. "I'll show you."

My father looked around but, as always, he showed more faith in me than my mother had. He clapped Buck on the shoulder and gave mine a pat, as well. "This place looks fantastic! You'll have these units sold in no time."

The Hartleys were the next to join the party. I took them on a tour of the pool area, the clubhouse, and the spec unit.

Mrs. Hartley put a hand to her chest and gaped.

"Whitney! I can hardly believe my eyes. This place is beautiful!"

Mr. Hartley concurred. "Incredible what you've done with limited space. The mirrors were an especially smart idea." He gave me a wink. He and I both knew I'd hung the mirrors to make the rooms appear larger. It was an old decorating trick.

Shortly thereafter, Owen, his wife, and their young daughters arrived. After hugs were exchanged, I directed them to the food trailer and drink table. "Yummy!" shouted their oldest after Colette treated her to a triangular piece of watermelon with sliced strawberries and blueberries on top, what she termed "fruit pizza."

Buck's parents, my aunt Nancy and uncle Roger, arrived next. While Aunt Nancy *oohed* and *ahhed* over the design elements, Uncle Roger knocked on the walls, tested the door trim, and inspected our handiwork on the cabinets. "Good carpentry work, you two. Hard to believe y'all are rehabbing big properties like this. Seems like just yesterday I was teaching you how to make birdhouses."

"Yep," Buck agreed, "and we were hammering our thumbs."

Uncle Roger winced at the thought. "That's a lesson every carpenter has to learn the hard way. A purple thumb is a rite of passage."

When we emerged from the unit, I saw that three more people had arrived, all women. *Thank goodness.* Relief lowered my shoulders by several inches. While Collin walked over to join my parents in enjoying Colette's appetizers, Buck, Presley, and I greeted the guests, who were realtors with one of the most prestigious Nashville agencies.

"Would you like the grand tour?" I asked.

"Of course!" one said.

The three repeated many of the same sentiments we'd heard from the others. We'd done a great job making the most of the space. Staying true to the mid-century style gave the place an authentic yet unique appeal. The view of the Titans' stadium, the Cumberland River, and the downtown skyline was nothing short of spectacular. They also commented on Sawdust, how cute he looked overseeing the festivities from the window of Jimmy's room.

One of the women texted our website link to a client, and received a response less than a minute later. "They'd like to schedule a showing for first thing Monday morning."

Woo-hoo!

Other people arrived, many filtering in and out. More real estate agents. Investors. A few lookie-loos who weren't on the guest list, but we weren't about to turn anyone away. Even Gia Revello and Rex Tomlinson stopped by.

T-Rex hiked a thumb over his shoulder to indicate the SoBro area. "A new band I'm managing was playing a gig at Tootsies. Gia came to hear them too. Once they wrapped up, I convinced her she needed to come take a look this place, so we hoofed it over here."

I was glad Gia didn't hold a grudge. "Welcome," I said, extending my hand to her. "Why don't I show you around?"

After I took them on the tour, Gia took one final glance around the condo and said, "My husband and I have been thinking about downsizing. Our kids are grown and we're empty nesters. Our house in Brentwood is much more than we need. The commute keeps getting worse too. A two-bedroom unit here just might work for us."

"Wonderful!" I handed her one of the design notebooks and held out a hand, inviting her to take a seat on the couch. "These are the standard options we're offering, but custom upgrades can always be negotiated if you have something specific in mind."

T-Rex gestured out the open door of the spec unit to the parking lot. "I'm gonna go outside and grab me a beer."

I sat down on the sofa next to Gia while T-Rex went out the door and strolled over to the metal trough. He picked a bottle out of the ice and glanced around as if looking for an opener. He didn't seem to notice the promotional guitar-shaped openers on the table next to him. I recalled his keychain with the bottle openers at either end, and wondered why he didn't simply pull it out of his pocket and use it to remove the top from his beer. Luckily, Buck noticed the man's dilemma and walked over, plucking a bottle opener from the table and handing it to T-Rex.

Gia had only made it to the third page of the notebook when T-Rex returned with his beer. I stood to allow him to take a seat on the sofa. "Make yourself comfortable."

"Don't mind if I do."

I excused myself and circulated, greeting newcomers and answering questions as the crowd grew and grew. While some took a quick look and left, many opted to stay and hang out around the pool to enjoy the pleasant evening temperatures, fun atmosphere, and breathtaking views, as well as Colette's scrumptious appetizers and the refreshing drinks. Their lingering proved the rehabbed motor court would be a welcoming, comfortable, and impressive place to call home. Not only was the night proving to be a smashing success for Buck and me, but Colette's food was getting rave reviews. Two of the attendees had asked whether she was for hire for events. Many more asked where they might find her food trailer around town.

I was speaking with a potential buyer near the food trailer when Buck wandered up to the trailer's service window with fresh cups of iced tea for Emmalee and Colette.

He held them out. "You ladies looked like you could use a drink."

Colette took the cups from him, handed one to Emmalee, and gave Buck a smile in return. "First a food trailer, now an iced tea. Careful, Buck. You just might ruin me for other men."

He cocked his head and cut her a sideways glance. "Maybe that's exactly what I'm trying to do."

I fought a groan. *How long will these two keep dancing around each other?*

Apparently, Colette was done with the dancing. She set her tea down, crossed her arms over her chest, and skewered my cousin with her sassiest expression. *Here it comes.* Knowing Colette as well as I did, I could almost read her mind. In light of the grand gesture Buck had made by buying the food trailer, Colette decided to muster the courage and lay things on the line. "Are we going to do this thing, or what?"

Buck replied in true form with a simple nod and a "Yep." But while his mouth might have said little, his eyes said everything. They sparkled in elation. He was overjoyed to learn his feelings were reciprocated, and thrilled to be starting a romantic adventure with Colette.

I couldn't help myself. I called over to my cousin. "Kiss her, dummy!"

Laughing, Colette leaned out the window and puckered her lips. Buck stepped closer, put his mouth to hers, and the two sealed the deal with a quick but meaningful kiss that took their relationship to a new and exciting level. I was beyond happy for the two of them. They'd make a perfect couple. Colette would keep Buck in line and feed him to his heart's content, while Buck would reciprocate with security and protection, and make sure Colette always knew how special she was.

As wonderful as this new development was, duty called and we were all forced to return to our respective tasks. I continued to mingle and answer questions, expounding ad nauseam on the many amenities the Music City Motor Court would offer its residents.

A few minutes later, as Presley and I were jointly addressing a real estate agent, Buck came over. "We're running dangerously low on Lynchburg lemonade. The Lynchburg part, anyway. There's plenty of lemonade, but we need more whiskey."

"Mind taking over the tour duties?" I asked Presley. "Collin and I can run down to the Poison Emporium and grab another bottle. Won't take us but a minute."

"I'd be happy to," she said.

Collin and I hotfooted it down to the liquor and tobacco store. As we aimed for the whiskey display, we passed the large humidor. The accessories next to it caught my eye. There were lighters, ashtrays, and cigar cutters. These cutters were specifically designed for a single purpose, much more elegant than the pocketknife and shears Jimmy and Buck had used to cut their cigars the night of Beckett's vigil. But one cutter in particular caught my eye and stopped me in my tracks. The cutter was attached to a keychain. It was oblong, with open parts on either end. *Just like the keychain T-Rex carried.*

My blood rushed through my veins like whitewater rapids, roaring in my ears. *Could T-Rex be the one who'd smoked the second cigar found at the murder scene?*

CHAPTER 29

WINDOW SEAT

SAWDUST

He'd been looking out the window all evening, having a great time watching the people. They were such curious creatures, so different from cats. For one, they made noise all the time. Cats were generally quiet. For another, they could go hours without a nap. *How in the world could they do that?* They also moved around on just their back legs. Sawdust had seen Whitney walk off a few minutes ago, doing just that. He wondered where she'd gone and when she'd be back. She hadn't forgotten about him, had she?

He put a paw to the window to make a request. A woman walking by laughed, came over, and put her hand to the other side of the glass. *Can you get Whitney for me?*

The woman must not have understood. She walked away without bringing Whitney to him. He knew he was worrying unnecessarily, anyway. Whitney would come back to him eventually. She always did.

CHAPTER 30

A DEADLY GAME OF MARCO POLO

WHITNEY

"Collin!" I cried, nearly hyperventilating with the epiphany.

He turned around, a puzzled look on his face as he came back to stand by my side. I pointed to the cutter I'd discovered. He breathed a sharp intake of air. "Tomlinson's keychain."

We exchanged a knowing glance. Maybe Rex Tomlinson was the one who'd introduced Beckett to the fancy Montecristo cigars. Maybe his DNA was on the cigar butt that had been found in the muck at the bottom of the swimming pool. Maybe he was the one who'd killed Beckett.

The gears in my mind turned, grinding out more epiphanies.

The locals in the music industry and Beckett's fiancée from back home had provided two very different versions of the young man. According to his fellow musicians, Beckett was an arrogant rising star who cared only for himself and the almighty dollar. According to Bess, Beckett was a young man of simple values struggling with his newfound fame, but at heart one who simply wanted to make a decent living at what he loved, and to be free to love the woman he chose.

I recalled my first impression of T-Rex, that the deep laugh lines flanking his mouth made him look like a ventriloquist's dummy. But perhaps he wasn't the dummy. Perhaps he was the ventriloquist, putting words in other people's mouths. After all, my impression of Beckett was largely formed by things other people claimed Beckett had said. If I recalled correctly, most of it was hearsay, funneled through T-Rex, who handled the bulk of Beckett's communications with the other musicians and his record label. Rex Tomlinson could have had been an evil puppet master, lying to others about what Beckett had said.

Sawyer, Wylie, and Shep had all indicated that T-Rex had told them, under no uncertain terms, not to raise their issues directly with Beckett. Had Beckett truly been the one who hadn't wanted to hire Sawyer and Wylie on full time, or had T-Rex made that decision to further distance Beckett from the others so he could better control and manipulate his proverbial golden goose?

Gia Revello said Beckett had seemed confused and surprised when she'd confronted him at the Ryman, asking why he hadn't accepted her generous offer. Had T-Rex even told Beckett about the offer, or had he kept his client in the dark, making Beckett seem greedy and unreasonable when, in fact, it was T-Rex who had been so? The voice mail Beckett had left Bess the night he died seemed to support this theory.

I shared my thoughts with Collin, told him my ventriloquist theory, that T-Rex had put words in Beckett's mouth.

He concurred with my conclusions. "I think you're on to something, Whitney."

As I reached out to pull the keychain from the peg for closer inspection, something else dawned on me too. Though my hands and feet had the same number of digits—*five*—a human handprint and footprint were distinct. I'd assumed the footprint of a Tyrannosaurus rex would match its handprint, just as Sawdust's front and back paws were similar, though the foot would be on a much larger scale. But maybe that was an incorrect assumption. I whipped out my phone, quickly typing in a search.

"What are you doing?" Collin asked.

"Looking at this." I held up my phone. On the screen was an image of a T-Rex footprint. Though its feet were thicker than a bird's, it was very similar. The foot contained three claws, not two like its hands.

Collin's eyes sparked. "Jimmy might have mistaken the imprint on Tomlinson's belt buckle for a bird's foot, when it actually belonged to a T-Rex. We've got to get back to the motel. ASAP."

We grabbed a large bottle of whiskey, paid for it, and rushed back down the street. When we reached the motel, we found Buck and Jimmy standing at the drink table. We hurried over and I showed Jimmy the T-Rex footprint I'd found online.

Keeping my voice low, I asked, "Could this be what you saw on the man's belt buckle the night Beckett was killed?"

"Darn well could have been," he said. "If I didn't see the words below that picture right now identifying it as a dinosaur footprint, I would've thought it was a bird's."

Collin handed the whiskey off to Buck, and led the charge as we returned to the spec unit. Sawdust watched us from the window of Jimmy's room, putting a paw on the glass as if to ask *Where are you going so fast?* We entered the condo. Only now, Gia Revello sat alone on the sofa, slowly turning the pages of the notebook. A plastic cup half filled with lemonade sat on the coffee table in front of her, along with an empty beer bottle.

Collin asked, "Where's T-Rex?"

Gia looked up from the book. She gestured to the empty bottle. "He finished his beer and left. Said he needed to get home and get some sleep. He's driving out to Memphis tomorrow for a show."

Gia watched with interest as Collin pulled an evidence bag from his pocket, opened it, and draped it over the bottle, careful not to disturb any fingerprints and DNA left behind. He wrapped his hand around the bag, gripping the bottle inside, and turned it upside down so he could seal it.

Gia's brow furrowed. "What are you doing with that?"

"Just cleaning up," Collin said.

"Thanks," I said, playing along. I knew good and well he was gathering the bottle for evidence. No doubt he planned to take it to the police lab to see if it matched the DNA on the cigar butt that had been retrieved from the muck at the bottom of the pool. Gia's skeptical expression told me she, too, knew exactly what was going on here.

The DNA sample obtained, Collin returned his attention to Gia. "How often did you speak with Beckett Morgan? Directly, I mean."

She looked up in thought for a moment, before returning her gaze to Collin. "Other than our argument at the Ryman, I can only recall us saying a handful of words to each other, and it was all during recording sessions. Most of our communications came through T-Rex. It wasn't surprising. A manager is the musician's representative. That's how it's done."

He nodded, bade Gia goodbye, and cut me a look that said he was off to see if the DNA was a match and if it was, to confront T-Rex.

After Collin left, Gia held up the notebook. "May I take this with me to show my husband?"

"Of course," I told her. "We've got several copies. If your husband would like to come take a look himself, I'd be happy to work around his schedule and give him a showing at his convenience."

"Perfect."

I saw Gia out to the gate.

A half hour later, Presley, Colette, Buck, Jimmy, Emmalee, and I were the last ones left. We gathered for a moment to celebrate.

I held up the clipboard where people had signed up for information about the bidding process for the units. "There's eighty-seven names on this list! Eighty-seven!"

Colette was ecstatic too. "Emmalee and I were hired to cater an anniversary party in July!"

Things were looking up for all of us. We traded high fives all around.

A few minutes later, Colette and Emmalee rolled out in my SUV, the Voodoo Vittles trailer rolling along behind them. Buck, Jimmy, and I waved goodbye from the parking lot.

Now that the party was over, the three of us glanced

around. There was quite a bit of trash, cups, and bottles lying around outside that needed to be rounded up. A glance through the windows of the clubhouse and spec unit said they could use at least a cursory cleaning too. We'd save the more detailed cleaning for tomorrow.

Buck pointed to the clubhouse. "Why don't Jimmy and I tackle the spec unit and the clubhouse? Whitney, you can clean up outside."

"Okeydoke."

We all moved to our appointed stations. I gathered up the cups, bottles, paper plates, and napkins, and tossed them in the proper trash or recycling bin. I dismantled the makeshift drink table. I hooked up the high-pressure nozzle to the hose and power-washed the parking lot, washing away the food and drink spills. All that was left to do now was tidy up the pool area.

Buck and Jimmy emerged from the spec unit, garbage bags in hand, and locked it behind them. They headed into the clubhouse, closing the door behind them to prevent moths and other bugs from flying in.

Knowing that Sawdust would be unable to slip through the narrow bars or jump high enough to make it over the six-foot fence that enclosed the swimming pool, I retrieved him from Jimmy's room and carried him out to the pool area with me. I set him down on the deck so he could explore the space. He set off, sniffing about and chasing bugs, while I grabbed more cups, bottles, and trash that had been left about.

The *clang* of the gate behind me said that someone had entered the pool area. I turned around. T-Rex walked toward me. I gasped involuntarily, but tried to cover my expression of alarm by forcing a smile. "Hi, T-Rex. I didn't see you come back."

Sawdust watched the man from a secret hiding place

among the hydrangeas as T-Rex pointed to the spec unit. "I realized after I'd gone that I didn't have my hat. I think I might have left it in the spec unit. I tried the door, but it's locked. Mind if I go in there and take a look?"

I hadn't seen T-Rex wearing or holding a hat all night. Had he realized he'd left DNA behind on the beer bottle? Was he making up an excuse to get back into the unit so he could retrieve the beer bottle he'd left behind? If he was Beckett's killer, the last thing I wanted to do was let him into the condominium and find myself in an even more confined space with him. The fenced pool area was bad enough. My fight-or-flight instincts were on high alert, and they were telling me that flight would be a difficult proposition with T-Rex standing between me and the exit gate.

"I don't recall you wearing a hat tonight," I said, "but I'll call Buck and Jimmy, have them go in and take a look."

It was a ploy to get them out here to help protect me, and the narrowing of T-Rex's eyes told me he knew it. As I pulled out my phone, he strode forward and slapped it out of my hand. It clattered to the pavement. If I hadn't thought T-Rex was guilty before, I sure as heck did now.

Before I could collect myself, he grabbed my hair in his fist and yanked my head down. "Let me in the unit now!"

I opened my mouth to scream but he slapped a hand over it. I struggled to get out of his grasp, but couldn't break free. My neck was contorted in agony. I feared he would break it. I did the only thing I could think of to try to get free. I twisted and dropped sideways, falling into the pool. *Splash!*

Refusing to release his hold, T-Rex fell in with me. We surfaced, sputtering. Sawdust rushed out from the bushes and ran to the edge of the pool, stretching out a paw as if offering it to me in rescue. The next thing I knew, T-Rex had forced my head under the water. Instinctively, I opened my mouth and screamed, a futile sound that would never reach the surface. Large bubbles bounced about my face as I cried out. Wrapping his hands around my neck, T-Rex immobilized me in a chokehold. I struggled and struggled, but I couldn't get out of his grasp. My feet slipped and slid along the bottom of the pool in their ballet flats, gaining no purchase.

Instinctively, I reached down for the big wrench, realizing too late that I was wearing a dress, not my usual coveralls, and I didn't have it on me. My lungs were in agony, desperate for air. I had to do something, and quick. *Think, Whitney! Think!*

I employed the same logic I used when doing demolition on a building project. When I couldn't force something to move one way, I tried the opposite. Instead of trying to move forward away from T-Rex, I put my back against his belly, my feet on the bottom of the pool, and shoved backward with all my might. I got lucky. We had been close enough to the edge of the pool that I'd been able to slam him back against it. I took advantage of his momentary surprise to twist out of his grip. I put my feet on the bottom and propelled myself upward with all my might, breaking the surface, knocking the floating guitar aside, and desperately sucking in air. *UHH-UIIII-UIIII!* I sounded like a barking seal.

Sawdust ran back and forth along the edge of the pool, desperately trying to figure out what was going on. T-Rex grabbed me again and pulled me under once more. This time, I went to the bottom, made a fist with my right hand, and covered it with my left for extra power. I jammed my elbow back against his knee. The action didn't have nearly the force it would have had if we hadn't been underwater, but it was enough to cause him to ease backward and give me a chance to come up for another breath.

As I surfaced, my eyes spotted the air pump I'd inadvertently forgotten about earlier. Gasping for air, unable to holler for help, I reached out to pull myself up onto the deck. I managed to get my upper body onto it. I stretched out my hand for the pump, which was still plugged into the electric outlet near the fence. Pulling the device into the pool would be suicide, but it seemed clear that T-Rex was going to end my life, regardless. *If T-Rex is going to kill me, he's going to die too.*

I grabbed the pump and pulled it toward the pool, fully intending to drag it into the water with me. I managed to get it to the edge before it slipped out of my grip.

T-Rex got me down again, and I did a flip, just like I'd done when I'd been a kid. It was a genius move. I straightened my legs upward. With my feet out of the water, I could kick the bastard in the face with far more force than I could muster under the surface. I flailed my legs as if I was dancing a frantic two-step, kicking him in the teeth and nose with my heels, feeling a satisfying crunch of cartilage and bone.

T-Rex let go of me to defend his head. It was just the opportunity I needed. I reached out for the ladder, yanked myself to the side, and pulled myself up and out of the water. I collapsed on the deck, gulping air, a puddle of pool water forming around me.

Blood gushing from his upper lip and nostrils, T-Rex called me a choice word and lunged for me. But he was too late. Sawdust stared down at the electronic air pump, his paw at the ready. He did what any cat would do in the situation, what their feline DNA told them to do. He put his paw to the pump and pushed it over the edge. The device entered the water with a *plop*.

A *ZZT-ZZT* split the air, which filled an instant later with a burning smell. The entire motel went dark. The pool lights went out. The lights inside the spec unit and clubhouse went off. So did the guitar-shaped neon sign.

A few seconds later, I was clutching Sawdust to my wet chest and still making sounds like a seal barking as I fought to refill my lungs. Buck and Jimmy opened the door to the clubhouse.

"What happened?" Buck called.

I wasn't able to speak. I grabbed my phone from the deck where it had landed when T-Rex slapped it out of my hand. I activated the flashlight app and lumbered to my feet, dripping like mad and slipping on the deck despite the sand we'd added to the paint. Seeing the light, Buck and Jimmy rushed over.

Buck helped me up. "Are you okay?"

"I will be," I managed on a breath.

"He's not." Jimmy pointed into the pool, where T-Rex floated facedown, his arms dangling limply into the water below him.

With the electricity out and no longer conducting a current, we could pull the man from the swimming pool without getting electrocuted ourselves. Jimmy grabbed the skimming net and used the pole to move T-Rex's body to the stairs, where Buck grabbed the back of his shirt and hauled him out, just as T-Rex must have done with Beckett's body weeks before.

Jimmy dropped to his knees next to the man's torso and began chest compressions, all the while singing the Bee Gees' classic "Stayin' Alive," as CPR training classes suggested. A pink stream of blood trickled from

Tomlinson's lip and nose, growing darker as the ratio of blood to pool water increased.

Meanwhile, Buck rounded up zip ties and secured Tomlinson's ankles and wrists. I stood aside, cradling Sawdust in my arms, soaking him with my wet dress. I'd never before liked the smell of wet cat, but it smelled wonderful now. I kissed my little hero on the head. He looked up at me, gave me a slow blink, and began to purr. The vibration soothed me, even as my body began to shiver and shake so much from the adrenaline that I could barely keep a hold of my precious cat.

While Buck dialed 9-1-1 and then placed a call to Collin, Jimmy continued the chest compressions. T-Rex came to life, coughing up water and sputtering. Jimmy turned the guy onto his side. He lay there for a few seconds trying to gather his wits before realization struck him. He attempted to get up, but with his hands and feet bound, all he could do was wobble back and forth like a walrus on a beach.

"Hit the breaker," I told Buck. The dark was too good for this man. I wanted his shame fully illuminated, for all the world to see.

Buck scurried to the fuse box in the laundry room. A few seconds later, we were back in business. The pool area was completely aglow and the Music City Motor Court sign flashed a prophetic message: NO VACANCY.

CHAPTER 31

PAWSITIVE REINFORCEMENT

SAWDUST

Sawdust thought Whitney would scold him for pushing the little black plastic thing off the edge of the pool. After all, she usually got upset anytime he pushed an object off a table or countertop or dresser. He hated to disappoint her, but he just couldn't help himself. This time, though, Whitney had given him hugs and kisses and treats, so many treats, in fact, that he'd actually lost interest in them. *Maybe later.*

Cleo sniffed at his still-damp fur, her nose twitching in distaste. Sawdust didn't like the smell either. It was too strong. It smelled like the stuff Whitney used for cleaning. *Ick.*

While he didn't normally like to take a bath and merely tolerated them for Whitney's sake, tonight he actually appreciated it. He could tell the warm water was washing away the bad smell of that other water that had been on Whitney's dress. Cleo walked along the edge of the tub, looking down at him, wondering what was going on. She'd better be careful or—*oops!* The kitten lost her footing and ended up in the water with Sawdust. Frantic, she put her paws on the side of the tub and scrambled to gain purchase. It was a futile effort. Sawdust knew because he'd been there before himself.

A few minutes later, both he and Cleo had survived a bath and lay atop a towel on the living room floor. Sawdust crouched and gyrated, showing Cleo how to shake water from her fur. She followed his lead, crouching and doing the same, most of the water she'd shaken from herself landing on Sawdust. *Oh, well.*

He licked water from both himself and Cleo. Soon, they began to look like their fluffy selves again.

When they finally got to bed late that night, Sawdust curled up against Whitney's chest, comforted by the vibration of her human heartbeat against his back. *Thump-thump, thump-thump.*

Life didn't get any better than this.

CHAPTER 32
STARS

Over the next few weeks, things developed on all fronts.

Our grand opening had led to a closed case. After being treated at the ER for electrocution, T-Rex was released into police custody. Collin said the man seemed to have acquired an odd, random twitch from getting zapped in the motel pool, but it served him right. He'd killed Beckett Morgan there and had very nearly done me in too. If not for Sawdust coming to my rescue, I would've been floating in the pool along with the inflatable guitar.

Though T-Rex wouldn't talk, it wasn't difficult to figure out what had happened. As we'd suspected, he'd manipulated Beckett for his own gain, failing to share information with the singer and spreading falsehoods about him. We surmised that T-Rex had been the one to come across Shep Sampson's song notes on the napkins, realize their commercial potential, and steal them for his client. Beckett's family, who'd inherited the copyright, agreed to give Shep all rights to the song, plus a share of royalties on Beckett's recording. It was the fair and right thing to do.

While a belt buckle with a T-Rex footprint was never actually found at Tomlinson's home, his online shopping history revealed that he had ordered one the year before. He'd likely thrown it away after wearing it the night he killed Beckett, worried that someone might identify him by the unique design. Of course, someone had. Jimmy, Collin, and I. Not right away, but eventually.

T-Rex's attack on me had been recorded on the motel's security system—at least until the electricity short-circuited. Between the violent footage of T-Rex's attempt to murder me, and the knowledge that a jury was likely to include fans of Beckett who'd give T-Rex the maximum sentence, the man's attorney agreed to a plea deal requiring him to serve twenty years in prison.

With the murder resolved, the renovation complete, and his pockets now flush with cash, Jimmy decided to say goodbye to the Music City, climb back on his motorcycle, and see where the wind might blow him next. On his last night in town, we threw him a going-away party at the motel. He ended the evening by performing a perfect cannonball into the pool. We got up early the next morning to see him off. He promised to get in touch the next time he rolled through the area.

Collin extended his hand to Jimmy. "Happy trails, man. Beers on me next time you're in Nashville."

Jimmy took Collin's hand and gave it a shake. "I'll take you up on that offer. Thanks."

The bids we received on the condominium units were, as Beckett's hit song put it, "past your wildest dreams." Buck and I made so much bank, in fact, that we were able to pay Presley her share of the market price for both a one-bedroom downstairs unit and a two-bedroom upstairs unit that Buck and I kept to lease out ourselves. The units would generate a consistent rental income that would help fund future flip projects. While my liquid assets were still mostly in the form of WD-40 and turpentine, my net worth increased tenfold thanks to the real estate I now owned. Never again would I have to grovel for a bank loan.

We paid Presley her share of the profits, and agreed to let her buy one of the ground floor units at cost. It was a ridiculously good deal for her, but we'd never have snagged the place if it wasn't for her joining in with us at the tax sale. The deal also eliminated any residual guilt I felt over her former boss selling me my home on Sweetbriar Avenue rather than offering it to her first. We were even now.

Gia Revello and her husband bought an upstairs end unit and were among the first to move in. They were often seen sitting in chairs on the balcony with glasses of wine in their hands, gazing happily across the river at the downtown skyline. The other units sold to record label execs, rising country-western stars, a surgeon, and a defensive end for the Tennessee Titans, among others. Yep, the Music City Motor Court was a wildly successful flip.

In light of the frantic pace with which we had worked on the motel, Buck and I held off jumping into another flip project just yet. We took a few weeks off to focus on other things, including putting another bathroom in my house and helping out on carpentry projects with my uncle Roger's business, which tended to be busy during the summer months. Of course, Buck was also focused on Colette. They'd been officially, and happily, dating since the grand opening.

Colette signed up for vendor-booth space for her food trailer at various festivals in the Nashville area. Word spread at the festivals that Voodoo Vittles served the best Cajun food outside of New Orleans. The line at her trailer was longer than the line at any other food truck. In only a short time, she amassed dozens of stellar ratings on Yelp.

Shortly after the Fourth of July holiday, Collin took me and his new telescope out to Natchez Trace State Park, which sat a hundred miles southwest of Nashville. With few towns in the vicinity, the area was exceptionally dark, a great place for stargazing and for Collin to snap photos of stars, nebulae, and other astronomical objects. A shooting star caught my eye, and I pondered how it was much like Beckett, a bright flash extinguished too soon.

Cleo continued to grow by leaps and bounds, and Sawdust continued to teach her new age-appropriate skills. She could now climb to the top of the cat tree all by herself, walk around the edge of the claw-foot bathtub without falling in, and spin a roll of toilet paper like nobody's business.

Come August, though, I was itching to get back to work. I searched the real estate listings and the tax sale rolls, and drove around, taking a look at the properties. Finally, I found one worthy of our attention. I cornered Buck when he and Colette were watching a movie on TV at our house one Saturday night. "You ready to do another flip?"

"You got something in mind?"

"I do." I plopped down on the sofa next to him and showed him pictures I'd taken on my phone.

"That looks like an old country church."

"It is," I said, "for now. Of course it's no longer in use. But look at those stained glass windows. Most of them are intact. What do you say?"

Buck grinned. "I say glory hallelujah."